MURDER
at the
ENGLISH
MANOR

BOOKS BY HELENA DIXON

HELENA DIXON

MURDER
at the
ENGLISH
MANOR

bookouture

Published by Bookouture in 2025

An imprint of Storyfire Ltd.
Carmelite House
50 Victoria Embankment
London EC4Y 0DZ

www.bookouture.com

The authorised representative in the EEA is Hachette Ireland
8 Castlecourt Centre
Dublin 15 D15 XTP3
Ireland
(email: info@hbgi.ie)

ISBN: 978-1-83525-777-7
eBook ISBN: 978-1-83525-776-0

For all my wonderful readers.

PROLOGUE

Torbay Herald May 1937

Situations Vacant

Live-in general maid required for large private establishment near Dartmoor. Must be clean, efficient and of good character. Experience preferred. Wages and description of duties on application from Mrs Putnam, housekeeper, Bovey Tracey 312.

Forthcoming Marriages

The engagement is announced between Sebastian Montague, eldest son of Sir Henry and Lady Amelia Faversham of Markham Hall, Bovey Tracey, and Miss Ruby Margaret Conway, only daughter of Mr Stanley Conway and the late Mrs Pearl Conway of Chicago, Illinois, USA.

CHAPTER ONE

The stone paved patio of Mrs Craven's house in Dartmouth was flooded with early summer sunlight as Kitty and her grandmother sipped their tea on the terrace. A silver-gilt tiered cake stand laden with tiny crustless sandwiches and delicious dainty pastry delights stood on an immaculate white-linen tablecloth.

The sky was a clear blue and the birds were tweeting happily in the laurel shrubbery at the far end of the neatly mown and rolled lawn. Mrs Craven was the perfect hostess, dressed in a fine cotton summer-blue-and-white print dress. The diamond brooch she always wore on her bosom glistening in the sunshine.

Kitty shifted slightly uneasily on the padded seat of her rattan-caned chair and wondered what was afoot. She had never been Mrs Craven's favourite person and the invitation to tea was unusual. Her grandmother appeared to sense her unease.

'Millicent, my dear, perhaps you should put Dora's problem to Kitty? It is really why you have invited us here today.' Her grandmother gave their hostess a meaningful look.

Mrs Craven, former mayoress of Dartmouth and her grand-mother's oldest friend, gave Kitty's grandmother a sharp glance.

'This matter is most delicate. It will require extreme discretion and tact,' she said with a sniff as she poured herself more tea through the metal strainer into the delicate bone china cup.

Kitty suppressed a sigh and helped herself to another tiny strawberry and fresh cream tart. She had a feeling that more sugar could only help her with whatever issue she was about to be roped into.

A pair of white butterflies danced over the table, weaving in and out of the floral-decorated crockery. Kitty waited for Mrs Craven to finally tell her why she had been summoned for afternoon tea on the terrace. She sincerely hoped it wasn't going to be yet another request for her to assist with the Dartmouth Ladies Guild jumble sale. The last one had left her feeling quite traumatised from having to sort through piles of distinctly dubious and odd-smelling garments.

'This matter is really to do with my maid, Dora.' Mrs Craven lowered her voice in a theatrical fashion and glanced about the terrace as if she suspected someone might be listening to their conversation.

'I don't understand. Whatever is wrong with Dora?' Kitty was bewildered. Mrs Craven's maid, Dora Jones, had been with Mrs Craven now for several years. A pleasant woman in her early forties, Kitty always thought she managed Mrs Craven extremely well. Although, the maid had seemed on edge when she had opened the door to them on their arrival earlier.

Mrs Craven frowned when Kitty failed to lower her voice. 'It concerns Dora's sister, Agnes. She is some years younger than Dora. Agnes was a late blessing to their parents and Dora feels responsible for the girl since their parents passed away.'

'Is this Agnes in some kind of trouble?' Kitty asked. She was unclear about quite what Mrs Craven wanted from her.

'It seems she has disappeared. Vanished into thin air,'

Kitty's grandmother said, setting her cup down firmly on its saucer and returning it to the table.

'She has run away or gone off without a word to anyone. To make matters worse, I recommended the girl to her position.' Mrs Craven huffed as she added more milk to her own drink.

'When did this happen?' Kitty couldn't quite understand why Mrs Craven was so concerned. Maids left their employers all the time and often didn't give notice before leaving. Even if Mrs Craven had vouched for the girl, any employer would understand that a servant would often up sticks if they found a better position.

'That's the thing. Apparently, Agnes left about a month ago and no one has seen hide nor hair of her since. She hasn't sent for her trunk, and she hasn't contacted Dora or anyone else that we know of,' Mrs Craven explained.

'Oh, that is rather odd. Especially not sending for her things. Was her trunk packed, do you know?' Kitty asked. It did sound peculiar that the girl hadn't taken her belongings.

A mildly exasperated expression crossed Mrs Craven's face. 'I have no idea. I presume not. Dora is most upset and concerned for her sister's welfare.'

'Who is the girl's employer?' Kitty asked. 'You said you recommended her for the post? Surely the housekeeper or someone might be able to shed some light on the matter. Was she employed locally?'

Her grandmother and Mrs Craven exchanged a look which aroused Kitty's suspicions that this might be the point where she was about to be persuaded into something she would rather not do.

'Agnes was employed by some friends of mine, Lord and Lady Faversham at Markham Hall near Bovey Tracey on the edge of Dartmoor. A most prestigious household. Actually, they are also distant relatives of mine by marriage.' Mrs Craven avoided Kitty's gaze by helping herself to a fruit scone from the cake stand.

Kitty's grandmother looked as if she were about to interject but held her peace. This sounded stranger with every piece of information she was being given.

'Has Dora spoken to anyone at the house about her sister and what may have happened to her?' Kitty asked.

'Yes, she contacted the housekeeper, Mrs Putnam, when Agnes didn't send her usual weekly letter and didn't arrive for their regular fortnightly meeting. They meet up on Agnes and Dora's half day off for tea at Newton Abbot. Dora went there to meet her, thinking she would see her sister and get an explanation for whatever was going on. Needless to say, Agnes never arrived at the tea room.' Mrs Craven took a sip of her tea before starting to apply clotted cream to her scone.

'Forgive me if this sounds indelicate, but was there a boyfriend? Could she have eloped? Or perhaps been disgraced?' Kitty was careful about how she phrased the question. If Agnes had become pregnant or run off with some beau who her older sister might not have approved of, then this could easily be the reason behind the girl disappearing.

'No, no boyfriends so far as Dora is aware, and Agnes was apparently quite frank with her about such matters. Mrs Putnam was apparently quite baffled as to where the girl might have gone. She had assumed she had returned home to Dora. Agnes was good at her work and provided satisfactory service in the household, so had not been dismissed.' Mrs Craven was now liberally applying strawberry jam on top of the cream.

'I see. I presume that Dora and her sister hadn't argued or fallen out over anything?' Kitty asked. She was still quite baffled about why her grandmother and Mrs Craven were dragging her into the matter. If they wished to employ Torbay Private Investigative Services, Kitty and Matt's business, then they could just have said so and made an appointment. Or, rather, Dora could have made the appointment and employed them.

'Dora assures me that she and Agnes were on excellent terms,' Mrs Craven said.

'Then, I don't know what you would like me to do? Does Dora wish to retain mine and Matt's services? Or would she like advice? Perhaps she should really go to the police,' Kitty suggested.

Once again, she became aware of the uneasy exchange of glances between her grandmother and Mrs Craven.

'The matter is a little delicate, Kitty, darling,' her grandmother said.

Kitty leaned back in her seat and looked at the two elderly women. 'Well?' So far she hadn't particularly heard anything that could be sensitive or that needed extra discretion.

'I have known the Dowager Lady Faversham for a very long time. Her husband, the late Lord Norman Faversham, and my own dear late husband, Peregrine, were cousins. Henry, Lady Sarah's son, who is the current Lord Faversham, was the second son and obviously shouldn't have inherited the estate. His older brother, Arthur, was however killed during the war and the death duties were considerable. This, coming soon after Norman's death, was terrible for the family. Henry is also not a good manager, so the Markham Estate's finances are somewhat parlous to say the least. Disastrous investments and high maintenance bills have hit the estate hard. Anyway, Lady Sarah has arranged an advantageous match between Henry's eldest son, Sebastian, to a Miss Ruby Conway, an American heiress. The engagement has recently been announced. A ball is being held at the house this coming weekend to introduce the girl into local society ahead of the wedding,' Mrs Craven explained between bites of her scone.

Kitty was still none the wiser about how this affected her or had any bearing on Dora's missing sister. 'I'm afraid I still don't understand, what has any of this to do with Agnes disappearing?'

Her grandmother gave an apologetic sounding cough. 'Dora is very concerned about her sister's welfare. Millicent is attending the ball this weekend at Markham Hall to try to discover where Agnes may have gone. The Favershams cannot afford to have any kind of shadow falling over the event or possibly derailing the wedding plans.'

'I have arranged for you and Matthew to also be invited to stay at Markham Hall for the weekend. Miss Conway is a very wealthy young woman and she and her father are obviously also going to be staying at the house. I suggested to Lady Sarah that some security for the event would be in order. The family are keen to impress Mr Conway, Ruby's father. Then you can make discreet enquiries whilst you are there about what may have become of Agnes. Then Dora's mind may be put at ease without any unpleasantness. With my assistance, of course.' Mrs Craven looked smugly at Kitty.

Kitty was taken aback at having her life organised for her by her grandmother's friend. She also suspected that by unpleasantness, Mrs Craven and the Favershams had no intention of reporting the missing girl's disappearance to the police. 'We do have other cases, you know,' she said. 'And what about Bertie?'

Bertie, Kitty and Matt's beloved roan cocker spaniel, was not always the best-behaved dog and Kitty was wary of asking for too many favours when it came to arranging for someone to care for him when they went away.

'Lady Sarah has said he would be welcome at the Hall. I assured her he was well trained and had assisted in previous cases,' Mrs Craven did have the grace to look a little embarrassed at this, knowing she had slightly overstated Bertie's case. 'I shall, of course, as I said, be assisting you myself in this investigation. I feel very responsible having put Agnes forward for this post in the first place. My own experience and connections with the family will no doubt have this mystery solved both quickly and *discreetly* in no time at all.' She emphasised the word discreetly.

'I am very happy to look after Rascal,' her grandmother added, her eyes twinkling.

Since her grandmother always jumped at any excuse to care for Rascal, Kitty's cat, that offer was not unexpected.

'Why does Lady Sarah feel security is required for the engagement? Surely it is not just to impress this Mr Conway?' Kitty asked. She also couldn't see that the Dowager Lady Faversham would be terribly bothered about a mere maidservant disappearing either. A house of the kind Mrs Craven had described must have many servants. No, there was something else afoot, Kitty was sure of it.

'Lady Sarah needs everything to go smoothly over the weekend. Her grandson, Sebastian Faversham, can be something of a handful and his younger brother, Rupert, is also rather a wild card. Their mother, Lady Amelia, is, well, vague at best. One of those artistic types. Lady Sarah has also said that someone attempted to break into Mr Conway's safe a couple of weeks ago while they were staying in London. It's left him quite paranoid. The Markham Estate is literally hanging by a thread and the money from Ruby and Sebastian's wedding would solve a great many problems for them.' Mrs Craven's gaze slipped away from Kitty's.

'And?' Kitty asked. There was something else behind Mrs Craven's sudden concern for her maid's missing sister and the fate of a distant relation's estate.

'On a personal note, and I expect you to keep this to yourself, Lady Sarah owes me a considerable sum of money. Money which will be paid back to me once the wedding has taken place. Or when Sir Henry and Mr Conway have signed the financial documents for the marriage. The financial institutions who hold the debts for the estate will look much more favourably upon a loan once they are assured of the prospect of money coming into the estate's coffers,' Mrs Craven confessed. Her cheeks had reddened and she looked quite uncomfortable.

'I see.' Kitty was taken by surprise. She would never have thought that Mrs Craven would have been foolish enough to lend money even to someone who was related, albeit by marriage. It was becoming clear now that not only were she and Matt to investigate Agnes's disappearance, but their presence would no doubt convince Lady Sarah Faversham to cough up the money she owed to Mrs Craven.

'Why did you loan Lady Sarah Faversham money? Is it a lot?' The question blurted from her lips before she could stop herself.

Mrs Craven stiffened. 'My personal financial decisions are not open to discussion, Kitty. Lady Sarah is both my friend and also a relation by marriage. Peregrine would have wished me to assist her in her time of need. Suffice to say I was badly advised, and I am anxious to see the return of my money. Dora also wishes to find out what has happened to her sister. Mr Conway requires a feeling of security. This weekend provides us with an excellent opportunity to achieve all of those aims.'

'I know you and Matthew are both busy, my dear, but I should be most grateful if you could assist Millicent with this matter. Think of poor Dora, she is desperate to discover what has happened to her sister.' Her grandmother rested her hand gently on Kitty's arm. 'It is just for a couple of nights and attending a ball cannot be such a hardship, can it?'

Ordinarily, attending a ball would have been fun. This weekend at a country house with the prospect of Millicent Craven 'assisting' them in an investigation somehow didn't sound terribly enjoyable. She wasn't sure either quite what Matt would have to say on the matter.

He was deeply involved in researching a case from his own past. A man who had seemingly faked his own death to avoid returning to the trenches of the Great War. It was a troubling investigation that had stirred up painful memories of Matt's own past at that time.

Kitty sighed. 'I'll speak to Matt. Perhaps I could first have a word with Dora. She does know, I suppose, that you intended to ask for our help finding her sister?'

Mrs Craven bridled indignantly. 'Of course she knows, she is in the kitchen now.' She picked up a small silver handbell that was standing next to the cake stand. Dora appeared a moment later in response to the summons.

The older woman stood somewhat awkwardly next to the tea table twisting her hands into the bottom of her starched white apron. Her plump, pleasant face was lined with worry.

'Now then, Dora, I have put your dilemma to Mrs Bryant and she has kindly agreed to assist us in discovering what has become of your sister,' Mrs Craven announced.

Hope flared into the woman's tired-looking eyes and Kitty immediately felt a little guilty at being so curmudgeonly about offering her help to find Agnes.

'Oh, thank you, Mrs Bryant. I can't tell you how relieved I am to have some help to find my sister.' Dora smiled tremulously as she finished speaking. 'I'm right worried about her. It's so unlike her to just disappear like this.'

'Mrs Craven said that you usually exchanged weekly letters and met up every fortnight?' Kitty asked.

Dora nodded. 'That's right. Sometimes she would telephone me as well if she could go to the village. She wasn't allowed to use the one at the Hall. That's why when I didn't hear from her, I started to panic. I thought as perhaps she was ill or her letter was lost in the post. I went to meet her at our usual tea room thinking as she'd be there or there would be some message, but she didn't turn up. I telephoned the Hall then and spoke to Mrs Putnam. She's the housekeeper, and that were when she told me as Agnes was gone.' Dora whisked a plain white-cotton handkerchief from her apron pocket and dabbed fiercely at her eyes.

'When did your sister take up her position at Markham Hall?' Kitty asked.

'September gone. She always seemed very happy there. Settled, although it was a bit isolated being near the moors,' Dora said.

Kitty went through similar questions to those she had already asked of Mrs Craven and received the same responses. It seemed that Agnes had disappeared a month ago and no one had seen or heard from her since.

'Was there anything unusual the last time you saw or spoke to your sister? Anything in her letters?' Kitty asked. 'A boyfriend, perhaps?'

Dora shook her head. 'No. No young men in her life. I've asked around her friends and they haven't heard from her neither. She did seem a bit excited about something though, but she wouldn't say what it was. They must think as she's gone for good as they've advertised her position and I was told as they've packed up her things.' She bit her lip as if trying not to cry in front of her mistress.

'I told the housekeeper if they had her trunk ready we would bring it back with us at the end of our stay,' Mrs Craven said to Kitty.

'I see. Thank you, Dora. Well, I'll speak to my husband and we'll do our best to get to the bottom of things.' Kitty watched as the woman retreated back to the kitchen. The business of the girl not having taken her belongings or sending for them was peculiar. It sounded as if the girl hadn't even packed. That, to Kitty, sounded the most troubling part of the whole affair.

CHAPTER TWO

Matt was at home when Kitty arrived back at their smart, white modern house at Churston. She had taken her grandmother back to the Dolphin Hotel on the embankment in Dartmouth on her way. The hotel was jointly owned by Kitty and her grandmother. Although her beloved Grams had retired from the business, she retained a large apartment within the ancient black and white half-timbered building. She also kept a close eye on the day-to-day running of the hotel, despite having appointed a charming and most efficient manager.

Kitty had taken the opportunity of the short drive from Mrs Craven's spacious home on the hill above the riverside town to the embankment to quiz her grandmother. She particularly wanted to know more about the loan Lady Sarah Faversham had received from Mrs Craven. It had sounded so odd and Mrs C's reluctance to speak about it added to the mystery.

Her grandmother had declared that she knew no more than Kitty on the matter. Kitty highly doubted that this was true, but it was clear her grandmother's lips were sealed. She was forced to abandon the subject and cross over the river on the ferry back to Kingswear still no wiser on the matter.

'Did you have a delicious tea with Mrs C?' Matt looked up from the notes he was making in a large book when she entered the sitting room. 'What has she persuaded you to help with this time? Not a jumble sale again?' He grinned at her.

Kitty drew off her thin pale-pink cotton gloves and flung herself down on the end of the black-leather sofa. Bertie roused himself from where he had been lying at Matt's feet to look at her.

'Oh dear.' Matt continued to smile at her, as if sensing her mood. 'Not a bonny baby contest? Or organising the village show?' Kitty had previously been coerced into helping with both of those events in the past.

'Did you have any plans for this weekend?' Kitty asked.

Her husband replaced the cap on his fountain pen and closed his notebook. His smile replaced by a cautious expression. 'That sounds rather ominous. What exactly has Mrs C roped you into now?'

'Not me. Us,' Kitty clarified.

Matt immediately sat more upright in his seat and Kitty enjoyed seeing alarm replace amusement in her husband's bright-blue eyes. 'Oh dear, I don't like the sound of this. What does that mean exactly?'

Kitty told him everything that had gone on during tea.

'That does sound concerning, that the girl seemingly left all of her possessions behind. Do they know if she was in her uniform when she left or if she had said anything to the other staff?' Matt asked.

Kitty shrugged. 'It seems no one at Markham Hall took much notice. Dora has attempted to find out more from the housekeeper, a Mrs Putnam, but has been given short shrift. Everyone there seems to be focused on this engagement.'

'And Dora has obviously not yet gone to the police?' Matt looked at Kitty.

'No. I did suggest it, but it was pretty clear that was unlikely to happen. I think Mrs Craven would have probably had a fit if I had pushed the matter. The whole thing seems to be complicated by this money the Dowager Lady Sarah owes to her. I can't work that out at all. She seems to believe her only hope of being repaid is if this wedding takes place. It's like something from the last century. Mrs Craven said Lady Sarah's husband had been a cousin of Mr Craven's. I rather think that is complicating matters.' Kitty folded her gloves and dropped them inside her cream-leather summer handbag.

'What do you know of Markham Hall and the Favershams?' Matt asked.

Kitty shrugged. 'Not much. I asked Grams about them as I was taking her back to the Dolphin. She has met Lady Sarah and the late Lord Faversham, years ago when Mr Craven was alive. She said it was a large estate, and the house had been very grand back in the day. The Favershams have owned the estate for at least five hundred years.'

Matt eyed her curiously. 'Do you recall Mr Craven at all?'

Kitty smiled. 'Peregrine? Yes, a little, I was only young when he died. He was always kind to me. He'd slip me a silver sixpence when Mrs Craven wasn't looking. He once told Grams I was spirited.'

Matt chuckled. 'He sounds like he was a nice man.'

'I suppose he was. He was quiet and always let Mrs C do all the talking.' Kitty rolled her eyes. 'You know Mrs C loves to talk.'

'Then I think we need to go to Markham Hall. It's very worrying that no one seems concerned about this missing maid apart from her sister. It sounds as if we shall have an interesting weekend though.' Matt leaned back in his chair.

'Oh, and one more thing. Did I mention that Mrs Craven will be assisting us with the investigation?' Kitty added somewhat naughtily, before promptly leaving the room to go and see what their housekeeper had planned for their supper.

* * *

Matt raked his hand through his hair as Kitty skipped out of the room. A weekend near the moors attending an engagement party in the company of Mrs Craven was one thing. Having her assistance to solve the mystery of a missing maidservant and act as security in some fashion was quite another.

Bertie flopped his head back down on the rug and sighed deeply. Matt knew how his dog felt. The prospect of Mrs Craven ordering them around for a weekend while they tried to solve the mystery of Agnes's disappearance was quite a wearisome thought. Still, like Kitty, he was troubled by the circumstances that seemed to be surrounding the girl's disappearance.

Kitty returned a few minutes later with Rascal, her tabby cat, walking behind her, his tail in the air. Matt gave her a baleful look.

'You do remember what happened before whenever Mrs Craven has fancied herself as a detective?' he asked.

Kitty perched herself back on the sofa while Rascal leapt gracefully up onto the windowsill and settled himself in a pool of sunlight.

'Of course I do. She was even more insufferable than usual. I don't see that we have much choice, however, and I am worried about what may have happened to Agnes. Dora is clearly extremely distressed.' Kitty frowned as she spoke. 'It sounded most out of character for the girl not to have been in touch.'

Matt could see that she was concerned for the missing girl. 'I suppose a couple of days in a country house and dancing at a ball shouldn't be too great a hardship. Even if it does come with having to put up with Mrs Craven. I have a feeling though that this may well end up with the police being involved. We shall just have to hope for the best,' he said.

Kitty flashed him a grateful smile. 'Thank you. I'll pack in the morning, and we can leave at lunchtime. It's not too far away so we should arrive in time for tea. Mrs Craven said she would let Lady Faversham know to expect us if we were able to take the case. The ball is the following evening on the Saturday.'

Matt nodded. 'Very well.'

'How did you get on today while I was out? I see you were making notes.' Kitty waved her hand towards the notebook which he had closed and set aside on the small chrome-and-glass side table beside his chair. She hoped he had been able to make progress on the case from his past.

'I made quite a few telephone calls to various people trying to trace the two orderlies who worked on the wing at Dellingbole when I was there.' Dellingbole House had been turned into a hospital and recuperation centre during the Great War and Matt had spent quite some time there recovering from his wounds.

It was also where he had met and married Edith, his first wife. She and their daughter Betty had been killed less than a year later. Now he was trying to find anyone who might have assisted a fellow officer, Redvers Palmerston, to fake his own death. At the time, Matt had believed the man had succumbed to infection and had attended his funeral.

Now, many years later, when he and Kitty had arrived back in England from America in January, he had spotted a man identical to Redvers in the crowd as they had disembarked from the ship. After giving chase at the dock, he had become convinced that Redvers was not dead. A belief that had been reinforced recently by Redvers's widow, who also believed she had seen him.

'Did you have any luck?' Kitty asked.

'The one fellow I thought may know something has sadly passed away. I spoke to his sister while you were with Mrs C. The other man is Samuel Jobbins, another of the orderlies, always a rather sketchy sort of chap. He has moved around quite a lot since he left Dellingbole. I wrote the other day to the place where he was last known to be living,' Matt said.

'Do you think he will know anything about Redvers?' Kitty asked.

Matt sighed. 'I think he might. Of the two, he was the one I think would be most likely to have assisted him in a deception. Jobbins was always running favours in return for a cigarette or a few shillings. I think if anyone could have been bribed to aid Redvers to fake his death, then Jobbins would be the one.'

Someone had to have helped Redvers to escape. He would have needed clothes and medical supplies. There was also the matter of placing some other poor deceased fellow in his bed to take his place. Otherwise no death certificate would have been issued and a funeral could not have been held.

'Hmm, even if he wasn't the one who helped him, I think he may well know something useful,' Kitty agreed.

Matt hoped she was right. When he had first caught sight of Redvers, he had thought he was hallucinating or going mad. He had attended the man's funeral. Had taken his watch and ring to his widow to pass on to their son. At the time of Redvers's death he had not even considered that they could be burying someone else.

Redvers's widow had since remarried a solicitor and was now Mrs Hayden, living a respectable life. Her son, Peter, was grown up and also married to the daughter of a local landowner. The implications of Redvers not actually being dead could be quite far-reaching. Yet for his own peace of mind, and at Mrs Hayden's behest, he had to discover the truth.

* * *

Kitty rose early the following morning and tempted Rascal into his wicker cat basket with the aid of a treat of sardines. Once he had been safely deposited at the Dolphin in the eager care of her grandmother, she returned home to commence packing. As she did whenever they went away on an investigation, she packed enough clothes for longer than the weekend, just in case they needed more time to determine what had happened to Agnes.

The fine weather seemed set to continue, and the air was warm. Perhaps the weekend would be pleasanter than expected and they could get to the bottom of Agnes's disappearance. She hoped for Dora's sake that nothing bad had happened to the girl and it would all turn out to be something and nothing.

Her packing skills had improved since the days when her friend, Alice, a former chambermaid at the Dolphin, used to pack for her. Alice now had her own business in the nearby town of Paignton. There she sold various small items of haberdashery and other goods. She also did custom mending, repairs and tailored clothing to fit.

The business had done well, and Alice had recently taken on a young girl to assist in the shop so that her time was more available for the custom sewing side of her business. Kitty sat back on her heels as she carefully placed the last article inside the trunk. It struck her that Alice might be a good person to consult on the subject of Agnes's disappearance.

Alice might be able to shed some light on what might have prompted the girl to leave and why she had not taken or sent for her things. She would also need to cancel their planned trip to the cinema for the evening. On Friday evenings they usually met up to see a film and eat a fish and chip supper together.

Kitty closed the lid of the trunk and headed downstairs to the telephone in the hall. Matt had taken Bertie for a brisk walk to burn off some of his energy before they set out for Markham Hall.

'Hello, Miss Miller's establishment, Rose speaking. How may I assist you?' The careful tones of Alice's young assistant greeted her. Kitty knew that Alice had coached the girl on the art of answering the telephone and taking messages.

'Hello, Rose, may I speak to Alice. Tell her it's Kitty.'

She waited while the girl went to find her employer.

'Oh, good morning, Kitty, is everything all right?' Alice sounded a little flustered and Kitty hoped she hadn't telephoned at an awkward time.

'Oh yes, everything is perfectly fine. I just called to say I won't be able to meet you this evening. Mrs Craven has arranged for Matt and I to accompany her to Markham Hall for the weekend. It's for a case. I'm afraid it's all rather last minute.' Kitty felt quite awful at letting her friend down. She looked forward to spending time with Alice.

'A weekend with Mrs Craven will be penance enough for depriving me of your company tonight.' Alice giggled as she spoke.

'I think you may be right. Do you know Dora and Agnes Jones at all? Dora is Mrs Craven's maid and Agnes is her sister, much younger than her,' Kitty asked.

'Yes, of course. They used to live three doors down from us. I don't know Dora that well, but I know Agnes. Is there something wrong?' Alice asked in a concerned voice.

'It seems Agnes has gone missing from her post at Markham Hall. She's not taken her things or sent for them and no one has heard from her since she left,' Kitty explained.

'Dear me, that doesn't sound like Agnes at all. She's a nice girl, very pretty and hard working. Not the flighty sort,' Alice said.

'Can you think of a reason why she might have done that? Left her post without notice? And not sent for her trunk?' Kitty knew Alice would understand the circumstances around a maid's employment better than she did.

'I don't know. It's odd. The upping sticks, well that can happen, but it's peculiar about her things. I suppose maybe she met someone better off than her and she could have gone off with him. He might have told her not to bother with her old stuff. That he would kit her out with all new clothes and such,' Alice suggested in a hopeful tone.

'Thanks, Alice, that's a possibility I hadn't considered. I had best let you get back to work, you must be busy.' Kitty could hear the hum of conversation in the background and guessed customers must be in the shop.

'Yes, there are some people just come in, Rose is trying hard but she's still learning. Let me know about Agnes, won't you? It sounds very odd,' Alice asked.

'I will, and thank you.' Kitty ended the call. The possibility of a wealthy suitor for the maid hadn't entered her head before. She hoped Alice was right and they would find Agnes safe, well, and living a more luxurious life. That foreboding feeling, however, was still in the pit of her stomach.

CHAPTER THREE

The drive to Bovey Tracey was a pleasant one and Kitty had the folding roof down on her red Morris touring car. The sun shone and the fields were greenish yellow with the ripening crops. Primroses gleamed in pale-gold clumps in the hedgerows. In the woods, bluebells added colour, while white wild garlic scented the air as they sped along the lanes. Bertie was sprawled happily on his rug on the rear seat, his tongue out and his eyes bright as he watched the world go by.

'Do you think Alice may be right?' Kitty asked as she navigated her car across one of the many narrow, grey stone-built bridges.

'About a mysterious wealthy suitor spiriting Agnes away, persuading her to leave all her worldly goods behind? It's a possibility, I suppose. You said that Alice said Agnes was a very pretty girl.' Matt glanced at Kitty. 'The mystery though is why she wouldn't have told her sister or have been in touch since. It sounded as if they were close.'

'I know, it's all very odd. Hmm, well let's hope it's something like that which has happened to the girl,' she said as she took the turn away from the town and headed towards the edge of the moor.

They drove on following the map that Matt had spread out on his lap. Soon they were travelling alongside a small wood before reaching a turn leading them onto the Markham Estate. They passed a small, dilapidated stone gatehouse, which was clearly uninhabited and followed the track towards another grove of trees in the distance. Kitty thought she could see a red-tiled roof and some tall chimneys above the trees.

The road became more rutted, and Kitty was forced to slow her pace as they entered a more formal avenue. Sheep were grazing in the distance, and she thought she glimpsed a flash of brown deer at the edge of the woodland. They passed a large, handsome Queen Anne style house at the side of the road leading to the main house.

Kitty guessed this must be the dower house where presumably Lady Sarah Faversham now resided since her husband's death. As they drew closer, however, Kitty saw it appeared run-down and the windows and roof were in need of some repairs.

A moment later they emerged through the wooded area to see Markham Hall itself. A large, venerable building. The centre of the house looked ancient, probably dating back hundreds of years. The wings to either side appeared to be of a more recent origin. Even so they had to be a few hundred years old. The render on the outside of the building was cracked and worn and tendrils of ivy seemed to be trying to climb inside the small leaded-pane windows.

A couple of cars stood to the side of the house in front of a red-brick building with a clock tower above it. Kitty assumed this would once have been the coach house judging by the size and shape of the large wooden doors. She parked her car beside a rather dilapidated dark-blue Rolls-Royce, which in turn was flanked by a much newer and smarter model.

Kitty hopped out of her car as Matt took Bertie from the

back seat to let the little dog sniff freely about the driveway. There was no one else in sight as she ensured the roof was up and Matt unstrapped their travelling trunk and bags from the rear of the car.

The front door of the house was under a stone portico on a flagstone terrace which seemed to wrap around the house. Below the stone balustrade down a flight of steps lay a large lawn bordered by a rather neglected-looking shrubbery and some rose beds. A wooden summerhouse was on one side and a few croquet hoops stood forlornly on the overgrown grass.

Kitty clipped Bertie to his leash and accompanied Matt to the dark-blue painted front door. As they drew nearer she saw the paintwork was peeling, revealing glimpses of the rusty-red undercoat and there were cobwebs around the frame.

Matt set down the trunk and pressed the tarnished-brass bell push at the side of the door. A minute or so later the door was opened by a somewhat sour-faced looking woman of about fifty years of age. She was dressed in a rusty-black dress and a bunch of keys hung from a chatelaine at her waist.

'Captain and Mrs Bryant, we are expected,' Matt said.

'Of course, sir, madam, please come in.' She gave Bertie a slightly disparaging look as they followed her into an impressive hallway, leaving their trunk on the step to be collected.

The centre of the hall was dominated by a huge carved-oak staircase which led up to the first floor. A suit of armour stood holding a sword on either side of the staircase as if guarding the stairs. A worn, red carpet runner led the eye upwards. The walls were hung with various oil paintings of mostly pastoral scenes. Here and there, however, Kitty noticed it looked as if some pictures had been moved leaving a line on the wall where they used to hang. The resulting gaps had been filled with modernist paintings in bright colours and patterns similar to some Kitty and Matt had seen at Christmas in the New York galleries.

There were also clay sculptures of strange, distorted figures placed on stands. The whole effect was somewhat strange and jarring as the figures clashed with the older white, Grecian-style statues and busts.

'I'll have your bags sent to your room. If you'd like to follow me, the family are about to take tea in the drawing room.' The housekeeper gave them little opportunity to take more notice of their surroundings.

They followed in her wake along the hallway towards the drawing room. Bertie sniffed interestedly along the walls at the skirting boards and Kitty hoped that he had not detected mice.

The housekeeper opened the oak-panelled door to the drawing room to reveal a large, somewhat shabby room furnished with a motley collection of furniture. Mrs Craven was seated on the sofa deep in conversation with an elderly grey-haired lady clad in dark green who occupied a very upright oak-framed chair.

A plump man in his fifties attired in tweed was conversing with an expensively dressed florid-faced gentleman of a similar age. Two good-looking younger men were sat with a plain, bespectacled young woman at one of the side tables. A woman with faded-auburn hair clad in a brown artist's smock which seemed to be covered in splashes of clay rose from her seat to greet them.

'Captain and Mrs Bryant, milady,' the housekeeper said tersely and disappeared as their hostess came to shake their hands.

'Welcome to Markham Hall, I'm so pleased you could join us. It's terribly good of you to offer to help us out. I'm Lady Amelia Faversham.' She glanced around vaguely at the other people in the room. 'You know dear Mrs Craven already, of course. This is my mother-in-law, Lady Sarah Faversham. Oh, and my husband, Sir Henry.' She waved a hand in the direction of the man in tweed.

'Delighted.' Matt and Kitty shook hands with Sir Henry, while Lady Sarah favoured them with a smile and a gracious nod of her head.

'This gentleman is Mr Stanley Conway, and his daughter, Ruby. My sons, Sebastian, my eldest, and Rupert. Now do come and take a seat. Tea should be here in just a moment,' Lady Amelia said as she looked around as if expecting to see a tea trolley.

Kitty and Matt took a place on one of the rather lumpy sofas after greeting the other occupants of the room. Kitty was relieved to find Bertie sitting nicely, for once, at her feet. Sebastian and Rupert, having shaken hands with them, settled back down to their conversation with Ruby. It appeared to be a debate about cars and Kitty thought the girl looked bored rigid.

The drawing-room door opened once more, and the housekeeper entered wheeling a gilt trolley containing all the accoutrements for afternoon tea. Lady Amelia appeared to relax at its appearance, before immediately jumping back up to begin serving her guests and family.

Lady Sarah Faversham eyed her daughter-in-law disapprovingly and continued to converse with Mrs Craven while Lady Amelia dealt with her guests. Bertie sniffed the air hopefully when he realised the tea trolley contained a selection of biscuits as well as hot beverages.

Kitty accepted her cup of tea and gazed around the room with interest. Matt fed Bertie his biscuit. It felt rather odd being treated as a guest whilst also clearly being considered hired help. Albeit that they weren't being paid by the Favershams. They were simply providing an illusion of security to reassure the very wealthy Conways.

'I suppose you'll want to look around the place, check the locks and things after tea? Rather good of you both to assist this weekend. Peace of mind having someone keeping an eye on things.' Sir Henry smiled congenially at Matt.

'Yes, sir, I think that would be most helpful,' Matt said.

'I'll give you a rundown too on what I have with me that needs to be watched. I'm pleased to see you have a dog with you.' Mr Conway looked at Bertie. His expression was doubtful, as if thinking the cocker spaniel wasn't an obvious choice for a guard dog.

Bertie's floppy ears lifted slightly at the word dog, and he looked hopefully at Mr Conway in case another biscuit might be heading his way.

'Mrs Craven said that someone attempted a robbery a few weeks ago?' Kitty asked.

'Yes, while we were in London. Not here. An attempt was made to jimmy the safe in our hotel room. I usually keep most of Ruby's jewels at the bank, but we had been attending several evening engagements.'

'Did they manage to obtain anything, sir?' Matt asked.

'No, thank heaven. It was an amateurish attempt. Ruby's diamonds and a pearl necklace that used to belong to her mother were in the safe that night. We were very lucky,' Mr Conway said as he set his empty teacup and saucer down on a side table.

'I presume the police in London have not yet found the person responsible for the attempt?' Kitty asked.

Mr Conway shook his head. 'I suspect one of the hotel staff. Still, you never know. I'm mighty glad Lady Sarah offered to get you guys in as an extra precaution while we're here. Ruby has some expensive stuff to wear to the ball tomorrow night.'

'For now, everything is securely locked away in the safe in my study. I'll be happy to show you round the place afterwards.' Sir Henry beamed genially at Matt and Kitty.

Bertie sighed and lay back down at Kitty's feet when no more biscuits appeared. As soon as they had swallowed the last drop of their tea, Kitty, Bertie and Matt accompanied Sir Henry and Mr Conway to Sir Henry's study.

The study was located at the front of the house, just off the hallway on the opposite side to the drawing room. It was a small, square room with dark-red walls and an air of neglect. The battered mahogany desk was piled high with what seemed to be estate papers and a brass paperweight shaped like an eagle held down a stack of brown envelopes. Kitty wondered how many of those contained bills.

The safe was a large, green-metal old-fashioned type of the kind Kitty had often seen before. It was secured with a combination and a key and seemed robust. Sir Henry kept the key on his watch chain and assured them that there wasn't another one.

'Thank you, that all seems in order. Perhaps you could show us around the rest of the ground floor?' Matt suggested.

Kitty privately thought the state of the windows meant that breaking into the Hall would be quite easy should anyone wish to do so. She, Bertie and Matt, however, dutifully traipsed behind Sir Henry and Mr Conway. Sir Henry extolled the history of the Hall and his family ancestry as he showed them the entry points into the house.

Mr Conway appeared to be lapping up Sir Henry's tales of his lineage. She thought the locks on the doors leading out to the terrace and through the kitchen seemed poor and in bad shape.

Since there seemed to be very little of value within the Hall, she could understand why Sir Henry had not been overly worried about security at Markham. Every room they entered appeared to have spaces where something valuable might once have been placed. A sculpture, painting or china.

There were, however, more modern, abstract sculptures and pictures hanging on the faded wallpaper. All of which seemed to have been created by the same hand. They concluded the tour and finished back in the drawing room. Lady Amelia had disappeared and so had the younger of Sir Henry's sons.

Ruby was now seated by the fire and Sebastian was lounging near the gramophone in the corner.

'I trust Henry has shown you around the house?' Lady Sarah asked as they approached the fireside.

'Yes, thank you, my lady,' Matt said as he and Kitty retook their seats on the sofa. Bertie subsided at Kitty's feet and gave Mrs Craven a baleful look.

'Everything in order?' Lady Sarah looked at her son as if she suspected it may not have been.

'Yes, yes.' Sir Henry sounded irritated by his mother's question.

'Excellent. Amelia has gone back to her studio. Something about making the most of the light and the clay drying out.' Lady Sarah lifted her shoulders in a small shrug.

'I take it you noticed Lady Amelia's work while you were looking around?' Mrs Craven asked.

Kitty realised their hostess must have been the producer of the abstract artworks scattered throughout the ground floor.

'Yes, they all seemed most striking,' Kitty responded politely, while Sebastian seemed to be attempting to turn a snigger into a cough at her response.

'Are you interested in art, Miss Conway?' Kitty addressed the younger girl who had been staring into the laid-up fireplace as if in a world of her own.

'Oh, Ruby has always appreciated the arts. She's had lessons from some of the finest drawing masters and can play the piano like an angel,' her father promptly answered for her, his chest puffing up with pride.

Ruby merely gave a smile which didn't seem to reach her eyes.

'Sebastian is rather less appreciative of art.' Lady Sarah looked at her grandson who sauntered over to join them.

'Mother's art definitely,' Sebastian agreed as he dropped into one of the armchairs, spreading out his long legs before him. 'I mean, those paintings she does are ghastly.'

'You prefer a more traditional style?' Kitty asked.

'I like to recognise what they are supposed to be pictures of,' Sebastian said.

'Really, Seb.' His father tutted reprovingly.

'It's true. That picture she did of you last Christmas, Granny, you have three eyes,' Seb protested.

Ruby stifled a giggle, immediately stopping when she caught the disapproving look in her father's eye.

Kitty noticed that Mrs Craven said nothing, which was odd since she normally didn't hesitate to offer an opinion.

'I'll admit it is an unusual piece.' Lady Sarah glared at her grandson. 'I think, however, your mother is making strides in her work.'

'I think you may need to get glasses, Gran,' Sebastian observed affectionately. He jumped back up again from his seat. 'Well, I suppose I should make a move.'

Lady Sarah looked at the china ormolu clock on the mantelpiece. 'Yes, we should start to get ready for dinner soon.'

Kitty remained seated next to Matt as the rest of the group drifted out of the drawing room and headed for the stairs.

'We need to find which room we have been allocated,' Kitty said.

'Hmm, we also need to try to talk to some of the staff about Agnes,' Matt agreed.

'I haven't seen a butler, so I suspect Mrs Putnam, the housekeeper, is fully in charge of the staff.' Kitty guessed that Markham probably retained only a small number of permanent staff. The signs of neglectful housekeeping had been visible in every room Sir Henry had shown them. It seemed Mrs Craven had not exaggerated when she had said the Favershams were in dire financial straits.

'Dora told you that Mrs Putnam hadn't been helpful when she spoke to her and she didn't seem terribly welcoming when we arrived,' Matt said.

'True, we shall have to be careful how we approach the

subject of Agnes.' Kitty rose from the sofa, while Bertie stretched and yawned ready to follow her. Matt chuckled and stood.

Mrs Putnam was passing through the hall as they left the drawing room.

'Excuse me, could you direct us to our room, please?' Kitty asked before the housekeeper could disappear into the dining room.

Mrs Putnam halted. 'Third door on the left as you go up the stairs. The hot water is unreliable so please do not overfill the bath. Your bags are in your room.'

Before they could say anything else, she hurried off.

Kitty exchanged a glance with Matt. 'Goodness, it seems this weekend will be fun.' She smiled at her husband, and they headed upstairs together.

CHAPTER FOUR

Given the housekeeper's demeanour, Kitty was quite apprehensive about what they might find when they reached their room. She couldn't help but feel a little relieved to discover they had been allocated a light, pleasant room with faded rose-pink curtains and shabby but clean furnishings.

The room overlooked the front of the house, offering a view of the terrace below and the untidy lawn with its abandoned croquet hoops. The sash window had been left open to air the room out. Despite this, Kitty's sensitive nose detected a slight odour of damp.

Their trunk had at least been unpacked and their evening attire hung up. Bertie had a long drink from the bowl of water which had been placed for him near the unlit fireplace. He then settled down with a sigh on the worn tapestry-patterned hearthrug.

'They seem to be very short of staff,' Kitty observed as she moved away from the window to perch herself on the edge of the bed. 'I've only seen the housekeeper since we arrived.'

Matt was busying himself arranging his shaving things beside the old-fashioned flower-printed jug and bowl which stood on a walnut stand near the dresser. 'Yes, Agnes's absence would have been felt. It's not as if they have other people to fill her post from what we've seen so far.'

'You would think then that they would have been more concerned about her leaving.' Kitty frowned.

'It does all seem very odd,' Matt agreed. 'Let's see what happens at dinner and if we can find out who else might be around.'

They had scarcely finished changing for dinner when there was the faint sound of a furtive tap on their bedroom door. Bertie let out a small protest woof at the disturbance to his pre-dinner nap as Kitty went to see who was there.

She hardly had a chance to open the door before Mrs Craven, resplendent in a dark-pink chiffon gown with grey feathers in her hair, barrelled into their room, closing the door behind her.

'I thought I had better come and see you to review our findings before dinner.' Mrs Craven cast a disparaging glance around the room.

Matt finished adjusting his bow tie in the mottled glass of the dressing-table mirror. 'Splendid idea, Mrs C. What have you discovered so far?' he asked.

Kitty gave him a hard stare.

'Well, I was going to bring Dora with me as my maid but then I thought it might antagonise the housekeeper. I also didn't wish to upset Lady Sarah. She may take our probing as criticism of how the house is run. Not to mention running the risk of Dora becoming distressed and possibly causing a scene.' Mrs Craven ran her forefinger across the top of the mantelpiece and frowned at the thin layer of dust.

Kitty continued to place items inside her small gold evening bag. 'And have you discovered anything more about Agnes's departure since you arrived?'

'You must have noticed the state of this place? I hadn't

realised until I got here that poor Lady Sarah has been forced to move here too since the dower house needs urgent repairs to the roof. I had thought she was still in her own home. They seem to have let a great deal of the staff go, but Agnes was not one of them.' Mrs Craven gave them a meaningful look.

'They clearly valued her work. Perhaps, however, the increased workload was not to her taste. I doubt they increased her wages if they were trying to save money,' Kitty said.

'Have you mentioned Agnes at all to either Lady Sarah or any of the staff?' Matt asked as he turned away from the mirror.

'Obviously, I apologised to Lady Sarah for Agnes's behaviour in leaving in such an impolite way. She seemed quite disappointed, but I wouldn't expect her to know what was going on with a maidservant. The staff are managed by Mrs Putnam,' Mrs Craven said.

'What about the rest of the staff? Have you spoken to any of them yet?' Kitty asked as she closed the clasp on her bag.

'I have not broached the matter with Mrs Putnam. In fact, the woman is so bad-tempered one hardly dare ask her anything. I shall leave that to you. I haven't yet seen anyone else about the house. No other servants at all. What have you discovered?' Mrs Craven gave them an eager look.

'We have only been here a few hours,' Kitty pointed out.

'We shall see what transpires this evening. Have you requested Agnes's trunk to take it back to Dartmouth with you?' Matt asked.

'I did mention it to Mrs Putnam when I arrived. She said she would see that it was put ready in my room by the time I was due to leave.' Mrs Craven gave an eloquent shrug of her shoulders and Kitty guessed the housekeeper had not been overly helpful. 'She said it had been packed.'

'I wonder who by?' Kitty mused.

'I suppose by one of the staff,' Mrs Craven responded dismissively.

'We really should go downstairs. I can hear voices outside, so I presume everyone has gone to the terrace for pre-dinner drinks,' Matt said.

Kitty peeped through the window and saw he was right. 'Goodness, yes.' She followed her husband and Mrs Craven out of the room. She hoped Mrs Craven was not going to make a habit of barging into their bedroom over the weekend. There didn't appear to be a lock on the door she noticed as she closed it behind her. She might have to resort to wedging a chair under the handle to secure it should Mrs Craven visit again.

* * *

Matt escorted Mrs Craven downstairs, leaving Kitty to follow behind and Bertie to continue his nap by the bedroom fireplace. Once they had gone through the drawing room and out of the French doors, he saw that Mrs Craven was seated before returning to Kitty.

'I hope Mrs Craven is not intending to make more clandestine calls upon us. That would start tongues wagging,' Matt observed with a grin as he rejoined Kitty where she was standing beside the balustrade.

The drinks trolley had been brought out onto the terrace, and it appeared that Rupert, the younger son of their host, was in charge of drinks.

'What can I get for you both?' Rupert asked as they approached the trolley. 'Martini? Sherry? Something more exotic, perhaps? I'm a whizz with the shaker.' He suited his words to his actions, jiggling the chrome cocktail shaker to make the ice inside rattle.

'A negroni would be marvellous,' Kitty said with a smile.

'Me too,' Matt concurred.

Rupert grinned at them. 'My kind of people.' He mixed the ingredients and poured them into the glasses with a flourish.

Matt glanced around the terrace. A few rattan tables and chairs had been placed outside along with an assortment of colourful cushions. An elderly looking man in a flat cap seemed to be begrudgingly tackling the overgrown shrubbery at the side of the lawn with an antique pair of shears.

'Big day for your family tomorrow,' Matt said as he picked up his drink. He noticed Ruby Conway sitting at a table with her future mother-in-law. Lady Amelia had changed into an old-fashioned shapeless silk frock in jade green. Ruby was dressed in an unflattering shade of dark-purple silk in a much more modern style.

'Yes, I suppose so.' Rupert glanced at Sebastian who was standing apart from everyone smoking a cigarette as he gazed out over the parkland.

'Ruby seems to be a very pleasant girl,' Kitty said.

Matt guessed his wife probably felt a little sorry for the girl who was clearly being bartered into marriage by her father. His money in exchange for a title and some social standing for himself and Ruby.

Rupert flicked a glance in Ruby's direction. 'Yes, she seems jolly nice. She'll have to be to put up with Seb.'

He smiled as he spoke, but Matt wondered if he was telling the truth rather than merely poking mild fun at his older brother. There had been something in his tone which hinted at more than the usual sibling rivalry.

'The marriage will be good for the estate I expect,' Kitty said as she sipped her drink. Her blue-grey eyes fixed guilelessly on Rupert's handsome face.

'The money will be a godsend. It's no good pretending. Everyone knows this isn't exactly a love match.' Rupert looked back at Ruby and swallowed his drink. 'Still, I'm sure everything will work out splendidly and there will be more little Favershams running around to inherit this place before we know it.'

Ruby seemed to overhear the tail end of Rupert's comments, and a dark-red flush appeared along her cheekbones. Mr Conway and Sir Henry appeared on the terrace looking very pleased with themselves and went to join Lady Amelia and Ruby.

Rupert sighed. 'Looks like they've signed all the papers for the marriage. I suppose I had better see what they want to drink. Do excuse me.' He strolled over to his parents' table.

Kitty and Matt took a seat nearby where they could observe everyone.

'Sebastian, do stop moping about and attend to your bride-to-be,' Lady Sarah admonished her grandson in a sharp whisper.

Sebastian extinguished his cigarette and dutifully obeyed. Lady Sarah returned to her conversation with Mrs Craven with a satisfied air.

Matt looked at Kitty who was clearly shamelessly eaves-dropping and he smiled to himself. It was certainly a very inter-esting situation to be in. He wondered how many people would be coming to the engagement ball the next day and how the Favershams were going to manage it all.

Mrs Putnam appeared through the French doors and announced that dinner was ready to be served. Sir Henry escorted his wife, and the rest of the group followed as they returned inside the house to take their places in the dining room.

The dining table was dressed in pale-pink linen with a centrepiece of early roses and lavender which perfumed the air as they sat down ready to be served. The silver plate had been polished and candles lit to add ambience to the occasion.

The light outside was starting to fade now and the golden light of the evening spread a mellow glow around the room. Ruby had been placed between Sebastian and her father. Matt had Kitty on his one side and Mrs Craven on his other side.

A very young girl dressed in an ill-fitting black dress and

overly large white apron and cap began to serve the soup under Mrs Putnam's watchful eye. Matt was quite hungry now since they had eaten an early lunch and there had only been biscuits served with afternoon tea.

The first course appeared to be French onion soup and smelled delicious. The Favershams might have no money, but they seemed to have a good cook if the first course was anything to go by.

He wondered if the young maid was Agnes's replacement or a girl they had promoted to take her place. It would be interesting to try to talk to her to see if she knew anything about the missing maid.

Conversation around the table was centred upon the ball and on arrangements for the wedding.

'It will be so lovely to have a wedding here at the estate. It's been far too long since we had something to celebrate,' Lady Sarah said as the maid collected up the now empty soup dishes.

'Oh yes, it will be simply super. Will you have many bridesmaids, Ruby, dear?' Lady Amelia asked as the second course began to be served.

'I'm not certain. Only possibly my one friend,' Ruby said.

'A nice quiet wedding. Classy, although it would be nice to have it at the cathedral in Exeter,' her father interjected.

'I think that may be too short notice,' Lady Sarah said firmly. 'The parish church is very old and has always been the venue for family weddings. I believe you wanted June as a date?'

June was not far away, and Matt thought the Favershams having secured Ruby's engagement did not want to give the girl a chance to back out before the wedding.

'A lovely time of year and so nice for the flowers, of course, for the bouquet and the church.' Mrs Craven added her voice to the discussion.

Matt noticed the groom was silent during the debate, as

indeed was the bride-to-be. Both of them appeared content to let their parents make all the decisions.

'Will you take a honeymoon?' Mrs Craven asked as she added mint sauce to the cutlets of spring lamb on her plate.

Ruby raised startled eyes in Sebastian's direction before dropping her gaze almost immediately.

'We haven't discussed a honeymoon. A holiday might be quite jolly. Is there some place you would care to go, Ruby?' Sebastian asked.

'Ruby has travelled extensively since she was a girl,' Mr Conway, as usual, butted in before his daughter could speak.

'Ruby?' Rupert asked this time.

'I've always wanted to travel to Egypt to see the pyramids,' Ruby said. 'Ever since I was a girl, I've always found them fascinating. So old, and Mr Carter's discoveries looked so amazing.'

Her father glowered at her from across the table. Matt surmised that he didn't share his daughter's interests in antiquity.

'Then, perhaps, that's where we should go. Maybe a Nile cruise,' Sebastian said. He was rewarded by a small smile from his new fiancée.

The lamb and spring vegetables were followed by strawberries and ice cream. Lady Sarah took great pride in explaining they were a special early variety grown on the estate. It seemed that much of the produce was grown in a small walled garden at the rear of the house.

The ladies withdrew back to the drawing room for coffee as Mrs Putnam carried in port and cheese for the gentlemen in the dining room. Sir Henry poured generous glasses and handed them around, while Mr Conway cut into the Stilton on the cheeseboard.

Once the housekeeper had gone, Sir Henry clapped his eldest son on his shoulder. 'Well, my boy, looking forward to tomorrow? Your grandmother has the ring all ready now that it's been resized.'

Matt assumed from this comment that Sebastian was giving his bride-to-be a family engagement ring.

'I've no doubt that everything is organised.' Sebastian was noncommittal and didn't seem to have great enthusiasm in his voice. Matt guessed that Ruby was not the bride he would have chosen for himself if money had not been such a large part of the equation.

Rupert merely raised his eyebrows and refrained from commenting.

* * *

Kitty was seated with the ladies back in the drawing room. The young maid had wheeled in the trolley containing the coffee cups and a selection of tiny, sweet pastries. She found herself sitting beside Ruby as the older ladies congregated together to discuss wedding arrangements.

'How are you liking this part of Devon?' Kitty asked once Ruby was seated.

The girl shrugged. 'It looked very pretty when we arrived. I studied it on a map when Father first said we were coming here. It's much different from London or Chicago. The moors sound very picturesque.'

'Perhaps you should get Sebastian to take you out for the day, have a picnic,' Kitty suggested.

Ruby smiled. 'Maybe. I don't really know what he would like to do.'

'Well, you have time to get to know each other better before the wedding,' Kitty said.

Ruby sighed. 'Not that much time.' She glanced over at the other women who were deciding on the flowers for the church.

'You can pull out of this arrangement if it makes you unhappy,' Kitty said in a low voice.

Ruby blinked and looked startled by the suggestion.

'I'm sorry. I don't mean to offend you,' Kitty added quickly.

'I'm not offended, Mrs Bryant. I love my father and want him to be happy. My money will always make me an object of interest to fortune hunters. I'm pragmatic enough to know that I'm no great beauty so there will always be a transactional element in any relationship. This way it's all upfront. Father has ensured the money, while benefiting Markham, will remain under my control. Once married I will have more say over my own life than I have ever had. Sebastian and I like one another well enough too. So, you see, it's not such a terrible exchange.' The girl smiled.

'At least your husband-to-be is good looking too,' Kitty agreed, and Ruby giggled.

Lady Sarah gave them a sharp, suspicious look and Kitty and Ruby returned to demurely sipping their coffee.

CHAPTER FIVE

The evening passed quite pleasantly but provided no further opportunity to discover what may have become of Agnes. The young maid removed the coffee things and promptly vanished and they saw nothing more of Mrs Putnam.

Matt went upstairs to check on Bertie and to take him out and discovered a dish which may have contained meat scraps had appeared next to the dog's water bowl. Bertie had licked it clean and Kitty was frustrated that she had missed an opportunity to visit the kitchen to talk to the staff. She was, however, very grateful that Bertie had been considered.

Kitty rose early the next morning, determined to try to talk to whichever of the staff she could find about Agnes. While the house was quiet she hoped for an opportunity to snoop. She dressed swiftly and took Bertie downstairs, leaving Matt to take his leisure with preparing for the day.

To her surprise, despite the early hour, the household was already quite busy. Mrs Putnam was in the ballroom supervising a team of what seemed to be gardeners and cleaners preparing the vast, empty space for the evening's festivities.

Chairs and pot plants were being unloaded from a large lorry and carried inside the room.

Matt and Kitty had only had a quick glimpse inside the room the previous evening when Sir Henry and Mr Conway had escorted them around the house. Then the great gilt-framed mirrors had been shrouded in dust sheets. The glass-paned doors which opened out onto the other side of the terrace had been shuttered, leaving the room in darkness.

Now, the shutters were open, the glass was being cleaned, the dust sheets removed and the wood-sprung floor swept. A piano tuner was at work on the grand piano. Kitty could see that she and Bertie would only hinder the workers by their presence. Besides which, she could tell these were unlikely to be permanent staff at the Hall but simply people employed to prepare the house for the ball.

She slipped outside through one of the open French doors and allowed Bertie to go meandering off along the terrace. The morning air was cool and fresh with the promise of a fine day ahead. Dew sparkled on the tall white heads of the daisies which lined the ground below the stone balustrade mingling with the early roses.

The gardener from the previous evening was now hard at work on the overgrown lawn and Kitty could smell the fresh-cut grass. A young lad of about fourteen assisted him as he worked, following with a rake and a wheelbarrow. Bertie romped happily around the border until Kitty called him to return inside the house.

She went back in through the other set of French doors into the drawing room. To her delight she discovered the young maid from the previous evening dusting and tidying the room. Flustered by Kitty and Bertie's unexpected appearance through the French doors the girl dropped the pile of magazines she had been collecting, scattering them across the floor.

'Here, do let me help you.' Kitty hurried forward to begin picking them up. 'That was my fault, I startled you.'

Bertie sniffed interestedly at the girl's shoes as she bent to gather the papers. 'Oh no, madam. I was in a hurry and got a bit clumsy.'

Kitty guessed the girl to be about fifteen, with dark curly hair and a smattering of freckles across a snub nose. She had a local accent and was clearly not very experienced.

'Here you are.' Kitty stacked the magazines neatly on top of a small rosewood side table. 'I'm Kitty Bryant, by the way, and this is Bertie.' She indicated her dog who was now eyeing the girl's feather duster with rather too much interest.

'I'm Tilly, pleased to meet you. I had best get on or Mrs Putnam will be after me.' The girl cast a fearful glance towards the drawing-room door.

'Did you know another girl who was working here as a maid? Agnes Jones?' Kitty asked. She was determined to try to discover something before the girl vanished into the kitchens ready to serve breakfast.

Tilly nodded. 'I shared a room with her before she left. She was kind to me, gave me one of her ribbons for my Sunday hat. I wish I knew where she went.'

'Did she say where she was going? Or if she had any notion of leaving her post?' Kitty asked as Tilly started to edge towards the door.

Tilly shook her head causing the pins holding on her neat white cap to slip. 'No, madam, she just went. She was here of the lunchtime but I didn't see her after that. She never did any of the evening jobs that day and she didn't come to her bed. I didn't know what to do. I thought p'raps as how she might have been called home urgent like or something. Then the next mornin', Mrs Putnam asked me where she was and if she had come back. Mrs Putnam were cross as she hadn't worked the evening to help with dinner and everything. Especially with having Mr and Miss Conway here for a visit. No one had seen her, not me nor Mrs Gray, the cook, nobody. She hadn't packed any of her things or left a note.'

'I see. Do you know if she had a boyfriend at all? Her sister, Dora, is very worried about her,' Kitty explained.

Tilly frowned. 'She never mentioned as she was courting but she seemed to have a bit more money the last few weeks before she left. I saw her counting it into her purse the one night after she thought as I was asleep.'

'Thank you, Tilly.'

The drawing-room door opened and Mrs Putnam appeared. 'Tilly, do stop dawdling and get to the kitchen.' She glared at the girl who blushed and scurried from the room.

The housekeeper was about to follow the maid when Kitty spoke up. 'Mrs Putnam, I wonder if I might have a quick word with you?'

For a moment Kitty thought the housekeeper was about to refuse.

'Of course, Mrs Bryant, but I am extremely busy today.' Mrs Putnam looked pointedly at the clock on the mantelpiece.

'Thank you. I will be quick. I want to ask you about a member of staff, one of the maids. Agnes Jones's sister, Dora, is very concerned about her. She has not heard anything at all from Agnes since the day she disappeared a month ago. She asked me to try to discover what may have happened to her. I know she has telephoned you on the matter.' Kitty saw no point in beating about the bush.

'Agnes walked out on her position. She left no message or note, no word of warning to any member of the household. We all naturally assumed she must have met someone. However, we have heard nothing from her. I recently had Tilly pack up her things as Mrs Craven intends to transport them to Agnes's sister. I'm afraid that's all I can tell you.' Mrs Putnam placed her hand on the door handle ready to leave.

'You haven't informed the police that she is missing?' Kitty asked.

Mrs Putnam pursed up her mouth at the mention of the police. 'Certainly not. I daresay the girl is off frolicking somewhere without a care in the world with some boyfriend or other. There seems no reason to involve the police in a respectable house. It wouldn't be my place to do such a thing.' She whisked her way out of the room before Kitty could ask anything else.

'Well really!' Kitty looked at Bertie who had his nose in the air sniffing the delectable aroma of sausages which was now drifting along the hallway from the direction of the dining room. He looked expectantly at Kitty.

'Very well, let's see if Matt is dressed.' Kitty rubbed the top of her dog's head affectionately and went out into the hall just as Matt was coming down the stairs.

'We were just coming to get you,' Kitty said.

'Did you find anyone to speak to about Agnes?' Matt asked as he kissed her cheek and greeted Bertie.

'Yes, but no one knows anything. They didn't inform the police or take any kind of action to try to find the girl,' Kitty explained as they walked towards the dining room.

There was no one else downstairs so they helped themselves to bacon, sausages, eggs and mushrooms from the metal-covered dishes which were set up on the sideboard. Kitty cut up several sausages and some egg for Bertie and slipped the plate under her chair.

'Tilly didn't know of a boyfriend but thought Agnes had come into some money,' Matt repeated when Kitty told him exactly what the young girl had said.

'A gift, perhaps, from an admirer or a win of some kind?' Kitty suggested.

Matt frowned as he ate his bacon. 'Or blackmail.' He looked at Kitty.

She set down her cutlery and pushed her plate away. 'I hope that's not the case. I feel that we do need to speak to the police about this if we don't find any clues to where she may have gone before we leave.'

'I agree. We have to avoid derailing the engagement party, however, so it gives us until Sunday to try to determine if something untoward has become of the girl.' Matt finished his breakfast and wiped the corners of his mouth with his napkin.

'That's not much time,' Kitty said. 'Today and part of tomorrow to try to discover what has happened to her.'

Lady Amelia entered the dining room as Kitty finished speaking and smiled vaguely at them. She was wearing the brown clay-and-paint-splattered smock she had worn the previous afternoon. 'Good morning. Isn't it the most marvellous day? I'm hoping to get an hour or two in at my studio before I have to start preparing for the ball.' She helped herself to eggs and took a seat at the table.

'Everyone seems very busy,' Kitty agreed. 'Is there anything we can do at all to assist?'

'Oh, that's frightfully sweet of you but Mrs Putnam has it all in hand, isn't that right, Mrs Putnam?' Lady Amelia said as the housekeeper carried in more toast and hot water for tea.

'Yes, my lady.' The housekeeper glared at Kitty before leaving again.

'Such a treasure. She and her sister, Mrs Gray, our cook. I don't know where we'd be without them,' Lady Amelia said.

Kitty's ears pricked up at this new nugget of information. She had been unaware that the cook and the housekeeper were related.

'It's such a shame that the maid, Agnes Jones, left. I understand from Mrs Craven that she was a good worker,' Kitty remarked as she added more hot water to the china teapot. 'It must have made a lot more work for the rest of your staff.'

Lady Amelia looked a little startled. 'What, oh yes, Agnes, a pretty girl. I think she went off with some boyfriend. These young girls can be rather reckless in that way.'

'Her sister, Dora, is very worried about her. She hasn't heard from her since she left,' Kitty said.

Lady Amelia looked puzzled. 'You know the family?'

'Yes, Mrs Craven recommended Agnes for this post, she is Dora's employer,' Kitty explained.

Lady Amelia appeared discomfited by this reminder. 'I had forgotten. My mother-in-law still deals with much of the organisation of the staff. Her and Mrs Putnam. It was never really my forte and Henry, of course, is much too busy managing the estate.'

'I suppose he must be. Still, I expect Sebastian and Rupert must be a great help to him,' Matt said as he helped himself to a slice of toast.

'Sebastian will inherit the estate so is learning all about the management of everything. Rupert will go into the army I expect, once he finishes at university,' Lady Amelia explained in a vague tone. 'It will be such a comfort having Sebastian married and settled here. Ruby is such a sweet, shy little thing. I think she must favour her mother in her nature.'

Kitty hid a smile. Certainly no one could think the rather loud Mr Conway was shy. 'She does seem a delightful young lady,' she agreed.

'My mother-in-law has had the family ring resized and cleaned ready for Sebastian to present to Ruby this evening. It's rather a nice ring, diamond cluster with a sapphire centre.' Lady Amelia smiled happily at them.

'Are many people coming this evening?' Matt asked.

'Around eighty, I believe. My mother-in-law and Henry have seen to the invitations with some of Sebastian and Rupert's friends coming too. Most of them are staying with the Boothes at Longchamps Manor. They have significantly more rooms than we do and are closer to the station for those who have come from London.' Lady Amelia didn't say so, but Kitty guessed the Favershams could not afford to host that number of guests.

'It sounds as if it will be a most joyful event,' Matt said politely.

Sebastian and Rupert arrived for breakfast and the conversation continued about arrangements for the evening. Kitty and Matt excused themselves and took Bertie outside once more.

The gardener was still hard at work on the large expanse of lawn. Before Kitty could stop him, Bertie decided some freshly mown grass would be perfect to romp and roll about on. The gardener's boy looked on as bits of grass flew everywhere.

'Bertie!' Kitty hurried down the shallow flight of three stone steps onto the lawn.

'Stay here, I'll get him,' Matt assured her and strode off after the naughty spaniel.

Kitty watched from the foot of the steps as Bertie danced around the lawn attempting to avoid both Matt, the gardener and the gardener's boy's attempts to capture him.

* * *

After a minute Matt and the gardener cornered the playful dog between the stone wall and the garden roller. Matt snatched up his dog's lead while an unrepentant Bertie shook grass clippings from his fur.

'He's a lively one,' the gardener remarked as Matt brushed bits of grass from the legs of his pale-grey flannel trousers.

'He is rather. I'm sorry about that.' Matt looked around the lawn. 'You have your work cut out here. It's a lot for one man. Lady Sarah said you have the walled garden to tend to as well.'

The gardener scratched his head and pushed his battered

flat cap further up from his brow. ''Tis that, sir. We used to have four full-time gardeners. Now it's just me and the lad there. Still, we can only hope as once Mr Sebastian is wed then we might see some more staff back on the estate.'

'Yes, we noticed that the house seemed short-staffed. I don't suppose you knew one of the maids who was working here? A girl called Agnes Jones, we know her sister, Dora, and she's quite worried about her,' Matt said.

'Yes, I know young Aggie. 'Tis right funny how she just went off without saying anything to anyone.' The man frowned.

'You don't know of a boyfriend or anywhere she may have gone?' Matt asked as Bertie sniffed at the garden roller.

'No, I saw her the day she left. She'd been a bit full of herself for a couple of days beforehand. Smiling a lot and looking pleased with herself. She had a row with Mrs Putnam the morning she went. I don't know what about. I seen her of the lunchtime and she seemed all right, so I didn't think much of it. Last time I seen her she was walking away on the path over yonder towards the woods. She would often step out for an hour on an afternoon if she could get away with it.' The gardener glanced in the direction of the area where Matt and Kitty had seen the deer the day before.

'And no one here has heard from her since that day?' Kitty asked as she came to join Matt on the lawn.

'No, not so far as I know. I thought as she'd gone home to her sister. I didn't realise as her sister hadn't heard from her neither.' The gardener looked troubled.

'Where does the path Agnes was taking lead to?' Matt asked.

'It all depends where you'm wanting to go. You can go down to the bus stop on the lane or walk on into the woods. There's the lake, the family mausoleum and the icehouse down there on different paths.' The gardener indicated towards the woods with a green-stained hand.

'Thank you,' Kitty said as she tucked her hand in the crook of Matt's arm.

'I take it we are going for a stroll in the woods?' Matt asked with a grin as Bertie trotted happily alongside them as they walked away from the gardener. He knew Kitty would be itching to take a look for herself to see what they could find in the woods.

She smiled up at him. 'Of course. It is the most delightful morning for a walk.'

Matt chuckled and they set off in the direction indicated by the gardener. They left the lawn by a smaller flight of steps. This took them through a small metal kissing gate at the side of the ha-ha, which was designed to prevent the deer from entering the formal gardens.

The grass now was taller and wilder, sprinkled with purple-pink clover, white daisies and yellow buttercups. The scent of the wild garlic in the woods was stronger. A trail seemed to lead through into the cooler shade of the trees. The deer had melted away as if by magic once they heard them approaching.

Bertie sniffed at the clumps of green bracken and acquired a stick which he carried in his mouth. His snuffling startled a grey squirrel which scampered swiftly up a nearby tree and chittered crossly at them as they passed by.

After a few minutes strolling in the dappled shade of the trees they arrived at a fork in the path. One direction seemed to Matt to run parallel with the lane they had driven in on and he guessed that would lead to the bus stop. The other path seemed to go down towards a body of water he could see shimmering through the trees.

'To the bus stop or down to the lake?' he asked, looking at Kitty.

Kitty frowned as she looked around. 'I would like to go to the lake and see if we can find the buildings the gardener mentioned. I suppose though we ought to at least investigate the bus stop first. After all, Agnes could have simply got on the bus and left.'

Matt nodded. 'The stop can't be far away. Although why would she have gone in her uniform without changing first, and left all her things behind?'

Kitty's pretty face was troubled. 'I don't know, but it is a possibility we need to check, however unlikely we think it might be.'

CHAPTER SIX

Kitty discovered the woods started to thin as they drew closer to the drystone wall bordering the lane. The trees were further apart and interspersed with rhododendron bushes, bluebells, wild garlic and bracken. The road was quiet with no traffic, and she could hear the birds singing in the woods.

After a minute or two they reached an old wooden stile which led out onto the side of the road. A metal post signifying a bus stop was attached to a stone shelter with a pantiled roof. Inside the bus shelter a tattered, sun-faded timetable was pinned to a board.

Matt extended his hand to assist Kitty over the stile, before he then lifted Bertie over.

'Where does the bus run to?' Kitty asked as she smoothed down the cherry-print fabric of her cotton summer dress.

Matt had hold of Bertie's lead and was busy studying the timetable. 'It looks as if the bus runs every hour and goes from Bovey Tracey and on to Ashburton. There are lots of other stops along the way. It seems to call all around the hamlets.'

'I presume that there is a bus from Bovey Tracey and Ashburton that then goes to Exeter and links with other routes.

If Agnes did take the bus, she could go on to catch a train or travel further. Surely though she would have changed from her uniform first if she planned to leave.' Kitty could see there was another bus stop virtually opposite which she presumed carried passengers going in the other direction.

'There may be a regular driver on the route. They would have noticed a girl wearing a maid's uniform boarding the bus,' Matt said.

Kitty nodded in agreement. 'It seems we may be able to find out. There is a bus approaching the stop now.'

Matt turned around and they waited for the bus to rumble to a halt. Only one passenger was on board, an elderly woman clutching a large wicker shopping basket.

'Excuse me, is this the bus to Bovey Tracey?' Matt asked the driver as he leaned into the open window of the bus.

'That's right, sir. You wantin' a ticket?' The driver looked at Kitty and Bertie who were standing back.

'No, not today. I wondered if you recalled picking up a young woman in a maid's uniform from this stop a few weeks ago in the afternoon?' Matt asked.

The driver frowned. 'No, can't say as I ever did and I allus have this run. Now, are you travelling or not? Only I have to get on,' the driver asked.

'No, but thank you for your assistance.' Matt stepped away and rejoined Kitty on the grass verge beside the stop as the bus continued on its way leaving a trail of dust in its wake.

'It seems that wherever Agnes went that day it didn't involve the bus. I suppose someone could have collected her from here in a motor car? They could have made arrangements so she wouldn't be seen leaving the Hall,' Kitty mused as Matt helped her back over the stile into the woods.

Matt passed Bertie's lead to her as he lowered the wriggling spaniel onto the path beside her before clambering over himself. 'A private motor car, you mean? It's a possibility but why wouldn't she have packed her things if it was prearranged that she was leaving? They could have driven to Markham to collect her and her things. Why just stroll off in her uniform with no note or message to say she was going?'

Kitty knew he was right. It looked increasingly likely that something bad had happened to Agnes that afternoon. A shiver ran along her spine as they left the bright sunshine to walk deeper into the green shade of the wood.

'We had better go back to the house. We can come down here again after lunch, but I think we need to be seen doing some work checking the security of tonight's arrangements and it will be lunchtime in less than an hour,' Matt said when they reached the fork in the path.

Kitty glanced down through the trees. In the distance the waters of the lake shimmered blue and enticing under the sun, and she reluctantly agreed. Matt was right, they needed to keep the Favershams happy if they were to discover what had become of Agnes. They also needed to keep an eye on Mrs Craven, Kitty thought wryly. Left to her own devices heaven only knew what the woman might say or do.

They walked through the wood back to the house. The gardener and his assistant had finished the lawn, leaving it in a much tidier state. Bertie trotted ahead on his lead as they crossed the grass towards the stone steps between the rose bushes and daisies. Sir Henry Faversham was engaged in supervising his sons and the hired staff as they set out more tables and chairs on the terrace.

Lady Sarah Faversham watched disapprovingly alongside Mrs Craven from their seats beneath a large ancient parasol at the far end.

'Rupert, put your back into it, boy,' Sir Henry barked as Kitty and Matt walked up the steps.

'These things are bally heavy, and Seb isn't doing his part.'

Rupert, red-faced and with rolled-up shirtsleeves, scowled at his father and his older brother.

'Well just get it done. It needs to be finished before lunch. Your mother is supposed to be supervising the arrangements in the ballroom, but I expect she's disappeared off to that confounded studio of hers again.' Sir Henry looked most unhappy.

Lady Sarah rolled her eyes. 'Don't worry, Henry, Mrs Putnam is taking care of everything. Millicent and I shall take over there after lunch. Frankly, Amelia is better off out of the way, she will only keep changing her mind on everything.' She muttered the last sentence in a much lower tone.

Kitty and Matt went to join Mrs Craven and Lady Sarah, not wishing to impede Sir Henry and his sons. Bertie flopped down under the table in the shade and immediately fell asleep.

'How are things going?' Kitty asked as she watched Sebastian and Rupert manoeuvre a rattan sofa into place with Sir Henry continuing to bellow instructions.

'About as well as one could expect,' Lady Sarah said with a sigh as the hired staff arrived with a bundle of cushions. 'At least the moths and the mice don't seem to have damaged the garden furniture. It's forecast to be very warm this evening, guests will probably wish to come outside for air. I thought we should get the furniture out of storage.'

Kitty thought she was probably right, and it would be pleasant to sit under the moonlight with a drink. If it were not for the worry over the missing maid, she would have been quite looking forward to the engagement ball.

Matt excused himself and roused Bertie to take the dog to get some water. Kitty guessed her husband also intended to check on the safe in the study and to see that everything appeared in order before any guests arrived.

Ruby Conway came out onto the terrace wearing a somewhat unflattering shade of pale-lemon silk. She had a large-brimmed straw hat to shield her from the sun.

'Oh dear, the engagement seems to have caused a great deal of work,' the girl said as she took the seat recently vacated by Matt. She winced as her future father-in-law shouted at her fiancé over the placement of a table.

'Nonsense, my dear. You are marrying into a great estate with a good deal of history. It's only right that the proper notice and attention is given to your engagement,' Mrs Craven assured her, drawing a nod of approval from Lady Sarah.

Ruby gave a weak smile, her gaze resting on her future husband and his brother sweating in the midday heat.

'Is your father not joining us?' Mrs Craven asked.

'No, Pa is working on some papers that arrived for him. Business things. He is using Sir Henry's study.' Ruby looked downcast, and Kitty assumed the girl's father was often consumed by his work.

Sebastian and Rupert disappeared inside the house while Sir Henry came to sit with them, fanning his crimson face with his panama hat. 'That looks better. Nice to offer guests a place to sit when the weather is so warm.' He beamed genially at Ruby. 'Are you looking forward to tonight, my dear?'

'I'm sure everything will be lovely,' Ruby responded in a meek tone.

Sir Henry seemed satisfied with this somewhat lukewarm and evasive answer and the conversation turned to the music and arrangements in the ballroom.

Kitty noticed that Ruby took no part in the chatter, merely smiling and nodding if anyone sought her opinion. The gong for lunch sounded a few minutes later and Sir Henry gallantly offered his arm to his mother to escort her to the dining room. Mrs Craven followed, while Kitty fell into step beside Ruby.

'Are you all right about this evening?' Kitty murmured once she was certain Mrs Craven was unlikely to overhear her.

'I'm just a little nervous. I don't like being the centre of attention,' Ruby confessed.

Kitty squeezed the girl's arm in a gesture of reassurance. 'If it feels a bit much, just look for me and I'll be a friendly face to support you,' she offered.

Ruby smiled at her and the girl's face changed. 'Thank you, Kitty, that means a good deal to me.'

They took their places at the lunch table. Matt slipped into his seat beside Kitty. 'I've left Bertie in our room for now. It's nice and cool in there.'

Lady Amelia arrived for lunch just as the first course was being placed on the table. Her brown artist's smock was gone but there was a faint telltale smudge of blue paint on her cheek. Sir Henry glared at her and Lady Sarah made a faint tutting noise as she shook out her linen napkin.

'Where did you and Kitty walk to this morning, Matthew?' Mrs Craven asked as she ate her watercress soup.

'We went through the woods to exercise Bertie. It was quite pleasant beneath the trees. We thought we might go back after lunch and explore the path that seemed to lead to the lake,' Matt said.

'The fishing is very good in the lake, fed by an excellent trout stream. You like fishing, Bryant?' Sir Henry asked.

'Yes, although I must admit I prefer golf,' Matt said.

'I'm a golf man myself,' Mr Conway said. 'A great place for doing business, the golf course.'

'Pa,' Ruby murmured a gentle reproof which went unheeded by her father.

'The lake is very pretty, although a little overgrown at present. All that wet weather we had earlier in the year. There are boats in the boathouse, however,' Lady Sarah said.

'The gardener said the icehouse and the family mausoleum were also not far from the lake.' Kitty placed her spoon down carefully in her empty dish.

'That's right. We used the icehouse up until just before the war. The gardeners used to haul the ice from the river and store it there. In a good winter with lots of frost it would last all year. It's not used these days, of course,' Lady Sarah said.

'The mausoleum is a most architecturally pleasing building in the classical style.' Mrs Craven pitched in her contribution as Mrs Putnam collected up the soup dishes, while the young maid started to pass out the white china dinner plates.

'There are most pleasant views from the front taking in the estate,' Lady Sarah agreed.

'I have used the views from there and the building itself in some of my paintings. The one in the billiard room came out rather well I thought,' Lady Amelia said.

'I'm sure we shall have a lovely stroll there this afternoon then.' Kitty eyed her lunch of seared salmon fillet with duchess potatoes and early peas appreciatively.

'Sebastian, you should take Ruby there, and show her the park. I don't think you've been there.' Lady Sarah looked at Ruby.

'A most splendid idea. You'd both still have plenty of time to get ready for the party afterwards. It would be relaxing before the excitement of this evening,' Mrs Craven agreed with her friend.

'Nice for you to get an idea of the land, honey,' Mr Conway added his seal of approval too. He declined Sebastian's suggestion that he might also walk to the lake, pleading business.

'A stroll might be nice.' Ruby looked at her fiancé. It seemed then that Ruby and Sebastian would be joining them on their walk.

After a dessert of iced lemon sorbet Matt went to check on Bertie before they set off once more into the woods. The heat of the afternoon would be too much for the little dog to go out again. As Kitty waited in the hall for Matt to come back downstairs it appeared that Rupert had decided to tag along with them too.

'It will be nice to have you join us. Matt and I would probably get quite lost on our own, now we shall have you and Sebastian to show us the way,' Kitty remarked to Rupert as she pinned her own straw summer hat in place.

'It's not too hard to find your way to the lake,' Rupert said. 'Not that it's that exciting. The water is probably too cold to use the diving platform just yet. Seb and I used to swim there a lot when we were younger. It all needs cleaning up and repairing now.' He glanced at his brother who was standing somewhat awkwardly beside Ruby.

Sebastian clapped his hand on his brother's shoulder. 'Those were the days, eh?'

Matt hurried down the stairs to join them. 'Bertie is safely asleep. I hope I haven't held us all up?' He looked at Kitty.

'Not at all,' Kitty assured him and took his arm to follow the Favershams and Ruby back outside into the bright sunshine.

Ruby walked alongside Sebastian as they entered the woods. Rupert had selected a large whippy stick and swished it periodically through the clumps of bracken as they walked. His actions heightened the scent of the garlic and decapitated some of the fading heads of the bluebells. The air was warm and still and Kitty wondered if a storm might follow in the next few days.

They followed the path Kitty and Matt had taken earlier but this time they ventured along the turn that led towards the lake. It was a little steeper since it went downhill, and steps had been cut into the soft ground. Kitty was glad of Matt's arm in places where the steps were worn and the wooden logs which had held back the soil had eroded away.

Sebastian assisted Ruby, calling a pink tinge to her pale cheeks as they drew closer to the water. Eventually they emerged onto level ground at the edge of the woodland. Now they were there, Kitty could see the lake was much larger than she had envisaged.

One end of the water was surrounded by clumps of tall reeds. Ducks, accompanied by squadrons of yellowish-brown fluffy ducklings, swam past. There was a ramshackle duck house on posts amidst the reeds and a wooden diving platform was out near the centre of the lake. At the very far end there was a wooden shed which she imagined must be the boathouse Lady Sarah had mentioned.

Ruby exclaimed with pleasure at the sight of the ducklings. Kitty saw Rupert rolling his eyes when he thought no one was looking. On a nearby grassy mound looking back across the estate was the family mausoleum, built of gleaming white marble in the neoclassical style. There was a stone bench outside beneath the porticoed entrance which Kitty guessed must offer the views Lady Amelia had spoken about painting.

Beyond the boathouse deeper in the other strand of woodland Kitty spotted the pantiled roof of a much plainer, squat, round red-brick building. That one had to be the icehouse or at least the entrance to it. She knew that most icehouses were built underground where it was colder to keep the ice from melting.

They strolled around the perimeter of the lake along a narrow path which had been worn in the meadow grass. Kitty could see there were fishing pegs sited at various points with small rotting wooden platforms.

She wondered if Agnes had come this way the day she disappeared. If she had, there were several places that would make good meeting points away from the house. Although the house could be glimpsed at different points it was surprising how hidden the lake and the area around it was. Had the maid gone there that afternoon to meet someone? Where else could she have gone?

As they drew closer to the boathouse the area became more shaded. The sun, which had been so bright, slipped behind a lone fluffy white cloud, throwing the space temporarily into darkness. Kitty shivered as the lake water turned black in the altered light.

The boathouse doors were open, sagging on their hinges to reveal a small rowing boat tied up inside. Kitty shuddered as she had a flashback of a previous case where she had been imprisoned in a similar place. Matt seemed to sense her discomfort. He placed his arm around her waist and they turned away to walk towards the mausoleum.

Kitty gave the boathouse a last glance and hoped that Agnes had not come to any harm there. The sun emerged once more and by the time they had ascended the steps to the stone bench it was quite hot again. Kitty perched herself on the end of the seat and Ruby sat beside her.

Sebastian took out his silver monogrammed cigarette case and proffered it around. Only his brother, Rupert, accepted his offer of a cigarette and a light.

'Well, what do you think then, Ruby?' Sebastian asked as the girl gazed out across the park.

'It's certainly a splendid view,' she agreed.

'Not like America?' Rupert asked with a grin.

'Not much like Chicago, no,' Ruby agreed.

'Are there any paths leading off the estate from here?' Kitty asked as she tried to work out where Agnes could have gone.

'Not if you come this way. You would need to go straight on in the woods, the way we came in. Then it takes you to the road and the bus stop.' Rupert blew out a thin stream of smoke. 'The only place this way would go is out onto the moors.'

Kitty exchanged a glance with Matt and the feeling of foreboding in her stomach grew stronger.

Sebastian threw down the stub of his cigarette and extinguished it with the toe of his shoe. 'We had better go back to the house. There's a lot to do before tonight and Father will start bellowing at everyone again if we are gone too long.' He offered Ruby his hand to help her up from the bench.

'Lord, yes, and you know how he gets when he's in a mood,' Rupert agreed with a grimace.

Kitty thought she and Matt would have to return after the ball to look around the icehouse and the mausoleum. Unless someone had met Agnes that day at the side of the road at the bus stop, the girl had to still be on the estate. If she was, then she was definitely dead, and this part of the park seemed to be the most likely spot to hide a body.

Tea was being served on the terrace when they arrived back at the house. Ruby's father looked disapprovingly at his daughter's flushed cheeks and untidy hair when she removed her hat.

'Ruby, honey, you look like someone pulled you through a hedge. I hope you're gonna make a better effort tonight. You have a lot of important people to meet.' He leaned back in his seat, a cigar in his hand.

'I'm sure Ruby will look lovely. A little colour suits her.' Kitty felt compelled to defend the girl.

Ruby gave her a brief, grateful smile as she attempted to pat her loose, mousey-brown hair back into place.

'Well, everything in the ballroom is almost ready. The musicians have just arrived and are setting up,' Lady Sarah explained as the faint sound of piano music drifted out through the open French doors. 'It promises to be a marvellous affair.' She smiled complacently at them all as she handed out cups of tea to the new arrivals.

CHAPTER SEVEN

Matt was quiet as he and Kitty dressed for the ball. His mind was running through all the possibilities of what could have become of Agnes. Kitty assisted him with his gold cufflinks and checked that his bow tie was straight. Bertie, who had finished his supper and now lay contentedly on the rug beside the fireplace, sighed. He knew the signs that his master and mistress were intending to go out.

'I'm really concerned about Agnes,' she said as she picked a tiny piece of lint from the front of his jacket.

'I am too. I'm starting to believe that she never left this estate and, if so, then she must be dead.' His gaze met Kitty's, and he saw her blue-grey eyes were clouded with a concern that matched his own.

'Finding her on a place this size, if indeed she never left, will be difficult if that is the case. We would need to go to the police and try to convince them to bring in dogs to search the woodland.' Kitty turned away to check her own appearance in the dressing-table mirror. Her new summer evening dress of pale-green silk had been expertly shortened by her friend Alice. The colour suited her and fit her slim, petite frame well.

Ordinarily he knew she would enjoy an evening of dancing and dining. With this concern over Agnes, however, that pleasure was gone.

'We need to at least check out the mausoleum and the icehouse first. The lake itself is another possibility, I suppose. There are a lot of reeds and overgrowth on the far side of the boathouse,' Matt said. He had been thinking about where the girl's body could have been hidden.

'I agree. The other thing that troubles me is that if she has been killed and is still on the estate, then it seems more than likely that someone here was responsible for her death,' Kitty said.

Matt's thoughts had been running along the same lines. 'We need to know for certain who was here the day Agnes disappeared. We know she argued with Mrs Putnam that day. The gardener and the lad assisting him were here. The other maid, Tilly, was present and the cook. Then we need to look at the family.'

'Mrs Craven may know something about that. She can tell us if they were all at home,' Kitty suggested.

'We'll see what she knows and then we'll need to find out the whereabouts of anyone she's not sure about,' Matt said as Kitty applied her lipstick.

She replaced the cap and dropped the tube into her small silver evening bag. 'Who would want to kill Agnes and why? Tilly, the young maid, said Agnes had more money lately. Blackmail of some kind, do you think?'

'Possibly, or a rich lover? Someone who was now tired of her and trying to pay her off?' Matt suggested.

He heard the sound of vehicles arriving and went to the open sash window to take a peek outside. 'The other guests are starting to arrive. I suppose we should go downstairs.'

'Dancing and detecting?' She gave a wry smile.

'Absolutely.' He followed her to the door. Bertie settled himself back to sleep on the rug.

* * *

The family were already in the hall greeting guests as Kitty and Matt made their way down the staircase. Ruby, looking very self-conscious in a pale-blue beaded silk dress, was next to Sebastian. Kitty noticed the girl was now wearing a large sapphire and diamond ring on her engagement finger. Diamond clips sparkled in her dark hair, and she wore a matching bracelet and necklace.

Her father stood on the other side of her smiling expansively at the guests as Sir Henry performed introductions. Lady Amelia assisted, wearing a gown of grey lace and a choker of pearls. Rupert appeared to be greeting his own friends and younger members of the party, before directing them towards the ballroom. One of the hired staff stood waiting at the doorway bearing a silver tray laden with champagne glasses.

Kitty and Matt slipped quietly away along the hall to the ballroom where they collected their drinks at the door. They took a moment to admire the transformation of the previously neglected space. Lady Sarah and Mrs Craven, both dressed to the nines in royal-blue and deep-purple satin respectively, were graciously greeting people as they entered.

The French doors were open to the terrace with the glass sparkling. The ballroom floor shone and small groups of tables with gilt and ruby-velvet upholstered seats surrounded the dance floor. On a small dais at one end a five-piece band with a glamorous young woman singer were providing the music. Fronded potted plants were arranged decorously, and the room was alive with music, chatter and light.

Mrs Craven spotted them as they entered and made her way over to them. 'Well? What have you discovered? I take it that was why you wanted to go to the lake this afternoon?' she asked after ensuring no one was within earshot.

'It seems increasingly unlikely so far that Agnes actually left the estate. We need to find out who was at home the day she disappeared. We know about the servants, but we need to find out who else was around,' Matt said.

Mrs Craven's brow wrinkled below her jewelled headband. 'Hmm, I know Lady Sarah was here because that was the evening she telephoned me to tell me of Sebastian's engagement.' She clicked her fingers. 'Yes, that's right, they were all here, the boys, Amelia, Sir Henry and Mr Conway.'

'And Ruby?' Kitty asked.

'Well yes, I think she was. I know that was the day Agnes vanished because Sarah was complaining about how bad it made them look to the Conways when dinner was served. They had come for the weekend.' Mrs Craven smiled complacently. 'I told you I would be an asset to this investigation. I really think I would make an excellent detective.'

Kitty was fortunately saved from having to respond by the arrival of Lady Amelia.

'Millicent, my dear, there is an old acquaintance of yours asking about you over there.' She waved her hand vaguely in the direction of the bar that had been set up at the side of the room. 'I believe they knew Peregrine.'

'Oh my goodness, it's Louisa and Peter Babcock, I haven't seen them in absolutely ages.' Mrs Craven waved at a plump older lady dressed in dark red accompanied by a thin man in over-large evening attire and immediately headed over to meet them.

'Amelia!' Sir Henry waved urgently at his wife, and she muttered an apology as she went to see what her husband wanted.

'Well, that was helpful of Mrs C.' Matt grinned at Kitty.

'If you would prefer her as a partner in the business, I can step aside,' Kitty offered with a matching smile.

'She's not as pretty as my current partner,' Matt said.

'Seriously, it doesn't help us in narrowing down who may have been responsible for Agnes disappearing if we are correct in our assumption that she is still somewhere on the estate.' Kitty's smile slipped from her face as she looked around the now crowded ballroom.

'No, I think it's time for more dancing and detecting.' Matt took her now empty glass from her hand and set it down next to his on a nearby table. He took her into his arms, and they started to dance.

'What's our plan?' Kitty asked as they waltzed around the room.

'We need to know who may have encountered Agnes and what they remember, or are prepared to say about her,' Matt said as he manoeuvred her skilfully past another couple.

'Shall we split up and tackle people separately? We haven't much time really since we are due to leave after lunch tomorrow. If the police do need to be informed then we really have to gather as much information as we can this evening.' Kitty could see Rupert laughing and talking to his friends in the corner of the room.

'We may find this is to our advantage. They may be more talkative now they are relaxed and enjoying the champagne,' Matt suggested.

Mr Conway and Sir Henry were busy with a group of well-dressed ladies and gentlemen near the bar. 'In vino veritas. Yes, you're right.'

'We need to be careful though, Kitty, not to arouse suspicion. One of these people may be responsible for whatever has happened to Agnes,' Matt warned as the song ended and the partygoers applauded warmly.

Kitty had been thinking the same thing. They each agreed

who their first targets were going to be and separated to go in search of their prey. Matt headed towards the bar as if collecting another drink. Kitty looked around to see who she could tackle first.

Lady Sarah had stepped out of the crowded room into the cooler air of the terrace so Kitty made her way outside. The sun was rapidly sinking below the trees sending streaks of pink and gold across the purple-blue sky. Kitty feigned feeling the heat and fanned her face with her hand as she wandered towards the older woman.

'What a glorious evening. It's so warm inside now that it's a pleasure to come out and cool down for a moment,' Kitty said as she joined the Dowager Lady Faversham by the stone balustrade. The scent of the roses and lavender mingled with the scent of freshly cut grass on the evening air.

'Yes, it is a little oppressive but gratifying to see so many of one's neighbours and friends joining in the celebrations. I think it was a sensible decision to place more seating out here for the evening,' Lady Sarah said.

Various chairs and tables were occupied by people chatting, laughing and smoking in the evening air. Fortunately none of them were particularly close to where she and Lady Sarah were standing.

'Have Sebastian and Ruby known one another long?' Kitty asked in a casual tone.

'About three months. We initially introduced them in London and they seemed to get along well together. Then Mr Conway and Ruby came here about six weeks ago to view the house and the estate. They enjoyed the first visit and returned a couple of weeks later to take a more in-depth look. That was when the engagement was agreed.' Lady Sarah glanced at Kitty who was still feigning feeling hot and fanning her face.

'Ruby seems a very nice girl and they appear well matched,' Kitty said.

'Yes, she is rather young but very sweet. Such a relief to have Sebastian settling down and feeling the estate will be secure. It's been such a worry to us all.' Lady Sarah switched her gaze to look back over the rapidly darkening parkland.

'Four weeks ago, that must have been around the time Agnes Jones disappeared. Mrs Craven told us her maid, Dora, was most upset. She's very concerned that she still hasn't heard from her. I'm sure Millicent must have mentioned to you that Dora is the girl's older sister,' Kitty mused.

'Yes, Millicent recommended the girl in the first place. Not that I blame her, of course, for the girl's behaviour. It was most inconvenient and thoughtless to take off the way she did. It was the day after Mr Conway and Ruby arrived. She was there on the morning and gone by afternoon apparently. It left Mrs Putnam in quite a pickle. Such selfishness.' Lady Sarah's lips pursed as she spoke.

'It does seem very strange. Mrs Craven said she hadn't been aware of any problems with Agnes's work before then,' Kitty said.

'Mrs Putnam deals with the household, and I believe she was most annoyed. The girl always seemed to work hard but was, well, fond of the gentlemen. Flirtatious. I think Mrs Putnam had to speak to her so perhaps it's a blessing she went.' Lady Sarah glanced across to where Sebastian and Rupert were standing with Ruby and Sir Henry.

'Oh dear, I hope there was no unpleasantness.' Kitty phrased her question delicately. It had sounded to her as if Lady Sarah believed Agnes had been flirting with either the younger members of the household or possibly even Mr Conway or Sir Henry.

'Not so far as I am aware, but I do think the girl was getting above her station. Aggie, the boys called her. Much too familiar. She was bordering on insolence shortly before she left. Good riddance I suppose, although the timing of her departure could have been better. Now, I really must get back to my guests. I hope you feel more refreshed now, Mrs Bryant.' Lady Sarah inclined her head in dismissal and sailed off back inside the house.

Kitty remained at the balustrade for a moment or two longer to digest this new information before being joined by Lady Amelia.

'Oh, Kitty, I thought I saw you with my mother-in-law? Millicent was looking for her, it seems another mutual acquaintance from their youth has arrived.' Lady Amelia looked around the terrace as if expecting to see Lady Sarah.

'I think she has gone inside to find them,' Kitty assured her. It was a real stroke of luck to have her next target seek her out. 'We were just talking about Agnes Jones, the maid who disappeared when the Conways came for their second stay a few weeks ago.'

'Agnes Jones?' Lady Amelia's face puckered in a frown. 'Oh yes, I remember, very pretty girl. It was most inconsiderate to leave us in the lurch that way. Lady Sarah was quite cross and it threw a lot of work on the other staff. These girls though, a young man comes along and turns their head and there's nothing one can do.'

'I didn't realise she had a boyfriend,' Kitty said.

'Well, she must have had, mustn't she?' Lady Amelia said. 'Why else would she have just gone off like that?'

Kitty had no real answer for this.

'Mother, are you doing your hostessing duties? Father is getting twitchy, you know how he fusses.' Rupert joined them, and Kitty noticed he was swaying a little on his heels.

'Oh dear, I had better go, do excuse me, Kitty.' Lady Amelia hurried off to find her husband.

Rupert remained and offered Kitty a cigarette, which she refused with a polite smile and a shake of her head.

'I don't blame you. Filthy habit really I suppose,' Rupert said as he lit up and stared out over the darkening lawn.

A servant carried out lanterns and placed them on the tables to provide illumination on the terrace.

'The engagement party seems to be going well,' Kitty observed.

'Yes, no expense being spared to secure the Conway dollars.' Rupert's lips twisted as he spoke. He glanced at Kitty. 'Do I shock you, Kitty?'

'No, I don't believe that anyone thinks the engagement is a love match. More a move born of practicality. Ruby seems a nice, sensible sort of girl and they do seem fond of one another.' Kitty could see Sebastian standing with Ruby further along the terrace.

'Yes, she's a good sort. Too good really for Seb. I just hope he doesn't muck her about.' Rupert blew out a thin stream of cigarette smoke.

'Does he tend to do that?' Kitty asked with an arch smile.

'He does have an eye for a pretty face,' Rupert said.

'It can be difficult for young women,' Kitty said. 'Your mother was just talking about the maid who left unexpectedly a few weeks ago.'

Rupert turned to look at her, a surprised expression on his face. 'I'm shocked Mother even noticed Aggie had gone. She's usually oblivious to anything, unless it involves daubing a picture of it in paint or sculpting it in clay.'

'Where do you think Agnes has gone? Her sister, Dora, is very worried about her, so Mrs Craven has said,' Kitty asked. She was keen to hear Rupert's view on the matter. He had clearly noticed Agnes enough to call her Aggie. Lady Sarah had also insinuated there had been flirting between the girl and Rupert and his brother.

'I don't know. I suppose I thought she must have met

someone and run off, eloped.' He moved his shoulders in a slight shrug and frowned. 'It is a bit queer, come to think of it.'

'Was she close to anyone in the house do you know?' Kitty thought she might be pushing things with this question but Rupert appeared a little inebriated so he might be more forthcoming.

Rupert's eyes narrowed slightly as he studied her expression. 'Depends on what you mean by close. Aggie was a flirt and a bit of a snoop. She'd drop out little comments letting you know she knew something and then giggle about it. You know, say she liked a picture in Seb's room or hint she knew I was going out with friends. That's all I know. I expect she'll turn up again somewhere soon.' He dropped his cigarette end on the stone flags and stubbed it out with the toe of his highly polished evening shoe before heading back inside the house.

Kitty frowned. Rupert had obviously taken notice of the maid, and she wondered what Agnes had found out about Rupert or his brother. That last comment signified to her that the girl had learned something that one of them might not wish to become common knowledge. Was that enough for them to kill her? Or for Agnes to blackmail either of them over?

The Favershams might be on their uppers but compared to a young maid like Agnes they would be wealthy. Then, with everything riding on Sebastian securing a wealthy heiress to save the estate, the stakes could be very high indeed.

CHAPTER EIGHT

Matt watched from the bar as Kitty began working her way through her list of targets. He looked around the room and set about talking to those on his list. He found Sir Henry first, red-faced and clutching a glass of champagne near the dance floor.

'It seems to be going jolly well, sir,' Matt said.

'What? Yes, I hope so. This is a big deal, Bryant, for Sebastian and for Markham. Lots at stake. Everything seem to be in order security wise?' Sir Henry asked.

'I believe so, sir. No signs of any problems. Miss Conway seems a charming young lady.' Matt had seen Sebastian and Ruby heading out onto the terrace a moment earlier.

'Yes indeed. It's high time Sebastian settled down and started taking over the estate. I shall be glad to take a step back. I've already transferred the deeds to his name.' Sir Henry downed his champagne and snagged another full glass from the tray of a passing waiter.

'I can imagine. It must be difficult managing such a large house and estate. Hard to get staff too, I imagine, with the house being rather isolated out here.' Matt took a sip from his own drink.

'Mrs Putnam is always complaining about it,' Sir Henry agreed as the housekeeper glided past them.

'Mrs Craven said you had a maid leave recently without giving notice.' Matt kept his tone casual and sympathetic.

'Oh yes, I rather think the girl came at her recommendation. Mother said Millicent was upset about her letting us down the way she did.' Sir Henry took another large gulp from his glass.

'It's rather odd that her sister hasn't heard from her since she left,' Matt observed.

Sir Henry gave him a sharp glance. 'A flighty young girl like that, it's not surprising. If you ask me there's bound to be a boyfriend involved somewhere. There usually is. Ah, excuse me, I must go and find Amelia, there are some people I want her to meet.' Sir Henry plunged into the crowd nearby.

It was clear to Matt that Sir Henry wasn't willing to think about what may have happened to Agnes. His tone had implied the girl was flirtatious. Matt sighed, he knew it was a possibility that Agnes had found herself in trouble and had left before her situation could be discovered. No one knew though who the boyfriend may have been if that were the case and the girl was pregnant. It also made no sense that she would have left all her meagre possessions and money behind.

If she had been pregnant and had felt unable to face the shame of it all, then surely she would have left a note if she had intended taking her own life. No one had said she seemed depressed, worried or unhappy. Tilly had told Kitty the girl had seemed quite the opposite, almost gleeful.

He glanced around the room looking for the next person on his list. Mr Conway was standing near the bar gazing around at the assembled crowd with a pleased expression on his face. Matt seized his chance and headed across to the American.

'A splendid party, sir, you must be delighted that your daughter has made such a good match,' Matt said as he joined Mr Conway.

'Ruby is a good girl. I can't tell you what it means to know my little girl will be Lady Faversham one day.' The American gave a satisfied smile.

'It's quite an accomplishment. Mrs Craven tells me the Favershams have been at Markham for over five hundred years,' Matt said.

'Sir Henry told us that when we first came here to look around. There is so much history in a place like this, it clear blows my mind. I'm just a humble man, Captain Bryant, self-made. I can't believe my girl is mixing with all these titled folk and being treated like one of them,' Mr Conway said.

'I presume Ruby will be assisting Sebastian with the management of the estate when they marry.' Matt chose his words with care.

'Oh well, the place needs some refurbishment, no one is denying that. Personally, I think that's a good thing, lets my Ruby put her mark on the place.' Mr Conway tapped the side of his nose with his forefinger. 'Mind you, I've made certain that my little girl keeps a good tight hold of the purse strings even after the wedding. Got to make sure she's treated right.'

'That's good to know. Ruby is a charming young lady, she appears very sensible. I can understand you wanting to look after her interests,' Matt agreed. 'I expect Ruby will oversee the household too, get more staff. Always a tricky thing in a remote area. Mrs Craven said they had a maid go missing when you and Ruby last visited here.'

Mr Conway raised his shaggy eyebrows. 'That's right. I remember there being a bit of a to-do at dinner. Harriet or Anna or something, just walked out I believe, left them all running around the place.'

'Agnes Jones, the girl was called. Mrs Craven said the girl's sister hasn't heard from her since she left, which is a bit odd.' Matt kept his tone casual as if just making light conversation.

All the time he was alert to any change, however slight, in the American's demeanour.

'Hmm, I guess that is mighty strange unless, of course, the girl has gotten herself in trouble. Then she might want to lie low until it's all over I suppose,' Mr Conway suggested.

'A possibility I expect. Young people, eh?' Matt said.

'Indeed, makes me glad that Ruby will be safely settled.' Mr Conway shifted his gaze out towards the French doors.

Mrs Craven came towards them accompanied by a couple of other older ladies all clearly intent on talking to Mr Conway. Matt made his excuses and escaped before he could be drawn into the conversation. He wondered how Kitty was getting on and decided to stroll outside to the terrace to look for her.

He soon spotted the shimmering pale-green silk of her gown near the balustrade at the far end and set off in her direction. He almost bumped into Rupert Faversham as he approached her. The younger man appeared to be a little worse for wear and Matt wondered how much champagne he had consumed.

Kitty smiled as he reached her. 'How have you got on?' she asked in a low voice.

He quickly told her what he'd discovered so far. 'Well done.' She reciprocated with everything that she had learned.

'That leaves us with just Sebastian to go then really,' Matt said.

'From the family, yes, although I think we may need to try and talk to the cook, Mrs Putnam's sister, too if we can. Although tonight is not the time for that,' Kitty said.

'Shall we tackle Sebastian and Ruby together? It looks as if their friends are moving back inside.' Matt offered his arm to Kitty, and they strolled along the terrace to where the newly engaged couple were standing.

'Oh, do show me your ring, Ruby,' Kitty asked as they approached.

Ruby shyly lifted her hand and spread her fingers to reveal the heirloom ring.

'It was my great-great-grandmother's. We've had it cleaned and made a little smaller to fit Ruby,' Sebastian said. 'She has dainty fingers.'

Ruby blushed at his comment.

'It's lovely,' Kitty said. 'What a fabulous party. Everyone seems to be having such a nice time.'

'It is rather pleasant to have so many friends over and to see the old place gussied up a bit.' Sebastian looked along the terrace at the row of lanterns twinkling on the tables. Couples were sitting around or leaning on the stone railing. Pale-yellow light streamed out from the open French doors, and everything looked elegant and tasteful.

'Are you getting to know everyone, Ruby?' Kitty asked.

'Seb has been introducing me but there are a lot of people here, so I don't suppose I shall remember who everyone is,' the girl confessed.

'You'll soon know all of them in time. Once the shooting season starts in the autumn and the hunting, then you'll find there will be a splendid social life for you here,' Sebastian announced breezily, not seeming to notice the brief flash of dismay on Ruby's face.

'I daresay Ruby will soon get to know people and make friends after the wedding, even if hunting, shooting and fishing aren't quite her thing,' Kitty remarked in a dry tone.

Ruby gave her a grateful smile.

'Well once the place is done up, I expect we shall be quite in demand socially. We can start having the balls at Christmas and New Year like we used to have,' Sebastian said.

'That sounds fun, my aunt and uncle at Enderley do much the same thing. Their house is near Newton St Cyres. I'm sure Ruby will have lots of ideas for the house and the gardens once you're married,' Kitty agreed. 'Although staffing can be difficult in a place as large as Markham. I know my aunt and uncle employ quite a few people. Mrs Craven was saying you had a girl leave unexpectedly a few weeks ago. A maid, Agnes Jones?'

Matt glanced at his wife. Kitty was cutting right to the chase pretty quickly.

'Agnes, by golly yes, that was a rum thing. She never said a dicky bird about wanting to leave and then Mrs Putnam said she didn't leave a note or pack her bags. I expect she must have had someone pick her up, a boyfriend or something. She was a pretty girl. No shortage of admirers, I don't suppose,' Sebastian said.

'It does sound odd if she didn't take her things. I mean, I think I remember a maid being here when we arrived but then at dinner there was a bit of a furore,' Ruby said. 'Mrs Putnam seemed very displeased. Do you think something has happened to the maid?'

'No one knows, but her sister is very worried about her, and no one has seen her or heard from her since the afternoon of the day she left,' Matt said.

'Gee, I can see why her family would be worried,' Ruby said.

'I expect she'll turn up,' Sebastian said. 'Now, how about a turn on the dance floor? I can see my grandmother watching us.' He took Ruby's hand.

'I hope she's found soon,' Ruby murmured apologetically as she was led away to be twirled around to the music.

* * *

Kitty watched the other couple depart for the dance floor. 'Well, that's everyone for now,' she said.

'I agree. I think perhaps we should also take a turn on the

floor and then I'll go and check on Bertie,' Matt suggested as he offered her his arm.

'More dancing and less detecting for a spell,' Kitty agreed as they re-entered the busy ballroom.

Kitty took notice of the rest of the house party as Matt steered her around the floor. She was keen to see if their questions had sparked any change in any of the members of the family or their guests.

Lady Amelia was accompanying Sir Henry while he regaled a group of people with some tale or other. Sir Henry was red-faced and cheerful, while she thought Lady Amelia seemed bored and restless.

Mrs Craven and Lady Sarah were seated at one of the tables enjoying some of the cold supper which was now being served to guests. Lady Sarah appeared to be watching Sebastian and Ruby closely. Rupert was talking to a young lady of around Ruby's age near the bar. He was clearly saying something flirtatious by the way the girl was giggling and blushing.

Mr Conway was surrounded by a group of ladies while he watched his daughter dance with her new fiancé. He looked very pleased with himself and was obviously enjoying the attention he was being given.

Mrs Putnam moved through the crowds, supervising the temporary staff with an eagle eye as they carried around trays of dainty sandwiches and savoury snacks. Her expression striking a dour note amongst the jollity of the other guests. Tilly, the young maid, was scurrying about collecting up empty glasses and used plates.

The song finished and Matt released her. 'I'll just go and see Bertie, take him out for a spell. Will you be all right here till I get back?'

'Of course, I think I might get some food. I'll get you a plate too,' Kitty agreed, and her husband slipped away into the hall. She duly acquired some food and managed to obtain a seat in a quiet spot partially hidden by one of the giant fronded plants.

She was just enjoying a dainty triangular roast beef sandwich when she realised Lady Sarah and Mrs Putnam were standing close by and they were having quite a heated conversation. Kitty discreetly parted the leaves of the palm and peered through.

'All I'm saying, my lady, is that we want our money. We've been more than patient,' Mrs Putnam said.

'Now is not the time or the place and it is Lady Amelia you should be addressing on such matters,' Lady Sarah retorted.

'Lady Amelia is not the one in charge of this house, my lady, and you knows that as well as me. I can't even get nobody from the village these days unless you pay them upfront first. Now, if my sister and I don't get our wages by next Saturday then we are leaving.' Mrs Putnam glared at her employer.

'If you do that, I shall see you are never employed anywhere again,' Lady Sarah hissed.

'We don't need your references, my lady, our work and our characters is already known. We wants to see Master Sebastian wed and the house restored but we don't work for charity. Next Saturday or we walk and you can fend for yourself.' Mrs Putnam swept away, leaving Lady Sarah with an angry red spot burning on each cheek.

Kitty hastily withdrew back behind the plant pot. It seemed that the Favershams were in a very parlous position indeed where their finances were involved. She hoped that Mrs Craven had not loaned her relative a large sum of money since it sounded unlikely that she would see it returned. At least not until Sebastian and Ruby were married. It did also explain Mrs Putnam's disposition if she couldn't even get help from the village.

Lady Sarah's place was taken a minute later by another squabbling couple. This time Sir Henry and Lady Amelia were conducting a brief argument. 'For heaven's sake, Amelia, make more effort to talk to people,' Sir Henry chastised his wife.

'I am exerting myself sufficiently, thank you. I would ask you to consider reining in your drinking and to have enough manners to keep your hands to yourself this evening. You are much more likely to mess things up for Sebastian than me.'

Kitty risked another quick glance through the leaves to see Lady Amelia shake her husband's hand free of her arm. The couple moved away, and she was unable to hear any more of the conversation.

Matt found her and took a seat at her table. 'Here, I got you some food.' Kitty slid a small china plate of sandwiches towards him.

'Thank you. I took Bertie out and did a quick check around the place while I was at it. I thought I should be seen to be doing some sort of security patrol.' Matt grinned at her as he picked up a vol-au-vent.

'It's been quite interesting sitting here.' Kitty told him what she had witnessed while he'd been gone.

'Hmm, it certainly gives us an insight into the dynamics of the household,' Matt agreed after he'd chewed and swallowed his food.

The evening progressed with more drinking and dancing until the first of the cars began to arrive at midnight to bear the guests away. By one thirty the guests had all gone and the hired staff were busy tidying up the rest of the used glasses and crockery.

Lady Sarah and Mrs Craven retired to their rooms and Matt accompanied Ruby, Mr Conway and Sir Henry to the study to place Ruby's jewels securely in the safe. Rupert and Sebastian were smoking on the terrace, so Kitty took her opportunity to also head upstairs.

Tomorrow morning was their best and possibly last chance to try and search the grounds for some clue of where Agnes might have gone that last day she was seen. Bertie greeted her happily before resuming his new favourite sleeping spot. Kitty quickly changed and slipped into bed, her eyes closing as soon as her head hit the pillow.

She didn't even hear Matt return to the room to join her sometime later.

CHAPTER NINE

The sun was shining through the threadbare fabric of the curtains when Kitty woke the next morning. The air in the room was already warm. Bertie instantly heard her stir and was soon on his feet, tail wagging ready to greet her.

A glance at her little travelling clock in its brown-leather case told her it was only seven o'clock. She doubted many in the house would be stirring yet after the late night of drinking and dancing. Matt was still fast asleep, so she rose and dressed quickly, deciding to take Bertie out before disturbing her husband.

The little spaniel happily charged ahead of her down the great staircase into the hall, where Kitty attached his lead. She made her way into the ballroom, the scene of last night's party, and unfastened one of the French doors. The air was fresh and cooler outside with a hint of heat to come. The sky was a bright unclouded blue, and the birds were chirping in the hedge at the side of the lawn as she walked Bertie down towards the edge of the wood.

The dew on the grass marked the sides of her leather shoes with water as she stepped off the end of the lawn through the gate into the trees. There was no one else in sight and the only sounds were those of the birds and the distant dry cough of a sheep.

Bertie forged ahead, his nose to the ground and his plumed tail waving in the air. Kitty followed, allowing him to take the lead on where they walked. If she could explore part of the grounds now, then it would make it easier for when she returned after breakfast with Matt.

Bertie took the turn leading to the lake and Kitty looked around her as she descended the rough steps to the bottom of the woods. There was no sign of anyone having left the path or of another path branching off in another direction. If Agnes had not gone from the estate via the main road, then she must have come this way. The gardener's sighting of her was the last one they had.

She walked along the edge of the lake making sure that Bertie couldn't get close enough to the water to alarm the ducklings. The spaniel, however, seemed to have more interesting things on his mind as he led her away from the water's edge and up the polished stone steps of the mound to the mausoleum.

Kitty followed Bertie up the steps and expected him to turn at the narrow terrace towards the marble bench where they had sat the day before. Instead, he led her to the closed, black-painted doors of the building, where he scratched at the woodwork and gave a small whine.

'No, Bertie, we don't go in there. I expect it's locked.' Kitty hoped he hadn't sniffed out a mouse or a rat hiding inside the building.

She tried to pull him away, but he wouldn't be diverted so she placed her hand on the brass door handle and tried it to see if it would open. To her surprise the door was unlocked, so she pulled it ajar, and Bertie immediately plunged inside.

The interior of the mausoleum was gloomy, and a dreadful undefinable aroma met her as she tugged at the dog's lead, anxious to get him back outside. It took a minute for her eyes to acclimatise to the gloom. A rectangular marble tomb topped by an effigy of a long-dead Faversham occupied the centre of the space. Lying just beyond it on the marble-tiled floor she glimpsed a girl's foot clad in a black stocking with a court shoe lying at a strange angle.

Kitty pulled Bertie out and reclosed the door behind her, her heart thumping as nausea rose inside her stomach. There was no doubt in her mind that she had discovered the fate of the missing maid. She crossed to the bench and sat down for a moment, sucking in the clean morning air while the contents of her stomach settled. Then she jumped to her feet and hurried back to the house as fast as she could, with the intent of letting Matt know what she had discovered.

Her husband was in the hall as she burst into the house. She rushed to meet him, Bertie trotting at her side as fast as his little legs could go.

'Matt, I've found her, Agnes. We need to call the police.' She could hardly get the words out she was so breathless from running back up the slope from the woods.

Matt caught her in his arms, holding her steady. 'Where is she?' he asked, his face grave and concern in his eyes.

'Dead, on the floor in the mausoleum. She must have been there since the day she went missing.' Kitty gasped and pressed her hand against her side to prevent the incipient stitch which had already started to stab at her.

'There's a telephone in the study.' Matt led the way, supporting her as they hurried into Sir Henry's study.

Kitty sank down on one of the dark-green leather-covered chairs and tried to stop herself from trembling. Bertie sat to attention at her feet.

Matt snatched up the telephone receiver and dialled. He asked the operator to connect him to Exeter Police Station.

Once connected he spoke briefly and succinctly to an officer there, before returning the receiver to the handset.

'They are on their way. Are you all right, old thing? Sir Henry seems to have some brandy in a decanter over here.' Matt went to a small, open crystal tantalus and extricated the liquor and a glass, pouring her a small shot.

'Thank you.' Kitty took a sip and coughed at the strength of the reviving liquor. 'I'm all right, really. It was just a shock. I hadn't expected to find the door unlocked and to see her there.'

'I can imagine.' Matt's expression was grim.

'We need to alert the house to what's happened.' She tightened her grasp around the glass trying to still the trembling in her fingers. The full horror of what she and Bertie had discovered threatened to overcome her.

'Will you be all right here for a moment while I see if Sir Henry is downstairs?' Matt asked. 'We need to tell him first since he is head of the house, especially as the police will be here shortly.'

Kitty nodded. Bertie sighed and lay down at her feet, while Matt hurried out of the study. Kitty took another small sip of her drink before placing the glass down on the blotter on top of the desk.

Her heart had slowed back to its normal rate now after her race back to the house. The nausea from her find had also diminished and she glanced around at the study while she waited for Matt to return.

Something about the large, square, green-metal safe in the corner of the room attracted her attention and she stood to go and take a closer look. At first she thought she had been mistaken, and it had been a trick of the light coming in through the sash windows. Then as she examined the safe more closely, she saw she was right. Around the lock were small telltale scratches gouged into the paint. Someone had attempted to pick the lock.

At the sound of approaching voices in the hallway she scurried back to retake her seat beside Bertie. She sat down not a moment too soon as Sir Henry bowled into the study, red-faced and worried. Matt followed behind accompanied by a weary and hungover-looking Sebastian.

'My dear Mrs Bryant, I can scarcely believe what your husband has just told me. The missing girl, the maid, is dead, in the family mausoleum?' Sir Henry took his seat behind his desk. Sebastian leaned against the Portland stone mantelpiece and lit up a cigarette. Kitty thought he too looked quite shaken by the news.

'I'm afraid so, Sir Henry. I didn't venture too far inside but there is definitely a body in there, which I suspect is that of Agnes Jones,' Kitty said.

'And the police are on their way, you say? Good heavens, what will Conway have to say about this?' Sir Henry looked at Sebastian in alarm.

Matt's brows rose at his host's concern for his son's future marriage rather than any worry over the dead maid.

'I'll talk to Ruby,' Sebastian said. 'She's a level-headed sort. She'll speak to her father. After all it's nothing really to do with us that Aggie is dead.'

Kitty glanced at Matt. The American girl might be jolly sensible, but it wasn't every day that one encountered a suspicious death. Agnes's death was definitely suspicious. Unless the girl had a note of some kind with her, then one had to assume that it was highly likely the maid had been murdered. Furthermore, it seemed to Kitty that someone in the household must be responsible. Sebastian's assertion that her demise was nothing to do with Markham was at best naïve.

Sir Henry's brow furrowed. 'I can't believe this has happened. How did you come to find her, Mrs Bryant?'

'Bertie was very keen to get inside the building. I noticed the door was unlocked and he pushed it open. I saw the girl's foot and of course noticed the, erm, smell.' Kitty glanced at her dog and didn't elucidate any further. Sebastian looked quite green even with the small amount of detail she had provided.

'I see, most unpleasant for you, my dear.' Sir Henry too looked shaken by Kitty's description of events.

'And, of course, you were both asking questions last night about Aggie.' Sebastian looked first at Matt and then at Kitty.

'Yes, her sister has been very concerned about her. Mrs Craven has also been worried,' Kitty said.

Sir Henry placed his head in his hands. 'Mother will be furious at having the police on the estate.'

'There is not really any other option, Father.' Sebastian finished his cigarette. 'I'll go and talk to Ruby before word starts to spread.' He left the study to go and find his fiancée.

'There is something else, sir,' Kitty said once Sebastian had gone.

Sir Henry raised his head to look at her. 'There is more?' he asked.

'While I was waiting for Matt to return, I noticed that it looks as if someone has been attempting to pick the lock on the safe.' Kitty inclined her head towards the corner of the room.

Matt immediately hurried over to take a look. 'I'm afraid Kitty is right. There are fresh marks around the key plate that were not there last night. I checked it when we put Ruby's jewellery and your wife's pearls away.'

Sir Henry's face paled, and he fumbled in the pocket of his paisley-silk waistcoat before producing a key. He went to the safe and turned the tumbler to release the first part of the combination, then inserted his key in the lock.

The heavy door swung open, and he peered anxiously inside, relief sweeping over his face when he saw the contents appeared to be intact. He opened a couple of the padded velvet jewel cases to check the contents before closing the door, resetting the combination and turning the key.

'Everything is still there, thank heaven.' He placed the key back inside his waistcoat pocket, before producing a handkerchief to mop his brow. 'A body and a burglary would have been too, too much.'

Outside the room in the hall there was the faint sound of the front doorbell followed by voices. A tap on the study door signalled the arrival of the police.

'An Inspector Lewis for you, sir,' Mrs Putnam announced as she held the door for the officers to enter.

Kitty was aware she was gaping and snapped her lips shut quickly as their least favourite policeman entered the room. Inspector Lewis wore his usual air of superiority and a slightly crumpled grey-flannel suit. He appeared equally appalled to discover Kitty and Matt were present in the study.

'Inspector Lewis, this is something of a surprise, rather off your usual patch,' Matt said as Mrs Putnam departed.

'I've been temporarily relocated to the Exeter station due to staffing shortages.' Inspector Lewis fixed his foxy gaze on Matt.

Kitty suppressed a sigh. They had worked with the inspector on a number of cases now and it never appeared to get any easier. The inspector had little time for private investigators and he especially disliked female detectives. Their last case in Cornwall together had been an especially distressing affair.

She had not been expecting Inspector Lewis to be working this far away from his regular area around Torbay. Kitty could only think that their friend, Chief Inspector Greville, had spied an opportunity to rid himself of his annoying colleague for a few weeks. It was just their bad luck to be stuck with him instead.

'Inspector Lewis, may I introduce Sir Henry Faversham, owner of the estate,' Matt said as the inspector advanced further into the study. A uniformed constable followed in his wake.

'Inspector, I'd appreciate it if this could all be handled discreetly. I have important guests staying at the house at present.' Sir Henry shook hands with Inspector Lewis.

'Naturally, sir. I understand that a young woman's body has been discovered in the family mausoleum?' The inspector pulled a black leather-bound notebook from his jacket pocket and flicked to a page.

'Yes, we believe it to be that of Miss Agnes Jones. She was working here as a maid and disappeared about four weeks ago,' Kitty said. 'Agnes's sister is Dora Jones, maid to Mrs Millicent Craven. She is also staying here at the estate at present.'

Kitty couldn't help feeling a secret spark of joy at the momentary expression of dismay and panic that flashed across the inspector's face at the mention of Mrs Craven's name.

'I see,' Inspector Lewis said. 'Perhaps you could show me where you found the body.' He tucked his notebook back in his pocket.

'I'll take you, Inspector. Kitty has had a nasty shock so it's best she stays here. No doubt she will be happy to answer any questions you have for her when we return,' Matt suggested.

'Very well,' the inspector grudgingly agreed and after bidding farewell to Sir Henry, followed Matt out of the study.

'I suppose I should go and see who else is around having breakfast. Far better to break this news myself, soften the blow and all that,' Sir Henry said.

'I expect everyone who knew Agnes will be quite upset,' Kitty said.

'What? Oh yes, I suppose they will.' Sir Henry rubbed his chin. 'I know my mother will not be at all happy. Having the police all over the estate, poking about. I had better speak to Stanley Conway too.'

Kitty could see that Sir Henry was still much more concerned about the impact of the news on the Conways' visit than concern that a member of his staff had been found dead.

'I should break the news to Mrs Craven.' Kitty rose from her seat, glad her legs no longer felt like jelly. Bertie promptly jumped up too.

Kitty accompanied Sir Henry to the dining room where they discovered Lady Amelia sipping an insipid cup of tea, while Mrs Craven was tucking into a hearty breakfast. They both looked up as they entered the room.

'Kitty, did I just see Inspector Lewis go past the dining-room window?' Mrs Craven demanded before Kitty could even say a word.

'Yes, I'm afraid you did. I went for an early morning walk with Bertie and unfortunately I found Agnes Jones.' Kitty took a seat at the table and pulled a clean china cup and saucer towards her. A cup of tea would be just the ticket now to settle her nerves after everything that had happened.

'Agnes, the maid who walked out? You were asking about her last night.' Lady Amelia looked at her husband.

'Mrs Bryant and her dog discovered the girl dead in the mausoleum this morning. The police have just arrived.' Sir Henry went to the sideboard and began to fill a plate with eggs, bacon and sausages.

Lady Amelia set her cup back on its saucer, her hand trembling. 'The maid is dead? Oh, Henry, how dreadful.'

'Quite so, my dear, quite appalling. I don't know how Stanley will take the news.' Sir Henry set his laden plate down at the table and took his seat as his wife gaped, open-mouthed at him.

'Oh dear, poor Dora, she will be most upset. You are certain it is Agnes, Kitty?' Mrs Craven set her cutlery aside and wiped the corners of her mouth with a linen napkin.

'I didn't go right inside. I only caught a glimpse of her foot, but I don't see who else it could be. I'm dreadfully sorry,' Kitty said as Bertie wheeled his way under the table, clearly hoping for a sausage to fall his way.

'Oh dear. I had better go and telephone her now to break the news. She will be at my house this morning to check all is well before she goes to church.' Mrs Craven stood up looking rather pale at the news.

'Inspector Lewis has gone down to the mausoleum with Matt. We may know more when they come back,' Kitty said.

'Well yes, I would think so. I mean if Agnes's death is not an accident or by her own hand, then I suppose it must be a murder,' Mrs Craven said and hurried away leaving an ominous silence in her wake.

CHAPTER TEN

Matt led Inspector Lewis and his constable out of the house via the terrace and down through the wood to the mausoleum.

'Heaven only knows why these posh families have these things. What's wrong with the village churchyard, that's what I want to know?' Inspector Lewis muttered as they made their way up the marble steps to the door of the white neoclassical building.

Matt fell behind the inspector, allowing him to go first. He didn't offer an answer to the policeman's question. Kitty had left the door slightly ajar and as they reached the porch Matt could already smell the odour of death.

Inspector Lewis pulled out his handkerchief and placed it over his nose and mouth before entering inside. Matt opted to wait on the portico with the nervous-looking constable. Inspector Lewis emerged back outside a minute later looking distinctly unwell. He staggered over to the marble bench and sat, pulling in lungfuls of fresh air.

'That fits the description you gave of the missing girl all right. She's been dead for quite a while I should say. It looks like she took a blow to the head,' the inspector said.

Matt's mouth settled in a grim line. That settled it, Agnes's death was definitely a murder. That meant that everyone who had been present at Markham at the time the maid had disappeared must be a suspect.

The constable was placed on guard at the entrance of the mausoleum and Matt returned to the house with the inspector. He took the time on the way to tell Inspector Lewis what they had learned so far about the occupants of the Hall.

'Right, well, thank you for that, Captain Bryant. Most informative. I need to telephone the police station to see if the doctor is on his way and to arrange for the girl to be moved,' Inspector Lewis said as they arrived at the terrace.

'Obviously, if there is anything more that Kitty and I can do to assist you, do please let us know,' Matt said.

Inspector Lewis's expression hardened. 'I'm sure you can leave it to us now, Captain Bryant, and we'll take it from here.'

'Of course, Inspector.' Matt knew there was no point in saying anything else to the policeman. There was little more he and Kitty could do anyway since they were expected to leave the house after lunch.

* * *

Kitty gave her statement to another constable before joining Matt and the rest of the household for lunch in the dining room. The mood around the table was sober as the celery soup was served.

'What was the girl doing down there?' Lady Amelia mused as she added seasoning to her bowl.

'Well, I expect it was an assignation of some sort. A boyfriend, that's what it will be, you mark my words,' Sir Henry huffed as he buttered his bread.

'It is quite isolated and private down by the lake.' Rupert languidly spooned up his soup.

'She was clearly dodging her chores. Quite disgraceful conduct.' Lady Sarah looked around the table as if daring everyone else to disagree with her.

'The poor girl, it's such a dreadful thing to have happened.' Ruby glanced at Sebastian.

'It sure is. You just don't expect this kind of thing in such a lovely spot. Now back in Chicago, well, that's a different story. Still, I expect your English police are up to the mark. I daresay they'll soon have the fella responsible behind bars.' Mr Conway set his spoon down with a clatter in his empty dish.

Ruby shivered. 'It's rather frightening though, isn't it? I mean knowing that whoever killed her must still be out there someplace.'

'Honey, I'm sure you'll be perfectly safe. This is obviously a lover's quarrel which went wrong. I bet the boyfriend is probably long gone,' Mr Conway reassured his daughter as Mrs Putnam moved around the table gathering up the crockery in readiness for the second course.

'I've spoken to Dora, Agnes's sister, and let her know what's happened. She's dreadfully upset, as one might expect. She says she doesn't know about any boyfriend. It was one of the things I asked her when Agnes first went missing,' Mrs Craven said as plates of pork chops were placed in front of them.

'I don't suppose the girl told her sister everything.' Lady Sarah looked at her friend. 'Really, Millicent, you should know by now what these girls are like.'

'It's possible, I grant you, my dear, but Dora was very close to Agnes. She was considerably older and more or less raised her. Even if Agnes hadn't told her directly, I do think Dora would have detected an omission.' Mrs Craven moved in her chair to allow Mrs Putnam to serve her with new potatoes.

Lady Sarah made a faint scoffing sound at this response.

There was a momentary silence while Mrs Putnam finished serving the spring greens, before leaving the room.

'What happens now about this business? I mean, I assume the police won't hang around here for days?' Sebastian asked.

'Dear heavens, I hope not.' Lady Sarah looked horrified by this suggestion.

'They will naturally wish to talk to everyone about what they remember about the day Agnes went missing,' Matt said as he helped himself to apple sauce.

'I suppose too they may want to take everyone's fingerprints,' Kitty suggested as she speared a slice of carrot with her fork.

'Fingerprints? Whatever for?' Lady Sarah looked aghast.

'If the weapon used to kill Aggie was left with her, then they'll try to see if anyone left any evidence there, I suppose. It's obvious really, Granny,' Rupert said.

'Rupert, I don't think this is suitable conversation for the dinner table.' Sir Henry glared at his youngest son.

Rupert shrugged and continued to eat his lunch.

'Surely though, the police will not consider anyone here a suspect?' Lady Amelia said.

'Oh, Inspector Lewis will consider everyone a suspect. You don't know what he's like.' Mrs Craven looked at Kitty and Matt. 'He'll poke into everything.'

'Is that true, Captain Bryant?' Mr Conway asked as he set his cutlery down on his now empty plate.

'Inspector Lewis always does things by the book. He likes to employ modern policing methods so he will no doubt be rigorous in determining who may have done this,' Matt said.

'That sounds reassuring to me,' Ruby said. 'I don't think I'll feel happy until they catch whoever killed her.'

'Captain Bryant, I don't suppose you and Mrs Bryant would consider staying on for a couple more days. You know, if Sir Henry has no objection, it might help my little girl feel safer having some extra security about the house, so to speak,' Mr Conway suggested.

'Well, if you are sure, sir, and if Sir Henry and Lady Amelia feel it's appropriate.' Matt looked at Kitty.

'Splendid idea! Should have thought of it myself, especially after the business with the safe,' Sir Henry said.

'What business with the safe, Henry?' Lady Sarah's voice was sharp. Everyone turned their gaze to Sir Henry, who shifted uncomfortably in his seat.

'There is some very minor damage to the safe. We noticed it this morning. It's quite secure, nothing has been taken but it does look as if there was an attempt to pick the lock,' Matt said.

'That settles it, then, Captain Bryant. I insist that you and Mrs Bryant stay to keep an eye on things.' Mr Conway glared at Sir Henry.

'This is what comes of having so many temporary staff in the house. I daresay one of them thought they would try their luck after seeing Ruby's jewels last night,' Lady Sarah said.

Mrs Putnam re-entered the room to clear the plates, and the conversation ceased once more while she cleared away. After they had all been served with fruit salad and cream and the servant had gone out again, Mrs Craven broke the silence.

'I shall be glad to have your company, Matthew, Kitty. I agree with Ruby, it's very unsettling knowing a murderer is at large. This business with the safe is also most concerning. I do hope you let Inspector Lewis know about it.' She looked at Sir Henry.

'Yes, Henry, you must tell the inspector. There could be a connection,' Lady Amelia said.

'Very well, if it makes you feel better.' Sir Henry sounded annoyed by all the fuss as he shovelled spoonfuls of his dessert into his mouth.

Once lunch was over everyone drifted off to various pursuits. Sebastian, Ruby and Rupert went to play croquet on the freshly cut lawn. Mr Conway returned to his business affairs, Lady Amelia to her art and Mrs Craven accompanied

Lady Sarah on a stroll around the walled vegetable garden. Sir Henry went to look for Inspector Lewis.

'It seems we are not going home after all, at least not for a while. We must let Mrs Smith and Grams know that we are postponing our return for a couple of days,' Kitty mused thoughtfully as she took a seat on one of the rattan chairs on the terrace. 'I'm glad I packed some extra clothes for us, just in case.'

'I don't know how Inspector Lewis will take the news that we are staying for longer. He seemed quite delighted this morning when I said we would be returning to Churston after lunch.' Matt smiled at her, the dimple quirking in his cheek.

'And now we shall be staying on here like thorns in his side.' Kitty's own smile widened.

'I'll go and telephone home.' Matt dropped a kiss on her cheek and strolled back into the house.

Kitty suspected he probably wanted to check on Rascal with her grandmother. Then he would speak to their house-keeper and enquire if they had received any post. Although the case here at Markham was keeping them busy, she knew his other case was still very much on his mind.

She leaned back in her chair, glad of the shade being offered by the slightly tatty umbrella above the table. The sun was high in the sky now and she could see the shimmer of a heat haze above the stone flags on the terrace.

The croquet players seemed to also be feeling the heat down on the lawn. They soon retired to sit on a tartan rug under the shade of the newly pruned shrubbery at the side of the grass.

Kitty wondered how the inspector was faring. The mausoleum wasn't visible from the terrace, and she was glad she wasn't down there by the lake. Although, she would like to know if they had found the murder weapon or any more clues to who may have killed Agnes.

The constable who had taken her statement had said that he

was going to talk to the servants. Kitty assumed this meant he would ask the gardener to confirm what he had told them about seeing Agnes go off along the path to the wood. She wondered if Mrs Putnam would tell the police about her argument with Agnes the day she died.

Matt came back out onto the terrace and took his place opposite her.

'Is everything all right at home?' Kitty asked.

'Yes, I spoke to your grandmother and Rascal is fine. Mrs Craven had telephoned her after she had spoken to Dora Jones. I checked on Bertie too before coming back here. He's sleeping in the cool upstairs.' Matt took off his panama hat and placed it on the table.

'Did you speak to Mrs Smith? Had you received any post about your other case?' Kitty asked.

'Everything is fine at home. There is a letter with a London postmark. I've asked Mrs Smith to forward it so it should arrive here tomorrow in the second post,' Matt said.

'Do you think it could be a lead to that orderly, the one you think may have assisted Redvers Palmerston to fake his own death?' Kitty asked.

'It's possible. I'm hoping Jobbins is still at that address I found. It would give us something to go on.' Matt looked down the lawn. 'I think Inspector Lewis is coming back up to the house.'

Kitty watched as the inspector plodded out of the wood and along the side of the lawn towards the terrace. The croquet players watched his progress curiously, but all stayed seated on the rug. Kitty suspected from his posture that Rupert was asleep.

'It's all right for some,' Inspector Lewis panted when he ascended the short flight of stone steps onto the terrace.

'You look very hot, Inspector. Do sit down for a minute, may we get you a cold drink?' Kitty was quite alarmed by the rosy flush on the policeman's face and the beads of sweat on his brow under the rim of his hat.

The inspector flopped down on a vacant chair and Matt disappeared into the house to get him a drink.

'It's not been an easy job down there. They've managed to transport her to the road by the bus stop to get her off the estate. We thought it better than hauling her up through the woods to the house.' Inspector Lewis removed his hat and used it to fan his face.

Matt returned with a jug of iced water and a tray of glasses.

'I'm sure Sir Henry will appreciate your thoughtfulness. Please let me pour you a drink.' Kitty poured a generous glass of water for the inspector.

'Did you discover the weapon used to kill Agnes inside the mausoleum?' Matt asked once Inspector Lewis had gulped down half a glass of water.

The inspector pulled a slightly grubby white-cotton hanky from his pocket and mopped his brow. 'No sign of the weapon. My men are searching around the exterior of the building.'

'You told Matt that you thought she had been hit over the head?' Kitty remarked in a casual tone as she refilled the inspector's glass.

'Yes, the doctor from Exeter certainly believes that to be the case. Some kind of blunt instrument.' Inspector Lewis picked his glass up once more and took another gulp of water. He eyed the group on the lawn who were just getting up from the grass ready to return to the house. 'I had better get on with interviewing that lot.'

'Your constable has been talking to the staff, I suppose,' Kitty said.

'Of course, not as I suppose they'll have much to say. Most likely case is either the girl went to meet a lover and he bashed her over the head, or she disturbed some vagrant and met her end that way.' Inspector Lewis finished his drink and set his empty glass back down. 'Still, I expect you'll be glad to get off back home. Leaving today, aren't you?' he asked, suddenly appearing more cheerful.

'Actually, Mr Conway has asked us to stay on for a few more days. He and his daughter are feeling quite unsettled by Agnes's death. There is also the matter of someone trying to get into the safe here last night,' Matt said.

A dark-red flush of indignation spread across the inspector's already rosy cheeks. 'What, an attempted robbery? Were there any signs of someone forcing an entry? Good heavens, why was I not informed of this sooner?' He glared at Matt.

'I take it Sir Henry hasn't told you. He did go to look for you, I believe, and you are rather busy with the murder. And, no, there were no signs of someone breaking in. The exterior doors were locked after the party but, to be honest, anyone could easily have opened them from the outside, the locks are very poor. Nothing was taken and the only signs that an attempt had been made on the safe were some scratches around the escutcheon plate,' Matt explained.

Inspector Lewis didn't appear to be at all mollified by this explanation. 'This could be of vital significance to the murder.'

'I don't see how, sir?' Kitty thought Inspector Lewis must be more affected by the heat than she had first imagined.

'If this girl Agnes did disturb some vagrant and he's been hanging about the place, then that could be who tried to get into the safe last night. I daresay this engagement party has been the talk of the village. Rich pickings for the right person.' Inspector Lewis glared at her.

The croquet party entered the terrace as the inspector was talking.

'You think whoever murdered Agnes may still be here and trying to rob us?' Ruby asked, a fearful expression on her face as the group neared the table.

'I'm just exploring all the possibilities, miss. Some of us are professionals and are trained to critically evaluate the evidence. Unlike amateurish guesswork and hunches.' Inspector Lewis stood and snatched up his hat from the table. 'Now, I had best get on. I shall be speaking to all of you in turn later so please stay near the house.' He stalked off, clearly most put out by what Kitty and Matt had told him.

CHAPTER ELEVEN

Ruby sat down on one of the vacant chairs, making the rattan creak. 'Oh dear, do you think I've upset the inspector? He seemed frightfully cross.'

'I think the heat may be affecting him and, of course, when a murder is involved it can make emotions run rather high,' Matt assured her.

Sebastian took a seat next to his fiancée. 'I wouldn't worry, darling. I expect if it is some vagrant that's been hanging about, they'll soon have him in custody.'

Rupert dragged a chair over from another table and sat down heavily on it. 'I wonder what he'll ask us all?'

'I expect he'll ask about the day Agnes went missing and anything anyone might know about her in the days running up to her being killed. You know, if anyone quarrelled with her and that sort of thing,' Kitty said.

'Do you think he's right about the possibility of whoever killed Agnes trying to rob the safe last night?' Sebastian asked, looking around at them all.

'I think it's unlikely. It's not impossible but it wouldn't have been my first thought. Agnes was killed four weeks ago,' Matt said.

'I wonder who did try and get into the safe?' Rupert asked.

'Granny thinks it was one of the hired staff come back to have a go.' Sebastian rolled his eyes.

'Granny always thinks the servants are up to no good.' Rupert idly traced his forefinger down the condensation on the exterior of the water jug.

Sebastian chuckled. 'That's true.'

Kitty thought Ruby still looked deeply uncomfortable. 'Still, with the estate crawling with policemen I'm sure whoever did it is unlikely to return,' she said.

'I sure hope you're right, Kitty,' Ruby said.

'Have Mrs Putnam and her sister worked here for long?' Matt asked, looking at Sebastian.

'About eighteen months I think, isn't it, Rupe?' He looked at his brother.

'Gosh yes, I expect it must be about that. Mrs P came first and then Mrs Gray a month or so later,' Rupert agreed. 'Granny had to let a lot of staff go. To be honest, we haven't really been fully staffed since the war. At least that's what Granny says.'

'Apart from Mrs Putnam and her sister, Tilly, and obviously Agnes, are there no other house staff?' Kitty asked.

'There used to be, but with one thing and another and such a small household, I suppose Granny just ran the numbers down. There's a woman comes from the village to do some of the stuff and Briggs, the gardener, has a young lad to help him but that's mainly it. We hire in when we need extra hands on deck,' Sebastian said.

'I presume you have an estate manager?' Matt asked.

'Oh yes, old Watts, a decent chap, lives in a tied cottage on the other side of the estate. He oversees all the tenant farmers and the land and so on. Father has been running that show but when Ruby and I are married he wants me to take it over. It's never really been Father's thing. He's fond of shooting, fishing and such but never had a head for business,' Sebastian said.

'Is that something that interests you?' Kitty asked.

Sebastian shrugged. 'One has to do it, I suppose. There is a lot that needs to be done, repairs to the cottages and woodland management, that sort of thing.'

'What about you, Rupert? What do you do?' Kitty had been wondering quite what Sebastian's younger brother did for a living.

'I finish at Oxford soon and then Father said he was going to speak to some chums of his about doing something in the city. Granny keeps suggesting I enlist,' Rupert said.

'You'll be moving away from Markham then.' Kitty thought he sounded unenthusiastic about both his father's plans and his grandmother's suggestion of the army.

'I expect so. Probably to London as I doubt there will be anything in Exeter. Although Father does have some connections in Plymouth. I really don't wish to join the army.' Rupert glanced at her, an amused glint in his eye. 'I assure you I am not a dilettante, Kitty.'

Kitty coloured. 'I hope I didn't imply that you were,' she said. 'I was just curious to work out how you all fit in around the estate.'

'It's a natural question. There's no need to apologise. I wonder who the inspector is interviewing first.' Rupert glanced towards the French doors.

'I expect it will probably be your father or Miss Conway's father,' Matt said.

'Pa? Why would he interview my father?' Ruby looked alarmed.

'He'll talk to everyone, and you and your father were here when Agnes disappeared,' Matt said.

Sebastian grinned. 'Don't worry, Ruby, he's probably speaking to Father first. Unless he's been collared by Granny.

Mother will be in her studio, I suppose. Good luck to him if he's trying to winkle her out of there.'

'Where is your mother's studio?' Kitty asked. She had been wondering where Lady Amelia did her artwork.

'She's commandeered the old orangery. It was in a bit of a state, but she managed to patch it up enough to house all her gear and she works in there,' Sebastian explained.

'Are those your mother's pieces in the hall?' Matt asked.

Rupert grimaced. 'I'm afraid so, they are pretty ghastly but she's terribly enthusiastic. She works in oil and clay. She keeps suggesting casting in bronze, but Father put his foot down.'

'Does she sell them?' Ruby asked.

Rupert laughed. 'If only she could, then we wouldn't have to live with them. No, she gives them to people and puts them on display here, but I don't think she's managed to actually sell any.'

Kitty felt rather sorry for Lady Amelia. Admittedly, she didn't care for any of the pieces she'd seen in the house, but it was clear the boys' mother was passionate about her art.

'Mrs Craven said that her late husband was a relative of yours,' Kitty said.

'Yes, a distant cousin of Granny's, I believe. Peregrine used to stay here in the summer when they were all young. Granny enjoys reminiscing about it, she has several albums of photographs of them all looking very Victorian. Sounds like they all used to have a high old time,' Sebastian said.

'Your grandmother has moved back into the Hall?' Matt asked.

'Only until the repairs are done on the dower house. Then she says she'll move back. I don't know if she will. Mother is hopeless at running the house and Granny adores bossing everyone around,' Rupert said.

'I suppose you and Ruby will also live at the house after the wedding?' Kitty turned to Sebastian.

'Oh yes, Mother and Father have said they'll move to the east wing so we shall have the main part of the house.' Sebastian patted Ruby's hand and Kitty thought she saw the girl's shoulders droop slightly at this announcement.

'Well, it's a large enough place for everyone,' Kitty said.

Mrs Craven and Lady Sarah stepped out onto the terrace as she spoke. 'Good heavens, it's so hot today. I've just spent half an hour being quizzed by that dreadful policeman.' Lady Sarah took a seat at a nearby table while Rupert jumped up to procure a chair for Mrs Craven.

'He has a job to do, Granny,' Sebastian said.

'That's as maybe, but the girl's death, tragic though it is, has nothing to do with anyone in this house,' Lady Sarah announced in a decisive tone. She took a black-lace fan from her small handbag and flicked it open to fan her face. 'I have asked Mrs Putnam to serve tea out here.'

Mrs Craven settled herself in her seat. 'How are your investigations proceeding, Matthew?' She looked at Matt. 'I assume you will be aiding Inspector Lewis?'

'Mrs C, you know that the inspector prefers that we leave murder to the police.' Matt smiled as he spoke, but Kitty detected an edge of steel in his tone. She hoped Mrs Craven would not start telling them how to investigate Agnes's death, especially since everyone else on the terrace had to be considered suspects.

There was a clattering of china from inside the house and Mrs Putnam appeared wheeling a large gilt tea trolley. She clattered it onto the flagstones with an ill-used air. 'I expect more cups are required, my lady.' She nodded stiffly to Lady Sarah and bustled away, leaving them to start serving while the housekeeper fetched more crockery.

'Well, it is all quite ridiculous.' Lady Sarah folded her fan and picked up her cup and saucer. 'I do hope you have all been discussing pleasanter things.' She looked at her grandsons.

'We were talking about where everyone would live after the wedding,' Rupert said, helping himself to a jam tart from the trolley.

'Well, I shall return to the dower house once the repairs are made. I may take young Tilly with me as my housekeeper. She's a bright little thing and properly trained she should do very nicely.' Lady Sarah frowned at Rupert.

Mrs Putnam returned with a jug of hot water and some extra cups which she loaded onto the trolley. 'That policeman would like to see you, Mr Sebastian. He's in the study,' she announced.

'Right ho.' Sebastian jumped up and followed the house-keeper back into the house, leaving Ruby to gaze after him, a worried frown on her forehead.

Lady Sarah gave a tut of disapproval and helped herself to a tart before Rupert could devour the lot.

'Will he wish to see me, do you think?' Ruby asked.

'I suppose so. As Matt said, you and your father were at the house when Agnes disappeared. I don't suppose it will take long though. I mean you barely saw her,' Kitty said.

'That's true,' Rupert said. 'Although I suppose you were talking to her when she helped you unpack your trunk.'

Colour tinged Ruby's pale cheek and she pushed her glasses back up her nose in a nervous gesture. 'Well, only to tell her where to put things and to ask her to press a couple of dresses.'

'She seemed to have quite a conversation with your father when you arrived. You remember, when she was assisting the gardener's boy with the bags from the trunk of the car. Probably hoping for a tip, I expect.' Lady Sarah tutted.

They drank their tea in silence for a few minutes. Ruby seemed uncomfortable and Kitty wondered if the girl was feeling the heat or if it was something more.

Sebastian sauntered back onto the terrace just as they were

finishing their drinks. 'You're up next, Rupert, old boy. Good luck too, he's a dashed impertinent fellow.'

Rupert rose to go and see the inspector and Sebastian settled into his brother's seat. He took out a silver monogrammed cigarette case and proffered them around. When everyone refused the offer of a cigarette, he returned the case to his jacket pocket.

'What did he say to you?' Lady Sarah demanded as Sebastian lit up his cigarette.

'Oh, the usual stuff I suppose. When did I last see Aggie? Had she a boyfriend? Then' – Sebastian blew out a plume of smoke and sat more upright in his chair – 'then he had the dashed impertinence to ask if I had a relationship with the girl.'

'And did you?' Lady Sarah asked drily. 'She was frightfully pretty.'

Kitty saw Ruby swallow and shuffle uncomfortably on her seat.

'No, I didn't. Aggie was a good sort but really, Granny, what do you think I am.' He looked at his grandmother and Kitty saw Ruby relax a little at her fiancé's protestation of innocence.

'I suppose the inspector has to consider all kinds of motives for Agnes's death,' Mrs Craven said. 'No matter how distasteful.'

Lady Sarah nodded her head in agreement and Kitty glanced at Matt.

Mr Conway stepped out onto the terrace. 'Phew, what delightful weather, it's gotten quite warm inside.'

'Do come and join us, Mr Conway. The tea will be cold now, but I can get Mrs Putnam to make a fresh pot.' Lady Sarah smiled expansively at her guest. She reminded Kitty of a fox eyeing up a particularly plump rabbit.

'No, that's fine, Lady Sarah, thank you.' Mr Conway moved another chair to sit nearer to their table.

'And have you been interrogated by the police yet?' Lady Sarah asked, unfurling her fan and using it once more to cool herself down.

'Yes, I had a chat with that Lewis fella. Not sure what help I could be to them though. I barely remember seeing the girl,' Mr Conway said.

'Rupert is in with them now. Then I suppose it will be Amelia's turn. Not that she'll be of any use. You know how your mother is.' Lady Sarah rolled her eyes as she looked at Sebastian.

'I don't know, I've seen that Lady Amelia can be most observant sometimes. Artistic people often are,' Ruby remarked in a thoughtful tone.

Kitty thought Lady Sarah was about to jump in to correct the girl but seemed to suddenly recall that she needed to keep on Ruby's good side. 'Well, perhaps you are right, my dear,' she conceded.

Sebastian looked amused by his grandmother's change of tone.

'I was thinking it might be nice, Sebastian, if you were to borrow a horse for Ruby and take her out for a ride around the estate tomorrow. One sees so much more on horseback. I take it you do ride, my dear?' Lady Sarah looked at Ruby.

The girl shook her head. 'I'm afraid I don't. Horses scare me a little. They are such large animals, aren't they?'

Lady Sarah was clearly astonished by this admission. 'Oh, my dear girl, you must learn. There is really nothing to be afraid of. Sebastian is part of the hunt, and you will, of course, have to learn to hostess the gathering.'

Ruby's face turned a deeper shade of pink. 'I don't think so, thank you, Lady Sarah. In fact, I'm not sure if I would like to have any part in the hunt. Chasing small animals with dogs seems unnecessary to me.'

Kitty thought Lady Sarah was about to have some kind of fit and Sebastian appeared quite alarmed by his fiancée's unexpected stance.

'Foxes are vermin, Ruby. They do untold damage to poultry and to game,' Sebastian said.

'Perhaps, but surely there are other more efficient methods of control,' Ruby said firmly.

The conversation subsided and Mr Conway looked uneasily at his daughter.

'I think I shall retire to my room for a rest before dinner. Come along, Millicent.' Lady Sarah commanded Mrs Craven to accompany her and the two older ladies departed.

Kitty thought they would no doubt complete an assassination of Ruby's character once they were out of earshot. Privately she was pleased and amused that Ruby was beginning to assert herself. If Sebastian and his family thought they were to have free rein spending Ruby's money after the wedding, then it looked to her as if they were mistaken.

Rupert appeared back on the terrace not long after the ladies had departed. He flopped down on a chair looking flushed and disgruntled.

'Mother has gone to see that wretched policeman now. What a fag that was, asking all sorts of questions. How was I supposed to know what a servant does on her time off?' he demanded, looking around the group for sympathy.

'The inspector has to ask questions, it is his job, and someone killed Agnes,' Kitty said.

'I'm inclined to believe it must have been a lover. I mean, the girl wouldn't go to that kind of place for no reason. I can only think she had some kind of meeting planned there that went wrong,' Mr Conway declared.

'I agree,' Sebastian said.

'Or she knew of others meeting there and went to spy on them,' Matt suggested.

Kitty watched the expressions on the faces of the people round the table. All of them looked uncomfortable at his remark.

CHAPTER TWELVE

Matt groaned as he slipped on his dinner jacket in their bedroom later that evening. 'I am so beastly hot. I wish we were back at home and sitting in the garden under the apple tree.' He looked at Kitty.

'I know, but we're stuck here for a little while longer now it seems. Either Inspector Lewis or ourselves will have to discover Agnes's murderer sooner rather than later.' Kitty clipped her ruby and diamond dropper earrings in place.

'Or Mrs Craven may have to solve it,' Matt muttered. Bertie stretched in his place at the foot of the bed and yawned in agreement.

Kitty smiled as she swivelled around on the dressing-table stool to face him. 'Mrs C is being remarkably restrained so far.'

'Yes, it's rather worrying,' Matt agreed as he fussed the top of Bertie's head. He was pleased to see that a large bowl of fresh cold water and an enamel plate of meat had been delivered to their room for the dog's supper. Not that the meat had lasted long.

'I'll just take Bertie for some air, and I'll see you downstairs,' Matt suggested. He was already starting to sweat in his evening attire, and he knew Kitty wasn't quite ready to go down.

'Good idea.' She turned back to the dressing-table mirror and started to powder her nose, frowning at her complexion as she did so.

Bertie ran down the stairs in front of him, clearly eager to go outside for a while. The burning heat of the afternoon had given way to a close, airless evening. Matt could hear the sound of music coming from the drawing room and he guessed someone must have turned on the radio.

Matt carried on along the hall to the ballroom, now deserted with only a trace of debris from the previous evening in evidence. The potted plants and gilt chairs were stacked ready to be collected by the hire company. He stepped out onto the terrace where they had been sitting earlier and watched Bertie gambol down the stone steps onto the lawn.

He remained on the terrace, not wishing to mark his evening shoes on the grass. Bertie sniffed around the edge of the shrubbery looking for signs of rabbits. The air was remarkably still, and Matt noticed that the previously clear sky now had a dull-grey tinge. Over the distant hills of the moors it was almost purple.

'It looks like we may get a spot of rain.' Sir Henry had come to join him. The scent of his cigar smoke mingled with the lavender and roses below the terrace.

'There's a storm on the way by the look of things,' Matt agreed.

'It might help with this confounded heat.' Sir Henry blew out a stream of pungent smoke and flicked some cigar ash over the edge of the balustrade.

'It is very close this evening.' Matt could see Bertie still roaming around the lawn.

'Amelia has invited this dashed policeman to join us for dinner. He's staying at the house since it's quite a trek from the village and the inn hasn't any rooms free. She says it's polite. Personally, I think it'll be like having a ghoul at the feast. Millicent tells me you and Kitty know this chappie, Lewis. He certainly seemed surprised to see you here. Is he any good?' Sir Henry asked. 'Thought you were a bit cagey about him at lunch.'

'Like I said before, sir, he is a great exponent of modern policing methods. He is not fond of myself or Kitty. We have locked horns before on several cases now, but he is very efficient, I believe.' Matt glanced at Sir Henry.

'And do you buy into this theory of a vagrant attacking the girl? And trying to get into the safe?' Sir Henry met his gaze.

'No, sir,' Matt said.

'Humph, unfortunately neither do I. It all makes a chap uneasy. We've never had this kind of thing here before. Murder, I mean. We've had the odd attempt at theft, that's why I got the safe in the first place. I caught the last chap red-handed bagging up the silver. That was back when we had silver, of course, not this plate stuff. Marched him off with my shotgun.' Sir Henry finished his cigar and stubbed it out on the wall before tossing the end into the rose bushes.

'Who do you think may have tried the safe last night?' Matt asked. He was keen to hear his host's views on the matter.

'Mother suspects the servants. Not Mrs Putnam, of course, she means the hired help who came to set up here yesterday,' Sir Henry said.

'And is that what you think too?' Matt persisted.

'It's a possibility, but no. I think it may be someone closer to home.' Sir Henry sighed. 'I don't care to think it but Rupert has been sailing rather close to the wind lately. Gaming debts. He thinks I don't know but word gets around.'

'Ah, I see.' Matt focused his attention on Bertie who was now exploring the area around the small shed where the croquet things were stored.

'This business with the girl, Agnes, there I think the inspector may have a point. I think the girl must have had a lover. Someone she was seeing on the quiet,' Sir Henry said.

'Someone local?' Matt asked. The house was quite isolated, and he had seen few candidates on the estate itself who could have been romantically involved with the maid.

'Perhaps a fellow from the village.' Sir Henry glanced at him again.

'I suppose the inspector will make enquiries there.' Matt personally thought whoever killed the girl was probably much closer to home. It seemed to him that the girl had gone to the mausoleum to meet someone without being seen. He whistled to Bertie to come up from the lawn.

Bertie took no notice of him and continued to snuffle happily around the shed.

'Needs a spot of recall training. I don't suppose you use him as a gun dog?' Sir Henry said, watching Bertie.

'Indeed no. We inherited him and I don't think his previous owner did any training with him at all.' Matt gave a wry smile and whistled again.

This time the spaniel lifted his head and reluctantly left the shed to come trotting back up the steps to Matt.

'I'd better get him back inside before dinner.' Matt bade farewell to his host and took the little dog back up to the bedroom.

The bedroom was empty and he assumed Kitty had already gone downstairs to the drawing room. Matt left Bertie inside and was just about to head down to join her when Mrs Craven came rustling along the corridor in a swathe of lilac silk and rose perfume.

'Well, how is it going? What have you found out? Has the inspector told you anything?' she demanded in an imperious whisper.

Matt suppressed a sigh, and much to Bertie's surprise reopened the door of the bedroom, ushering Mrs Craven inside.

'It's hard to say at present. There are lots of possibilities.' He quickly apprised her of most of what they had discovered so far.

'Lewis favours a boyfriend or a vagrant as his culprit. At least that's what I've gathered from Lady Sarah,' Mrs Craven said. 'I am not so sure. This business with the safe is rather odd too. You said Sir Henry thinks Rupert may have been responsible for that?'

'Yes, he seemed to believe Rupert has gaming debts,' Matt said.

Bertie gave Mrs Craven's black-patent evening shoes an interested sniff before subsiding back to sleep.

'Hmm, well leave that to me. I shall do some probing.' Mrs Craven held her hand up imperiously to ward off the protest Matt was about to make. 'Have no fear. I shall be very discreet.'

Matt was forced to comply since it was almost time for dinner, and they needed to be downstairs. He followed Mrs Craven out onto the landing and reclosed the bedroom door. He had a feeling that Kitty would not be too pleased when she discovered Mrs Craven's plans.

* * *

Kitty glanced at the clock on the drawing-room mantelpiece and wondered what could be taking Matt so long. She took a sip of the sherry that had been pressed upon her by Lady Sarah and wished it had been a nice refreshing cocktail instead.

Inspector Lewis wasn't present, and Kitty wondered if he was still in the house. She had seen one of the constables walking past the drawing-room window, presumably heading for the kitchens.

There was no air coming into the room through the open windows and Kitty was glad her pale-green silk evening gown had a low back and thin straps. The heat was stifling, and she was surprised they had not taken their pre-dinner drinks out on the terrace.

'Goodness me, it's so warm this evening.' Lady Amelia seated herself beside Kitty.

'Yes, although I expect it will break soon,' Kitty responded politely. 'Did you talk to Inspector Lewis this afternoon?'

Lady Amelia blinked. 'Oh yes. It was rather trying. I'm working in clay at the moment, and everything dries out so quickly in this heat. It quite ruined the one piece.'

'Oh dear, that must be most vexing. Did he ask you many questions about Agnes?' Kitty asked.

'Lots. Not that I was much help really. My mother-in-law manages the staff. Agnes always seemed a pleasant enough girl to me. Very pretty and polite but one always felt there was an edge of impertinence to her, especially the last few weeks. The inspector asked about her personal life but of course I know nothing about that,' Lady Amelia said.

'You've never seen or heard of a vagrant or tramp about the grounds either?' Kitty didn't expect that Lady Amelia would have noticed such a person even if there had been anyone.

'No, the inspector asked the same question. I expect he thinks that's who may have killed Agnes if it wasn't a boyfriend of hers.' Lady Amelia took a sip from her own glass of sherry.

'I wonder who may have tried the safe last night,' Kitty mused.

This earned her a surprisingly sharp glance from Lady Amelia. 'My mother-in-law as usual suspects a servant. One of the temporary staff, but they had all left in a car chartered by their agency. They aren't returning until tomorrow to finish clearing away and returning all of the hired glassware and things. I don't see how one of them could have done anything.'

'Then do you think it may have been someone inside the house?' Kitty asked.

'It did cross my mind that perhaps Mr Conway may have tried his luck. He could have been testing our security or trying to read some of the papers my husband keeps in the safe.' Lady Amelia paused and glanced in the direction of the American. 'This marriage business is very complicated.'

Kitty considered Lady Amelia's idea. It was a possibility, she supposed. The man did seem very nervous about his and his daughter's security. He had also said someone tried to rob them when they had been in London. Perhaps that had been a cover story of some kind.

Sir Henry entered the room and immediately went over to Mr Conway to talk to him. Kitty checked the time once more. Matt was certainly cutting it fine, and there was no sign of Mrs Craven yet either, which was in itself rather suspicious.

Mrs Craven entered a moment later accompanied by Matt. Kitty thought the older woman appeared smug as Matt came over to join her.

'Where have you been? Was Bertie being naughty?' Kitty asked as her husband greeted her with a kiss on her cheek.

'No, I was talking to Sir Henry on the terrace, then I ran into Mrs C on the way downstairs.' Matt glanced at Lady Amelia and Kitty guessed he probably had something to tell her once they were alone.

The dinner gong sounded in the hall, and everyone rose to file into the dining room. The dining room was even hotter than the drawing room. The temperature was not helped by the heated serving dishes on the sideboard.

They were just taking their seats when Inspector Lewis came to join them. Kitty discovered he was to be seated next to her. Something which she suspected pleased neither the policeman nor herself.

Mrs Putnam served the first course of a cold summer soup. Conversation around the table was desultory and mostly consisted of speculation about the weather. Inspector Lewis confined himself to silently devouring his soup.

There was an air of tension in the room which Kitty surmised was mostly due to Inspector Lewis's presence at the table. Lady Sarah was clearly unimpressed he was there, and Lady Amelia kept glancing anxiously at her husband.

'How is it all going, Inspector?' Stanley Conway voiced the question everyone was thinking as the soup bowls were being cleared to make way for the roast beef.

Inspector Lewis dabbed the corners of his mouth with his linen napkin before responding. 'It's early days yet, Mr Conway, but I daresay we shall have our culprit soon.'

'That's the ticket,' Sir Henry remarked approvingly as his roast beef dinner was placed before him. 'Can't have these villains running around the countryside.'

'You have an idea who could have killed her then, Inspector?' Ruby asked.

'I have a working theory, yes, miss. My men will be conducting more enquiries in the village tomorrow.' Inspector Lewis nodded to Mrs Putnam who spooned some minted peas onto his plate. 'We shall also be continuing our search for the weapon used in the attack.'

Kitty thought she detected a ripple around the table at this. She wasn't sure if it was alarm or excitement at this unexpected piece of news.

'What kind of weapon?' Ruby's eyes were wide behind her spectacles.

'I'd prefer not to say at this stage, Miss Conway, but rest assured my men have been fully briefed.' Inspector Lewis applied large quantities of mustard to his meat.

Kitty could only assume that perhaps the inspector was privy to some information from the doctor who had examined Agnes. Information that, as usual, he hadn't shared with either Matt or herself.

She had been giving some thought to the weapon. The murderer must have been holding it when they entered the mausoleum. There had been no signs that she had noticed to say the girl had been killed outside and then hidden there. No drag marks on the ground or the marble floor of the building.

That signified that either the murderer had been holding something already which had not alarmed the victim, or he or she had picked something up outside to use to kill the girl. A rock perhaps, or a large stick. The mausoleum, however, was surrounded by a terrace and any rocks or sticks would be in the wood, not readily to hand.

A walking stick, or umbrella perhaps, something of that nature. If the killer had used a rock or a stick from the woods then they could have simply disposed of it back there afterwards. Since Agnes had been killed there had definitely been some rain so even if they found something, any evidence may have been washed away.

Kitty added some new potatoes to her plate, her mind busy on the problem of the weapon. She was so engrossed in her own thoughts she didn't hear Matt the first time he asked her to pass the horseradish sauce.

He grinned at her when she did finally hear him and passed the condiment. Lady Sarah had diverted the conversation back to the wedding and was quizzing Ruby on the subject of a wedding dress.

'You could go to Paris, but there is not much time if you would like a June date. Or a London couturier might suffice unless, of course, you have a heritage gown, perhaps from your mother?' Lady Sarah asked.

'No, my lady. I thought perhaps I could simply go to someone perhaps in Exeter or Plymouth? They are both size-able places so I'm sure there will be a dressmaker there,' Ruby said.

'The lady who made my dress is in Torquay. She is a French

dressmaker and highly regarded. Mrs Craven, I believe you recommended her to Grams when our wedding was being planned,' Kitty said.

'Yes, that's right. She is very well thought of indeed. Lady Hazelmere's daughter had her dress from her.' Mrs Craven nodded in agreement.

'Then you must give us her details after dinner.' Mr Conway beamed at his daughter.

'It's a pity the gardens here have been let go but we should be able to get some lilies for your bouquet and for the church,' Lady Sarah continued.

'No. I mean, no thank you. I don't care for lilies. They remind me of funerals. I'd like roses, pink roses,' Ruby said in a firm tone.

'Oh.' Lady Sarah didn't pursue the matter, but her face suggested she disapproved of Ruby's floral tastes.

Sebastian smiled at his fiancée and Kitty sensed he approved of seeing his domineering grandmother being forced to rein herself in.

'What about attendants, Ruby? We have no young people in our immediate family but if you wanted a flower girl the gardener's granddaughter is a pretty little thing,' Lady Amelia said.

'I'd prefer not to have attendants, thank you. I might have my closest friend, Jennifer, as a bridesmaid. She's in London so it wouldn't be too difficult for her to get here,' Ruby said.

Kitty saw Mr Conway's smile slip from his face. 'Now then, Ruby, honey, you know how I feel about Jennifer Baden-Bradstock.'

'She's my best friend.' Ruby glared at her father.

'Then I'm sure we'll make her very welcome if you want her to come to the wedding,' Lady Sarah soothed.

The empty dinner plates were removed, and raspberry sorbet was served for dessert. Kitty was glad of something cool.

The light was starting to fade outside, and the sky had grown darker. Mrs Putnam lit the long white candles in the silver-plated candlesticks on the dinner table.

'Coffee on the terrace I think, Mrs Putnam, before it begins to rain. It may cool us off a little to be outside for a spell,' Lady Sarah directed as they finished eating.

Kitty hoped she might get the chance to grill Inspector Lewis about Agnes once they were outside. Much to her annoyance, however, he excused himself and escaped before she had a chance to pin him down.

CHAPTER THIRTEEN

The table lanterns on the terrace had already been lit when they went outside. The gentle yellow glow attracting small moths which fluttered against the glass. In the distance across the darkening lawn, banks of grey clouds were gathering over the distant dark-mauve hills of the moors.

The air was still and heavy and even the bedtime twittering of the birds in the shrubbery sounded muted. Mrs Putnam wheeled out a trolley with the coffee things and departed quickly with an air of one being ill-used.

Lady Sarah looked meaningfully at Lady Amelia, clearly waiting for her to take the hint to begin serving coffee. Sebastian, Rupert and Sir Henry had all lit cigarettes, while Mr Conway had produced a cigar. The scent of tobacco mingled with the perfume of the roses and lavender below the balustrade.

'Amelia, my dear, coffee,' Lady Sarah prompted when her daughter-in-law failed to move.

'Oh yes, of course.' Lady Amelia went to the trolley.

'I'll help you,' Ruby offered, jumping up from her seat to assist.

Lady Amelia dispensed the coffee in fine white bone china cups. Ruby offered sugar and cream as she passed the drinks around. Kitty had expected the tension she had sensed around the dinner table to have eased with the departure of the inspector. Instead, it seemed to be increasing.

'Do you think the police have finished now at the mausoleum?' Rupert asked as he gazed towards the lake.

'I would certainly hope so. The other occupants of that building deserve to be left in peace. The inspector and his constable have also ceased harassing the house staff and are presently talking to the gardener and the boy, I believe.' Lady Sarah sniffed.

'The gardener?' Rupert looked at his grandmother.

'He was the last person to have seen Agnes alive,' Kitty said. 'He told us he saw her walking off towards the wood that last afternoon.'

Rupert finished his cigarette and stubbed it out on the balustrade wall. 'How ghastly. Did he see anyone else around there then, do we know?' He glanced at the others on the terrace.

'I suppose that is what the inspector will be asking,' Lady Sarah pointed out with a touch of asperity in her tone.

'A vagrant perhaps, or the elusive lover. He would be well placed to know if some undesirable had been about on the estate,' Sir Henry remarked. He was hidden in the shadows of the terrace, the tip of his cigarette glowing red in the dark.

'No one seems to know anything about a lover.' Matt leaned back in his chair, making the rattan creak. 'Not her sister, her fellow servants, or indeed anyone in this household.'

An uneasy silence followed his statement.

'Then clearly it must be a vagrant, or someone the girl had slighted, from the village perhaps,' Lady Sarah said.

'The police are visiting the village tomorrow. I expect they will ask those questions there.' Sebastian put out his own cigarette and turned his attention to his rapidly cooling coffee.

'Well, there you are then.' Lady Sarah sat back with an air of satisfaction.

Kitty was not so sure that this was the right conclusion, but the conversations turned to different subjects. They hadn't long finished their coffee when an ominous distant rumble sounded above the moors.

'I think the storm is approaching.' Mrs Craven rose from her seat and the others began to follow suit.

'We should go inside.' Lady Amelia glanced nervously at the hills, now almost swallowed up by the dark sky.

Rupert assisted Kitty to wheel the trolley inside the house just as the first raindrops started to fall.

Within minutes there was a loud crack of thunder, and the rain began to hammer like fat, wet pennies onto the stone flags where they had been stationed a few moments before. Sir Henry pulled some of the French doors shut, assisted by Sebastian.

'That was in the nick of time,' Lady Sarah announced. 'I think we should adjourn to the drawing room.'

They abandoned the trolley inside the ballroom and made their way through the darkened corridors to the drawing room. Sebastian switched on some of the old-fashioned silk-shaded lamps. Rupert secured the French doors.

Outside the rain bounced up from the flagstones and pelted the windows as lightning illuminated the room, followed almost instantly by bangs of thunder. It seemed the storm was moving swiftly to above the house. Kitty saw Ruby wince at the sound and her father immediately patted her hand to reassure her.

Mrs Putnam entered the room and went to Sir Henry. Kitty watched as the woman murmured something to him. He nudged Rupert and Sebastian, and they all followed the housekeeper from the room. Lady Sarah watched them leave through narrowed eyes and she, in turn, spoke quietly to Lady Amelia.

Lady Amelia paled and hurried out after her husband and sons. Outside on the patio the rain was splashing out of the gutters and running like a stream down the stone steps leading to the lawn. Kitty wondered if the inspector had taken a coat with him to the gardener's cottage. If not, he was going to be very wet.

The Favershams didn't return, and Lady Sarah and Mrs Craven continued to entertain Mr Conway. Ruby kept glancing nervously outside at the weather and flinching when the thunder overhead was especially loud.

There was one spectacular clap of thunder and the lights in the room failed, plunging them into darkness. Ruby shrieked in alarm.

'Don't panic, my dear. The lights will be back on shortly. There are candles on the mantelpiece,' Lady Sarah admonished, and a second later Kitty heard a match strike.

Matt had found the silver-plated candlesticks and lit the candles. Ruby's face looked teary and frightened in the poor light.

'I assume the fuses have blown with that last strike,' Matt said.

'I expect so. Henry will have to go down to the cellar to fix them.' Lady Sarah tutted.

'Can I be of any help, Lady Sarah?' Mr Conway asked.

'Oh no, it's quite all right. A mere consequence of country living with the storm being so close,' Lady Sarah assured him.

'I'll go and see if I can help Sir Henry,' Matt offered and slipped out of the room.

'Such a nuisance,' Mrs Craven agreed. 'One gets so used to the convenience of electricity but in many ways the gas lamps and oil lamps were much more dependable.'

Ruby screamed. 'Oh, out there, there is someone out there!'

She pointed dramatically to the French doors which had been closed against the storm.

Kitty caught a glimpse of a man's rain-soaked face, his hair plastered to his forehead and jumped up from her seat. She hurried over to the door and opened it to allow a very wet Inspector Lewis to enter the room.

'Good grief, Inspector, you frightened poor Ruby out of her wits, and don't drip on the rug,' Lady Sarah admonished as the lights came back on.

Inspector Lewis was a very sorry sight indeed. Water ran in rivulets from his sodden jacket onto the polished wooden floorboards as he attempted to obey his hostess.

'I'll see if Mrs Putnam has any towels,' Kitty said.

'Stay here. I'll go.' Lady Sarah glared at the unfortunate policeman and moved out of the room at remarkable speed for a lady of her age in a dinner gown.

'Do take off your jacket, Inspector Lewis. It's completely soaked. Did you get caught out by the storm?' Mrs Craven asked.

'My car developed a flat tyre on the way back from the gardener's cottage. I had to abandon it in the lane and walk.' Inspector Lewis's teeth chattered as he peeled off his sopping wet coat and extracted his sodden notebook from the pocket.

He dropped the notebook down on the side table next to Kitty's seat. Lady Sarah bustled back into the room accompanied by a very harried-looking Mrs Putnam. The housekeeper was bearing a pile of towels. Inspector Lewis found himself being ensconced in fabric and bundled unceremoniously from the room. He was accompanied by the housekeeper with instructions from Lady Sarah that he was to borrow some things from Sir Henry so he could get dry.

Kitty picked up the inspector's notebook from the table and dabbed the black-leather cover dry with her handkerchief. She also mopped up the damp patch on the rosewood tabletop, not wishing the furniture to be damaged.

She glanced around to see if anyone was watching her. Ruby was by the drinks cabinet with Mrs Craven insisting she take a little brandy for shock, while Lady Sarah was calling for mops for the water on the floor. Mr Conway was assisting with the drinks, fussing over his daughter.

Aware she would have to act swiftly before anyone noticed what she was doing, Kitty unfastened the band keeping the notebook closed. She flicked it open to the latest entry and started to glance over the inspector's notes. Fortunately, the inspector had a fairly neat hand and she quickly found it quite legible.

She silenced her guilty conscience about reading the book by reminding herself it was all the inspector's own fault. After all, if he was more forthcoming with information she wouldn't have to resort to snooping.

The last entry was a transcript of his interview with the gardener. She leafed through that and found nothing new. The entry before that was with the gardener's boy. This was much more promising. It said the lad had heard raised voices in the woods the afternoon Agnes had disappeared. A man and a woman arguing.

Kitty hurriedly turned the pages to read the notes before that. This time to an interview conducted with Mrs Gray, Mrs Putnam's sister. She said she didn't know of a boyfriend but said Agnes had been hinting about bettering herself and she seemed to have come into some money.

Before she could read any more Ruby and Mrs Craven returned to their seats, so Kitty quickly replaced the band and dropped the book onto her lap.

'What have you there, Kitty?' Mrs Craven demanded.

'I was drying the inspector's notebook. I got the water off

the table too.' Kitty tried to look innocent. Mrs Craven eyed her suspiciously.

Lady Sarah entered just in time to overhear Kitty say she had dried the table and rushed over to examine it. 'Thank you, my dear. Really, that man has no thought. The furnishings in this house are very valuable. Fortunately, it seems no harm has been done.'

Tilly, the young maid, came in with a mop and bucket and began to get the water from the floor under Lady Sarah's critical eye. Kitty thought the girl looked exhausted and close to tears. It must have been a long day, especially after all the extra work yesterday with the party.

Matt and Inspector Lewis returned together. The inspector was clearly wearing borrowed clothing that was several sizes too large for him. It didn't appear to have improved his mood.

'Do sit down, Inspector. I'll get you a drink.' Matt indicated a vacant seat near to Kitty.

The policeman took it and immediately looked around on the tabletop. Alarm flashing across his face when he saw his notebook was gone.

'I've dried your book as best I could. It was completely soaked,' Kitty said as she passed it over to him.

'Thank you, Mrs Bryant. I'm most obliged, I'm sure.' He took it from her with a suspicious look and tucked it away inside the pocket of his borrowed jacket.

Matt handed him a drink. 'There you go. I'm sure you must have felt quite chilled after being so hot all day and then being caught in the rain. I hope your trip was useful?'

'It was very informative,' the inspector said before taking a sip of brandy.

'Any sign of a vagrant?' Ruby asked.

'Not as yet, Miss Conway, but we have more enquiries to make in the village before that possibility can be excluded,' Inspector Lewis said.

'Do you still think it was someone from the village who may have killed the girl?' Mr Conway asked. He too was nursing a crystal glass of something that looked like whisky. Kitty guessed he had helped himself at the bar whilst they had been fussing over Ruby.

'As I said, sir, we can't be certain at this stage. There is also a question of a motive.' Inspector Lewis's expression grew even more foxy.

'I guess she must have fought with someone. I don't suppose she was robbed. I mean you said she was in her uniform, and she wasn't rich.' Mr Conway looked at the inspector.

'Not rich, no, yet she had more money recently from somewhere,' Inspector Lewis said.

Lightning flashed once more outside the house.

'A gift from an admirer? A present from a relative? Even a small win at bingo could account for that,' Lady Sarah said dismissively.

Tilly had finished drying the floor with the mop and placed it in the metal bucket ready to leave. Outside the rain had started to slow a little and the thunder diminished to a menacing growl.

'Or money she made from blackmailing someone,' Matt suggested.

Tilly stumbled with the metal bucket, making the wooden mop clang against the handle.

'Oh, do be careful, girl. You'll have it all over the floor,' Lady Sarah chided.

'Sorry, my lady.' Tilly scuttled from the room and Kitty was left to ponder the expression that had appeared on the maid's face when Matt had mentioned blackmail.

Sir Henry and his sons entered as Tilly left, passing her in the doorway. They all looked slightly flustered and dishevelled.

'The dashed fuse had blown again. I had to go down to the cellar,' Sir Henry grumbled as he lowered himself into a seat.

Sebastian headed for the drinks cabinet accompanied by Rupert.

'What were you all talking about?' Sir Henry asked as Sebastian handed his father a whisky.

'Captain Bryant suggested that Agnes may have been black-mailing someone.' Lady Sarah rolled her eyes.

'The girl had seemed flush with money in the last few weeks. We were trying to discover why that would be the case,' Inspector Lewis said. He had more colour in his thin cheeks now the brandy was taking effect.

'I'm sure there is probably a much more straightforward explanation,' Mr Conway suggested.

'Maybe, sir, but until we know what that might be then we must consider everything,' Inspector Lewis said.

Once again silence filled the room until it was broken by Ruby suggesting she switch the radio on now the thunder appeared to have gone. There was a rush of voices agreeing to her suggestion and the remainder of the evening passed off with no further discussion of the murder.

CHAPTER FOURTEEN

Kitty snuggled up to Matt in bed later that evening in their room.

'What a very peculiar day this has been,' she said with a yawn.

The thunderstorm from earlier had finished and the rain had ceased. Bertie lay snoring gently at the foot of the bed.

'Extremely.' He frowned at her in the darkness, his expression barely visible. 'What is that infernal noise?'

Kitty listened. In the distant darkness she heard faint metallic pinging sounds. She began to chuckle. 'That odd plinking sound? I rather think it explains where the Favershams dashed off to when the rain started.'

Matt's brow cleared. 'Oh, you mean...'

'I think the roof of Markham Hall leaks like a colander and what we can hear is the sound of water landing in the many receptacles placed to catch the drips.' Kitty smiled as she replied. 'I worked it out when I heard the sound.'

Matt chuckled. 'I found Sir Henry on the stairs when I went to see if he could fix the fuses. He did look frightfully flustered. That would explain it.'

'Poor Inspector Lewis looked most uncomfortable in Sir Henry's clothes, didn't he? He frightened Ruby half to death when he appeared at the French doors like some spectre from the lake. I hope Mrs Putnam manages to dry his clothes out by morning or that he can have some fresh ones sent from his lodgings,' Kitty mused.

'I take it you read his notes before giving that notebook back?' Matt asked.

Kitty pulled back from him a little as if affronted by the question. 'Of course. Well, naturally I tried to get a peep.' She told him what she had managed to read before she had been forced to give the book back.

'Interesting.' Matt paused. 'Um, by the way, Mrs C is going to try and find out the truth about Rupert's gambling debts. It might be important, or it may not, but it would be helpful to know.'

'I suppose it's better to try and keep her occupied,' Kitty said once she had become accustomed to the idea. She hoped the woman would be tactful. 'Speaking of Mrs C, doesn't she have Agnes's box now? Tilly said she had packed up her things and that Mrs Craven was going to take them back to Dartmouth for Dora. I wonder if anyone has checked through the contents?'

Matt adjusted his position on the mattress. 'Yes, you're right. Surely the inspector will have done that, won't he?' He glanced at Kitty.

'Possibly, but we can ask Mrs C tomorrow,' Kitty said. Tilly hadn't felt there was anything out of the ordinary except the amount of money Agnes had in her purse. Still, it was worth checking. There might be an indication somewhere of where this money had come from that had been overlooked.

* * *

The air the next morning felt fresher and cooler when they went down to breakfast. It was a slightly grey start, but Kitty suspected the cloud would move away once the sun came back out.

Sebastian was already at breakfast when they entered the dining room. They had brought Bertie downstairs with them as he was eager to be outside and the scent of sausages and bacon was in the air.

'Morning, the rain seems to have stopped.' Sebastian gestured towards the window with his fork.

'I expect it will turn bright again later,' Kitty agreed as she went to the sideboard and helped herself to scrambled eggs from one of the trays on top of the spirit burners.

She joined Sebastian at the table while Bertie sat patiently at her feet waiting for Matt to return with a loaded plate. The dog wasn't disappointed as Matt cut up some sausage and placed it down for Bertie.

'What are your plans for the day?' Kitty asked, looking at Sebastian.

'I've a meeting with Ruby's father and old Watts, the estate manager, then I promised Ruby I would show her around the place a bit more.' Sebastian toyed with a mushroom on the edge of his plate. 'I suppose you will be assisting Inspector Lewis with this business of Agnes's death? I mean, Millicent Craven said you knew him well and you are private investigators.'

'I don't think the inspector would especially welcome our help, but we have promised to stay for a couple of days, as you know, to make Ruby feel more secure. The murder is bad enough but the attempt on the safe has left her feeling worried I think,' Kitty said as she applied butter to a rather cold slice of toast.

'That's true. The business with the safe does seem a bit peculiar. Ruby's jewellery is very valuable though so it may have tempted someone,' Sebastian said and frowned as he finished his breakfast.

'The safe would be more secure if your father's study were kept locked but he said he has no idea where the key to the door might be.' Matt slipped a bit of bacon under the table to Bertie.

Sebastian laughed. 'That key has been gone for years. It's like the ones for his desk drawers. The only key he has is the one to the safe and of course that has a combination as well. Security has never been at the top of Father's list.' His face sobered. 'Although, now this has happened to Agnes he may need to rethink things, I suppose.'

He drained the remainder of his tea from his cup and stood up from the table. 'I had better get a move on. I want to look at some things before Mr Conway arrives for the meeting. He always asks hundreds of questions.'

'He seems to be taking his new responsibilities very seriously,' Kitty said after Sebastian had hurried away.

'Yes, he does. I daresay Lady Sarah will be pleased,' Matt agreed.

Rupert arrived a few minutes after his brother had left. He was accompanied by Mrs Craven.

'Good morning,' Mrs Craven greeted them cheerfully while Rupert mumbled a hullo.

They both helped themselves to breakfast while Kitty rang for more tea and fresh toast.

'I have said I shall help Lady Sarah at the dower house this morning. She wishes to compile a list of repairs that need to be done before she moves back there,' Mrs Craven said once Mrs Putnam had brought in the things Kitty had requested. 'What are your plans for the day?' She looked at Matt while helping herself to the fresh toast.

'We wondered if you still had Agnes's box?' Kitty said. 'I'd like to look through it in case there's something that was missed when it was packed up.'

'Oh yes, of course. I should have thought of that myself. It's been delivered to my room. We can go up after we've finished eating.' Mrs Craven looked a little put out that she hadn't suggested the idea.

'Rupert, what about you? Do you have plans for today?' Kitty asked.

'I might go and see some friends who are staying at the rectory at Chudleigh. I think Seb is going to be busy with the Conways.' Rupert declined Mrs Craven's offer of a cup of tea.

'Yes, he mentioned he had a meeting with the estate manager,' Matt said.

'That'll be interesting.' Rupert's lips twisted in a grimace. 'Good luck if he's trying to sort out any of Father's record-keeping. It's little wonder the place is going to wrack and ruin.'

'Rupert,' Mrs Craven chided him gently. 'Your father has not had an easy time. He wasn't meant to be the one managing the estate, you know. I'm sure he has done the best he can over the last twenty years or so.'

'Possibly, but he has no head for business, you can't deny that,' Rupert said.

Kitty and Matt had finished eating so Matt said he would take Bertie outside again for a walk around. Kitty said she would wait in the hall for Mrs Craven to be ready to go and look at Agnes's box, once Mrs Craven had finished her breakfast.

Matt took Bertie out via the French doors in the ballroom while Kitty dawdled along the hall examining Lady Amelia's art. The door of Sir Henry's study was partly open, and she assumed Sebastian must be in there preparing for his meeting.

She paused by a sculpture which she thought might be that of a horse's head and tried to work out if she was correct. The murmur of a female voice talking on the telephone reached her.

'No, everything is all right, Jennifer. A change of plan, that's all.' Ruby must be talking to the friend her father disapproved of.

Kitty crept a little closer on the pretext of standing back to admire the art.

'Yes, I couldn't get it. I did try but there are detectives here and the police. There's been a murder in the grounds. One of the maids.' Ruby paused, and Kitty guessed her friend was talking.

'We don't know. I don't intend to try again. It's rather frightening. Listen, I have to go. I need to have breakfast.' There was another pause and Kitty prepared to move away quickly should Ruby come out of the study into the hall.

'Yes, I'll call again. I'm spending more time with Sebastian.' There was another short break before Ruby giggled. 'Yes, it's all going well, better than I expected so there may be a change of plan as I said. I guess you'll be a bridesmaid after all. I'll let you know but keep your diary clear.' There were a few words of farewell then Kitty heard the distinctive click of the telephone receiver being placed in its cradle.

She moved quietly and quickly along the hall and nipped into the drawing room just before she heard Ruby leaving the study. She waited for the girl to go past on her way to the dining room before she released a slow sigh of relief.

That had been an interesting conversation. She wondered what plans Ruby and Jennifer had been making and why having the police in the house might have changed them. There was clearly more to Ruby than she had first imagined and it was becoming obvious that the girl had her own hopes for this marriage with Sebastian.

She stepped back into the hall as Mrs Craven bustled towards her. 'Kitty, shall we go and take a look inside this box?'

'Has the inspector asked to see it at all?' Kitty asked as she accompanied the older woman up the stairs.

'No, I don't think he has even thought about it. Or he may believe it must have gone off weeks ago when Agnes first disappeared,' Mrs Craven said as they reached the landing.

'Tilly didn't notice anything unusual when she packed it.' Kitty stood back to allow Mrs Craven to enter the bedroom ahead of her.

The room was much nicer than the one Matt and Kitty occupied. Kitty suspected that was because Mrs Craven was family. She also would have complained bitterly had her accommodation not been to her satisfaction.

'Now then, I had Mrs Putnam place the box in the bottom of the wardrobe so it wouldn't be in my way.' Mrs Craven opened the double doors of an elaborately carved oak wardrobe.

Beneath the rail of evening gowns and day dresses Kitty saw a small pine trunk.

'You'll need to drag it out, Kitty, and do watch my shoes,' Mrs Craven instructed.

The box wasn't terribly heavy, so Kitty lifted it out and placed it on the low table in front of the bedroom fireplace. Mrs Craven flapped and fussed around her with unwanted instructions as she did so.

The box was secured with leather straps and a small brass plate on the lid was engraved with Agnes's name. Kitty unbuckled the straps and lifted the lid. Tilly was a neat and tidy packer. The dead girl's clothes, what few there were, had all been carefully folded. A few dried sprigs of lavender had been added to the small bundle of clean underwear and stockings.

A pair of shoes was at the bottom of the box along with a Bible bearing Agnes's name inside the cover. There was a cheap evening purse and some cosmetics along with some costume jewellery. Agnes's other handbag contained letters from Dora, a comb, handkerchief, lipstick and a purse with a surprising amount of money inside.

'Well, do you see anything important?' Mrs Craven looked at her expectantly.

'I'm afraid not. It seems Tilly was right.' Kitty began to replace the items back inside the box, taking care to check the dark-green cotton lining in case anything had been concealed inside.

She flicked the pages of the Bible, again checking that nothing had been missed.

'I really did think perhaps we might have discovered something interesting,' Mrs Craven said with a disappointed air. 'I must go and meet Lady Sarah. Put the box back in the wardrobe when you have finished, Kitty.'

She departed, leaving Kitty to finish placing Agnes's things away inside the box. She double-checked everything as she put the items back. She took one last look inside Agnes's handbag as she did so. There were three letters from Dora on cheap lined paper folded inside their envelopes.

Kitty had no desire to invade Agnes's privacy by reading the contents but thought she should check nothing else had fallen inside the open envelopes. As she pulled out the last one she realised there were two pieces of paper. One was clearly a letter from Dora on the same paper as the other letters. The other sheet of paper was different.

Kitty sat down on the edge of Mrs Craven's bed and opened it up. This letter or note was on thicker headed notepaper from a London hotel. It was dated a week before Agnes had died.

Dear Miss Jones,

Thank you for your information. I shall be pleased to remunerate you on our arrival at Markham.

Sincerely,

S Conway

'Well, well,' Kitty murmured to herself as she read the note again, before refolding it and tucking it into her pocket.

It seemed this might well be the answer to where the money in Agnes's purse had come from. She replaced the remaining items inside the trunk and secured the leather straps, before shutting it back inside the wardrobe. She smoothed the creases she had made on the bedcover while sitting on Mrs Craven's bed and went downstairs to look for Matt.

She found her husband out on the terrace watching Bertie racing around on the lawn.

'Matt, I think I've discovered who gave Agnes the money,' Kitty said as she hurried up to him.

She took the note from her pocket and passed it to him to read. His brows rose and he gave a low whistle of surprise. 'It sounds as if he and Agnes have been corresponding, probably since the Conways' first visit here.'

'It looks as if he was paying her for information, probably about the Favershams,' Kitty said.

'You know we will have to give this to Inspector Lewis.' Matt looked at her as he passed the note back over.

'I know, but not before we speak to Mr Conway ourselves,' Kitty said. 'And, while we are discussing the Conways, I overheard Ruby just now talking on the telephone to her friend.'

She told Matt what she'd heard while she had been in the hall.

'So, Ruby and this Jennifer had a plan that has been changed because you and I and the police are in the house,' Matt mused.

Kitty looked at her husband. 'Are you thinking what I'm thinking?'

Matt grinned, the dimple flashing in his cheek. 'I think you may have solved another small puzzle.'

CHAPTER FIFTEEN

Matt called a reluctant Bertie up from the lawn and they went back inside the house.

'Mr Conway has gone to attend a meeting with Sebastian and the estate manager. I expect he should be back soon,' Kitty said as they made their way to the drawing room.

'Once we've spoken to him about the contents of that note, we need to find the inspector,' Matt said as Kitty took a seat on the sofa.

Bertie flopped down at her feet and looked up at her expectantly, ready to be petted. Kitty smiled and stroked the top of her dog's head.

'Oh, Kitty, Matt, I was looking for Sebastian.' Ruby peered around the door of the room.

'I expect he'll be back soon. He and your father were meeting the estate manager. He said he was taking you around the estate today. Although not on horseback.' Kitty smiled at the girl, and she came into the room to take a seat on one of the armchairs.

'Yes, that's right. I'm afraid I'm not fond of horses,' Ruby admitted.

'Perhaps you'll grow more used to them once you and Sebastian are married,' Kitty suggested.

Ruby blushed. 'Maybe.'

'I mean you'll no doubt have the opportunity to learn to ride if you've changed your mind and intend to stay and go on with the marriage,' Kitty said.

The expression on the girl's face changed to one of alarm. 'I don't know what you mean?'

'Since you were unsuccessful at breaking into the safe to steal your jewellery,' Matt added in a casual tone.

'I... I...' Ruby's cheeks were dark red, and she flicked a scared glance towards the partly open door.

'That was the plan, wasn't it? You tried and failed in London, then tried again here. You were going to steal your own jewellery and run away to escape your engagement. Your friend Jennifer was going to help you.' Kitty looked directly at the frightened girl.

Ruby threw up her hands and covered her face. 'All right, yes. I don't know how you worked it out but that was my plan. At least it was what Jennifer and I originally cooked up together. I wasn't sure about marrying Sebastian and Jennifer thought if I had some money independent of my father then I could decide for myself what I wanted to do. The jewellery is mine. My mother left it to me in her will so it wasn't stealing.'

She pulled a small white-cotton handkerchief from her pocket and scrubbed at her eyes, moving her glasses aside to do so.

'And since then you've had second thoughts?' Matt asked.

Ruby sniffed and nodded. 'Seb and I get on really well and I can make this house mine. Father has assured me that I shall have full control of my money. Then when I tried to open the safe and failed it seemed like a sign.'

'So, the wedding is on and you have no more ideas of liberating your property from the safe? Or of running away?' Kitty asked.

Ruby resettled her glasses back on the bridge of her nose. 'No, I've been thinking a lot about it all. I know Seb's family need my money for the estate, but like Lady Amelia, I can be free here in a way I could never hope to be back in London or Chicago. Having the inspector staying in the house too was unnerving. I hoped he wouldn't realise it was me that tried to get my things. You won't tell him?'

'I presume it's not connected to Agnes's death so unless he takes a wrong track then your secret is safe for now. When you came here to Markham for the first time, do you recall much about the visit?' Kitty asked.

Ruby looked surprised and relieved by Kitty's words. 'Not a great deal. We came for the weekend. Sebastian had been courting me in London. We'd been to balls and out to tea, that sort of thing. The next step was to come here, meet the rest of the family and view the house. It was chilly when we arrived and the daffodils and primroses were barely out. We met the family and dined here. We only stayed one night. We came back a couple of weeks later for a longer visit.'

'Did you see your father speaking to Agnes at all?' Matt asked.

The girl frowned. 'Not really. Oh, only when he took something, his evening shirt I think it was, and asked her to press it for him before dinner. Why? Is this something to do with her murder?'

'We were just working out who was here then on that occasion,' Kitty reassured her.

'Just the family. On both visits it was just an intimate family weekend. Servant wise there was Mrs Putnam, Agnes and the young girl, Tilly. I didn't see anyone else. I guess the cook was here,' Ruby said.

The drawing room door opened, and Sebastian entered with Mr Conway. Ruby seized her chance to escape and jumped up so quickly even Bertie lifted his head to give her a surprised look.

'Right, we had better be off if we're to see around the park. See you all later.' Ruby tucked her arm in her fiancé's and whisked him out of the room.

Mr Conway dropped down on a nearby armchair. 'Good to see my little girl so happy,' he remarked as the couple disappeared into the hall.

'I take it you had a good meeting with the estate manager? Sebastian said he wanted to run through some of his ideas for the park,' Matt said.

'Yes, indeedy. It'll take some pulling around. Between you, me and the gatepost, Sir Henry has not kept his eye on the ball at all these last few years,' Mr Conway said.

'I think it's clear that Sir Henry is not a good businessman,' Kitty said. 'I think you already knew that though. After all, you had done your research.'

Mr Conway sat up straight, his genial smile fading as he gave her a sharp glance as if trying to work out what she was insinuating.

'You were paying Agnes Jones, the dead girl, to supply you with information about the Favershams. No doubt it gave you an extra edge when you looked at the figures Sir Henry provided.' Matt's own gaze grew keen.

'How dare you.' Mr Conway jumped up.

'We have the note you sent to Agnes from the hotel in London,' Kitty said.

The colour drained from the American's face and he sat down again slowly. 'It's not what you think,' he said.

'Oh?' Kitty asked.

'Well, I guess it is sort of what you think. I was trying to discover the extent of Sir Henry's liabilities. We'd already visited here and well, you can see for yourself that things are in a pretty perilous state. The repairs alone will set us back a fair amount of dollars. I was just looking out for my daughter. She and Sebastian seemed to like each other and to see her settled, a titled lady when anything happens to Sir Henry, well...' His voice tailed off and he scrubbed at his face with his hand as if trying to clear his thoughts.

'You got Agnes to snoop around. Probably reading Sir Henry's correspondence and listening in on the talk at the dinner table. She reported everything back to you so you could decide if you were happy for the match to go ahead. You paid Agnes for her trouble,' Kitty said.

'Yes, I paid her an advance. Then I sent the note you found to let her know I'd pay her for the last time when we arrived here for our second visit.' Mr Conway's shoulders slumped.

'What happened then? Did she demand more money to keep quiet?' Matt asked.

'No. I saw her when we arrived and paid her that morning first thing. I don't know, she hinted I suppose that more information might be forthcoming but I made it clear that her job was done and finished. There would be no more money from me unless she ever came across anything that could harm my girl,' Mr Conway said.

'What did Agnes say to that?' Matt asked.

'She laughed and said not to worry, she had plenty of other people who had things to hide. I suppose you'll tell that policeman all of this?' Mr Conway looked resigned.

'I'm afraid we must,' Kitty said.

'I didn't harm the girl. I had no need to. Her job for me was done and dusted.' Mr Conway looked at Kitty.

'You didn't arrange to meet her at the mausoleum to pay her?' Matt asked.

Mr Conway made a scoffing sound. 'No, why would I? I paid her when she came to my room to unpack my things. She took some things to press, and I tipped her as well as giving her the fee I'd promised. She seemed pleased. I had no need to go down to the lakeside or to harm that girl in any way.'

Lady Amelia drifted into the room, her pleasant face wearing a vague and faintly worried expression. 'Good morning, I don't suppose any of you have seen Henry anywhere? I need him to move some things for me in the studio.'

'Please, allow me to come and help you.' Mr Conway made his offer with some alacrity and disappeared with his hostess.

'He kept all that quiet, didn't he?' Matt looked at Kitty.

'I wonder what else Agnes found out while she was information gathering,' Kitty mused. 'I heard Mrs Putnam asking Lady Sarah for her wages. So, I'm guessing all of the staff are owed money, including Agnes probably. She may have decided to try a different way to supplement her income.'

'She would have been trapped here in many ways. No money to leave. Probably no reference if she did decide to go and she wouldn't want Dora to worry. It would have been tempting to gain some extra shillings,' Matt said.

'Very true. Now I suppose we need to find Inspector Lewis to tell him what we've discovered and to give him this note.' Kitty wasn't looking forward to seeing the inspector again. He would not be happy that they were interfering with his case.

There was no sign of the inspector in the house. A telephone enquiry to the police station at Exeter merely confirmed that he was busy with a case and was not expected back to the station that day.

'He is probably in the village with the constable talking to the villagers,' Kitty said with a sigh.

'He did say that was his plan. Perhaps he may appear at lunchtime,' Matt said.

However, when they gathered in the dining room for lunch the inspector did not appear. Sebastian and Ruby were also still out. Rupert too was absent, as was Sir Henry. Lady Sarah was clearly not pleased with her son not being present for lunch.

'It's too bad of Henry not to let anyone know he wouldn't be here for lunch. Millicent and I have compiled an up-to-date list of the repairs required to make the dower house habitable again. I would have liked his opinion.' She shook her linen napkin onto her lap and glared at Lady Amelia as if insinuating she was to blame.

'I'm afraid I have no idea why Henry isn't here. He said something to me about having to sort out some business matters and vanished.' Lady Amelia picked up her water glass and took a sip. 'I haven't seen hide nor hair of him all morning.'

'I do apologise, Mr Conway, for my son's absence. I hope you have plenty of things to entertain you until his return, especially since my grandsons are also out.' Lady Sarah nodded graciously in the American's direction.

'It's no problem to me, my lady, I have some business affairs of my own that require my attention. Sebastian and the estate manager met with me this morning so that was all dealt with then,' Mr Conway assured her, before giving his attention back to his lunch of salad and cold cuts of meat.

'Has anyone seen or heard from the inspector today?' Mrs Craven asked as they ate their lunch.

'No, he is another one that seems to be missing. Although, I must say in his case that may be a blessing if he has made progress towards catching whoever killed that girl.' Lady Sarah set down her cutlery neatly on her plate.

Mr Conway made no comment on this and avoided catching either Kitty or Matt's gaze.

'Perhaps he might update us at dinner,' Lady Amelia suggested as Mrs Putnam started to collect up the empty dinner plates.

'Have you invited him to dine here again?' Lady Sarah huffed in an appalled tone.

'He has to base himself somewhere, at least temporarily, and

I thought it might help Ruby to feel safer having a policeman in the house,' Lady Amelia protested.

'Most thoughtful,' Mrs Craven said.

Lady Sarah gave her friend a sour look.

Dessert was ice cream and tinned pears, after which everyone drifted off to do their own thing. Kitty and Matt ended up back in the drawing room.

'What should we do now?' Kitty asked.

Bertie had gone back to their room to snooze.

'We could drive to the village and see if we can spot the inspector,' Matt suggested.

'He may not appreciate that,' Kitty said. 'Especially if he thinks it makes him look less competent. If he is coming here tonight for dinner, we can always update him then.'

Mrs Craven popped her head around the door. 'Are you alone?' she asked in a dramatic whisper.

'Yes.' Kitty longed to ask who else the woman thought was in there with them. Instead, she decided discretion was the better option and waited for Mrs Craven to come and join them.

'I've been doing some sleuthing.' Mrs Craven looked very pleased with herself as she took a seat on the sofa beside Kitty.

'Did you discover anything about Rupert's so-called gaming debts?' Matt asked.

'Sarah was most informative while we were looking around the dower house this morning. Henry has confided in her about Rupert owing money. Apparently, he likes to play poker and is not terribly good at it. That's why he's been hiding out here. There are people looking for him to recover the money he owes them. They have kept it from Amelia since it would only worry her.' Mrs Craven leaned in as she spoke.

'I wonder if Agnes passed that piece of information on to Mr Conway,' Kitty murmured.

Mrs Craven gave her a curious look before continuing.

'There is no chance of the family paying off his debts, of course. They have sold everything they can that was of any value. The paintings, the bronzes, the silver, even most of the family jewels.'

'Did Lady Sarah mention how much these debts might amount to?' Kitty asked.

'I gathered that she thought it was close to a thousand pounds.' Mrs Craven arched her brows in disapproval.

'Whew, that is a lot of money,' Matt said.

'Did she say anything else?' Kitty persisted.

Mrs Craven tutted. 'Do hold your horses, Kitty, dear, I was coming to that. You young people haven't a scrap of patience.'

Kitty subsided and tried to hide her irritation while she waited for Mrs Craven to get to the point.

'As I was about to say, Sarah told me she is very worried about Henry. She thinks he may be in more trouble than anyone realises, financially that is. She told me that Amelia is very concerned. The banks have been making noises about fore-closing on his debts which means they could lose the Hall. This marriage is the only thing keeping them at bay.' Mrs Craven leaned back slightly.

'Hmm, that may be where Sir Henry has gone today, to placate some of his lenders,' Matt said.

'Mr Conway is clearly aware that money is a problem for the family,' Kitty mused. 'I wonder how much money is owed all round.'

It seemed to her that Sir Henry would not have wanted Stanley Conway to discover how much of Ruby's money might be needed to save the family's fortunes. It could be a far larger sum than anyone knew. If Agnes had found something out and threatened to tell, could that have been a motive for murder?

CHAPTER SIXTEEN

Matt heard the letter box rattle as the afternoon post arrived in the hall. He went to see if Mrs Smith, his and Kitty's housekeeper, had forwarded the letter from home with the London postmark. The ongoing mystery of his former army colleague's miraculous resurrection was still playing on his mind. Mrs Putnam had picked the mail up from the mat ready to sort and distribute it to the various inhabitants of the house.

'There is one here for you, Captain Bryant,' the housekeeper informed him and handed over a stiff, brown envelope.

'Thank you, Mrs Putnam.' He took the letter from her and wandered back into the drawing room.

From everything he and Kitty had discovered so far it was clear that Redvers had faked his own death. Now he had to try and confirm his suspicions. It was unlikely that his former colleague could have escaped from the requisitioned country house that was serving as a makeshift hospital without assistance.

It had taken him a while, but he had two suspects in mind as possibilities who could have been bribed to aid Redvers. Thanks to the call he had received before coming to Markham Hall he knew one of those men was dead. He hoped the letter he had been waiting for might lead him to the other one, Samuel Jobbins.

Mrs Craven had gone, leaving Kitty sitting on the edge of the sofa waiting eagerly to discover if the letter he had been waiting for had arrived. There was a letter opener on the side table near the fire, so he used it to slit open the top of the envelope.

As expected, it contained the letter Mrs Smith said had arrived which bore a London postmark. The envelope was white and cheap and the handwriting on the front barely legible. He used the opener again and extracted the letter.

'Well? What does it say?' Kitty asked as he scanned the thin sheet of lined paper.

'Here, take a look. It's a note from Jobbins's landlady. She says he is in hospital.' Matt passed the letter across to his wife.

Dear Captain Bryant,

I am responding to your question about Mr Samuel Jobbins who has been residing with me for the last twelve months. Mr Jobbins is in St Martin's Hospital this last month and is very poorly. He is not expected to return to his lodgings so you would be advised to come and see him soonest if the matter you have in mind is urgent.

Sincerely,

Mrs Letitia Bloom

'Oh dear, that doesn't sound at all good.' Kitty set down the letter and looked at him. 'What do you wish to do?'

'I'm going to telephone the hospital and make sure he is

there. If so, then I may need to go there to see him as soon as possible.' Matt was thinking quickly.

Jobbins was the last real lead he had to Redvers Palmerston. If anything happened to the man before he could speak to him it would make the task of tracing him almost impossible.

Matt left Kitty taking another look at the letter while he went to Sir Henry's study to use the telephone. After a minute the operator connected him with the switchboard at St Martin's. He vaguely remembered it as a small hospital situated in one of the poorer areas of the city.

There was another wait while the hospital operator looked up Jobbins's name on her list of patients and confirmed his presence.

'Mr Jobbins is a patient on Wren ward. Visiting times are Tuesday afternoons, two till three and Saturday afternoons two till three,' the operator informed him.

Matt thanked her and replaced the receiver. Tomorrow was Tuesday – if he caught the early train to Paddington he could make the visiting time. The only difficulty was that he would have to leave Kitty alone at Markham for the day until he returned.

He went back to find her.

'Was he there?' Kitty asked as he entered the room.

'Yes, the landlady was telling the truth. I need to go to London for the day tomorrow. I can get to see him in the afternoon for an hour. Otherwise, I may not get in till the Saturday and we don't know what state he is in or if he will live that much longer.' Matt paced about in front of the fireplace.

'No, I agree, you must go tomorrow. Let's look up the trains and I can drop you at the station in the morning,' Kitty suggested.

He remembered seeing a pile of timetables and maps in the library. 'You're a brick. Will you be all right here on your own for the day?' he asked as they headed out into the hall.

'I have Bertie, and Mrs C,' she said and gave him a wry smile.

The train timetable was with the other documents on a side table. Kitty picked up the timetable and opened it up. 'There's a train at seven which will get you in to Paddington for midday,' Kitty said. 'Would that work?'

'Perfectly. I can get the three o'clock train back and be here for around seven thirty. We may have to apologise for being slightly late to dinner,' Matt said.

'I'm sure no one will object. I do hope you can find something out from this man. It's such a puzzle.' She refolded the timetable and placed it back on the pile. 'Darling, how much longer do you think we need to stay here?'

Matt glanced at her. 'Why? Is something bothering you?'

He knew his wife well enough to know this was a loaded question. On the one hand Kitty's insatiable curiosity would want to discover who had murdered Agnes. On the other hand, Markham Hall and its inhabitants didn't make for the most comfortable country house stay they had ever had.

'I don't know what more really we can do here once we have spoken to Inspector Lewis. Mr Conway wanted us to remain because Ruby was worried about the murder. He was also worried about the attempts on the safe. Now that we know that Ruby was the one trying to get her own jewellery out to potentially run away, well, where does that leave us?' Kitty asked.

'I see what you mean.' Matt scratched his chin as he thought about what she'd just said. 'It's almost as if we're here under false pretences.'

Relief flashed across Kitty's expressive features. 'Yes, that's exactly it. Inspector Lewis will not be happy if we continue to dig around in what he sees as his investigation. Then, what happens if his leads all come to nothing? I have a horrid feeling that the key to Agnes's murder is much closer to this house than anyone dares to admit.'

Matt understood what she meant. He had the same feelings about who might have murdered the maid. There were quite a few people in the house who potentially had a motive for wanting the girl dead.

'I think you're right. I doubt the inspector will uncover any new information in Bovey Tracey.' Matt crossed to the library door and closed it before pulling up a chair.

Kitty took the seat opposite him. 'Let's go through it all. Start with the Conways,' she suggested.

'Ruby came here uncertain if she wanted to marry Sebastian. We know that it's a practical match rather than a love match. Although, they seem to be growing increasingly fond of each other. Ruby tried to steal her own jewels both in London and here so she could run away if she wanted to. Suppose Agnes got wind of Ruby's plans?' Matt looked at Kitty.

'Agnes could have asked Ruby for money to keep quiet and not tell her father or Sebastian. There's a lot riding on this wedding. Would Ruby have killed the girl though? She could just have come clean about her doubts. If the wedding doesn't go ahead, then the Conways are not impacted in any way. Possibly socially perhaps.' Kitty frowned.

'Unless that premarital paperwork that Sir Henry and Mr Conway were signing the other day ties the Conways into some kind of financial penalty? It's not unheard of in these kinds of arrangements if the bride-to-be gets cold feet about the wedding,' Matt suggested.

'I still doubt that it would be a great inconvenience to them. They are so wealthy it wouldn't really affect them. Mr Conway dotes on Ruby too. He would forgive her pretty much anything I think.' Kitty drummed her fingers on the wooden arm of her chair. 'No, that won't do. Now Mr Conway has already admitted to us that he was paying Agnes to spy on the Favershams.'

'He wouldn't want that to be made public, but Sir Henry is

hardly in a position to object. He needs Ruby's money to keep the estate from going under. Of course, we don't know if that was the only reason Mr Conway was paying Agnes money.' Matt looked at Kitty.

Her eyes widened. 'No, you're right. We do only have his word for that. It could have been that she had discovered something about him or offered him some kind of, well, other favour.' Kitty wrinkled her nose in distaste.

'He wouldn't want that to get to Ruby's ears or the Favershams,' Matt said.

'Very well, that gives Mr Conway a potential motive. Ruby, I'm not so sure, but she would protect her father.' Kitty's expression brightened. 'Yes, that would give her a motive definitely. She agreed to this engagement for her father's sake so it's not unreasonable to believe she might take drastic action to protect him if she thought he was being threatened in some way.'

'Then there are the Favershams. Lady Sarah is desperate to retain the estate and restore it back to its former glory. She's very proud and I could see her losing her temper and potentially striking down a mere maid if she thought Agnes might derail her dreams.' Matt shifted his weight in his seat. He could see Lady Sarah hitting the girl with her parasol or a walking cane.

'She is physically quite fit so could have lured Agnes to the mausoleum,' Kitty agreed.

He could see her turning the possibility of Lady Sarah being Agnes's killer over in her mind.

'I think she could be quite ruthless too where her family's interests were concerned. On that note, what about Sir Henry?' Matt asked.

Kitty's brows rose. 'Well, he has most to lose, doesn't he? I mean it's his poor business sense that has enhanced their misfortunes after he took over the estate. If his brother had not been killed then it would have been a different story. We don't know the full extent of his debts and from the conversation at dinner, I suspect he has a lot of secrets.'

'If Mr Conway were to discover them then it could well derail the wedding. He may also have learned that Agnes was in Mr Conway's employment and decided to silence her,' Kitty said.

'He could easily have gone to meet her by the lake on a promise to pay her off or something and then killed her,' Matt agreed. 'We aren't ruling anyone out it seems just yet. I suppose we must also consider Sebastian as a suspect?'

'I'm afraid so. This marriage to Ruby would save the estate. We don't know what Agnes may have had over him that she could have used, or it may just be he thought she was about to reveal something detrimental. If he had realised she was selling information to Mr Conway, and knowing what his father's debts might be, then perhaps he decided to strike. He also seems to be developing quite an attachment to Ruby. Perhaps he feels more for her than he's revealed. Rupert mentioned that Sebastian had an eye for a pretty face. Another girl, perhaps?' Kitty leaned back in her seat and sighed. 'Gosh, it's so complicated.'

'It is rather,' Matt agreed. He smiled at her slightly woeful expression. 'Let's keep going, Rupert is our next candidate.'

'Well, there is this business of his gambling debts. I wonder if he realises that his family seem to know about them?' Kitty asked.

'Sir Henry and Lady Sarah may know of them but not the amount he owes or the kind of people he seems to owe them to,' Matt responded.

'That's true, especially if he is lying low out here. I wonder if Agnes could have discovered this and threatened to tell Mr Conway, or even his father?' Kitty said.

'I think it might make him something of a liability if he is hoping to gain a job where he might be responsible for the funds belonging to other people. Potential employers would not be keen to take him on. He has said he doesn't wish to enlist so a city job is his best option.' Matt could see that might well be a motive for murder.

'Hmm, and he needs money badly. This wedding benefits him too because he and Sebastian seem quite close. I doubt his brother would see him struggle. He would probably get his debts cleared or at least his creditors might feel they stand a chance of seeing some money with Ruby being in the family,' Kitty said.

'What about Lady Amelia? Agnes may have found out something about her that she wanted to keep secret and was prepared to kill for?'

'Possible, I suppose, but rather tenuous, don't you think?'

'I do. Then we come to the staff.' Matt looked at his wife.

'You mean Mrs Putnam? We know all the staff are owed wages and she argued with Agnes the day the girl was killed. Depending on what's owed, then she and her sister may well be counting on Ruby to finance all their back pay.' Kitty sat forward again.

'We know money is a motivation behind most murders,' Matt said. 'It could make quite a difference to Mrs Gray and Mrs Putnam if they received what they were owed. It would also ensure their positions were secure when Ruby and Sebastian marry. Not to mention the house being properly staffed which would ease their workload. I can see they wouldn't want an upstart young maid to jeopardise that.'

'I suppose at least we can clear Tilly of suspicion.' Kitty smiled at him.

'Even I can't make a case against young Tilly,' he agreed.

'What about the gardener?' Kitty asked.

'I think he too can probably be ruled out. After all he was the one who said he had seen her that day. If he hadn't told us that we may never have discovered her. Although Bertie does get some credit for that.' Matt gave a smile. 'The boy said he heard a couple quarrelling in the woods that day. I wonder who that might have been.'

'It could have been anyone. It may not even have been Agnes. So, it seems everyone has a motive, even Mrs Craven. She's given Lady Sarah this money, which was to enable them to throw an engagement party and prepare for the wedding. If the wedding was to fail then she wouldn't get her money back.' Kitty flashed a mischievous grin at him.

'You aren't seriously considering Mrs C as the killer?' Matt returned his wife's smile. 'Although, I think I could see her doing it quite well.'

They both burst out laughing at the idea.

'All right, we'll add Mrs C to the definitely didn't do it pile,' Kitty conceded.

CHAPTER SEVENTEEN

Inspector Lewis was not at all happy when they sought him out on his return to Markham. He had apparently spent a long and frustrating day in Bovey Tracey and had not found any trace of a vagrant or a potential suitor for Agnes. Something they discovered when they went to meet him as he got out of his car.

'What do you mean, Mrs Craven has Agnes Jones's box in her room? Why wasn't I told about this?' Inspector Lewis's face turned red with rage, and he closed his car door with what Kitty considered to be unnecessary force.

'We only remembered the box this morning. Tilly, the young maid, had packed it when Agnes didn't return to the Hall,' Kitty said as Bertie started to sniff around the inspector's slightly muddy shoes.

'And it's been sitting here all this time and no one thought to mention it. Well, I think I had better go and take a look at it,' Inspector Lewis said.

'Um, I already did that after breakfast, and I found this enclosed inside a letter from Dora, Agnes's sister. It must have slipped inside the open envelope.' Kitty held out the folded sheet of hotel stationery.

Inspector Lewis snatched it from her hand and scanned the contents. 'Conway has been paying Agnes? That's why she had more money in her purse, and he sat there and never said a word. I've been out all day, traipsing round farms and cottages, getting chased by dogs and chickens. All the while you've had this and that Conway has been sat here looking like butter wouldn't melt in his mouth!' He scowled at Kitty.

'We did telephone Exeter Police Station to try to reach you, but they said you weren't expected,' Matt said, pulling Bertie away from the inspector's feet.

'I'd better see what Mr Conway has to say for himself then, or have you already quizzed him?' Inspector Lewis looked at the blush stealing along Kitty's cheeks. 'I might have known. You've interfered there too. Now he'll be on his guard, won't he? Have his story all nice and pat. What did he tell you?'

'He said he had been paying Agnes to pass on any information she came across about the Favershams. He wanted to make certain he was fully au fait with all their financial issues before Ruby's marriage went ahead.' Kitty suppressed a wince at the thunderous expression on the inspector's face.

'Gah! You amateurs have probably messed up my investigation. The trouble with you people is you can't tell the important from the irrelevant unlike professionals like me, trained in up-to-date proper policing methods.' Inspector Lewis glowered at Kitty.

Bertie sat down and gave a short, sharp bark of reproof to show his disapproval of the inspector shouting at his mistress.

'I'm glad we were of assistance.' Kitty gave the inspector an insincere smile and walked away before she was tempted to say a great deal more. Matt followed her with Bertie trotting alongside, his plumed tail wagging happily now they were walking again.

'That wretched man!' Kitty exploded as soon as they were out of earshot. 'He would never have found that letter or had any of that information without us. He is so ungrateful and rude.'

Matt nodded. 'I agree. He can be rather trying. Still, we did the right thing. He knows now so hopefully it may help him to solve the case.'

Kitty stopped and looked at her husband. 'Do you really believe Inspector Lewis is capable of finding Agnes's murderer?' she asked.

'Well, he has had some successes since he came to Devon,' Matt said in a mild tone.

Kitty could see her husband was trying to suppress his mirth at her indignation. 'He caught a Peeping Tom and solved the mystery of who was stealing the undergarments from Mrs Craven's neighbours' washing line,' Kitty said.

'Very well, I give you that he doesn't have the best record at solving murders.' The smile broke out on Matt's face, and he gave her a hug. 'It's a good job he has us mere amateurs to help him.'

Kitty sighed. 'Grr, he still makes me cross, but yes, it is a good job we found the note and talked to Mr Conway.'

'Come on, let's go and see if we can get some tea before we change for dinner.' Matt gave her another hug and they went back into the house.

Sebastian and Ruby were in the drawing room. Ruby looked anxious and Sebastian was pacing about near the French doors.

'The inspector has just called Daddy into Sir Henry's study, he seemed very angry about something,' Ruby explained when Kitty and Matt came to join them.

'I think the inspector has had a difficult day,' Matt said as Kitty rang the bell to request some tea.

'He certainly seemed to be in a foul mood,' Sebastian said.

Tilly came into the room to answer the bell. Her white cap was askew, and she appeared flustered.

'May we have some tea, please, Tilly?' Kitty asked, frowning slightly as she saw the girl's nervous state.

'Yes, Mrs Bryant.' The girl turned to rush back out.

'Tilly, is something wrong?' Kitty asked.

'No, not at all.' Tilly darted from the room before Kitty could quiz her about her insincere denial of a problem.

'I wonder what that was about?' Matt looked at Kitty.

'It's probably something to do with having the police all over the estate,' Sebastian said. 'Ruby and I saw them in the woods when we were out. It looked as if they were searching for something.'

Kitty thought the police must still be looking for a murder weapon but said nothing.

Lady Sarah bustled into the room accompanied by Mrs Craven.

'Has anyone rung for tea yet?' she demanded as she took her usual seat beside the fireplace. Mrs Craven took the chair opposite.

'Tilly has just gone to see about it,' Kitty assured the dowager.

'I thought I heard raised voices coming from the study. Is Henry back?' Lady Sarah looked around at everyone.

'Not as far as we know. Inspector Lewis is in there interviewing Mr Conway,' Matt said.

'Is he indeed.' Lady Sarah looked confused. 'Then why is he shouting?'

Ruby started in her chair as if about to dash off to rescue her father. Sebastian placed his hand on her shoulder.

'Don't be alarmed, Ruby, darling, it's probably something and nothing. Your father will no doubt join us for tea in a moment and you'll see that everything is all right,' Sebastian reassured her.

'I'm sorry. I just feel so on edge. Ever since they found that poor girl, I keep thinking that something else bad is going to happen,' Ruby said.

'Nonsense, my dear. I assure you we are not in the habit of discovering bodies at Markham, at least not since the Civil War. I'm sure the inspector has things in hand,' Lady Sarah declared as Tilly returned with the tea trolley.

'Good heavens, child, you look as if you've been pulled through a hedge backwards. Straighten your cap and tidy your-self up,' Lady Sarah commanded as the hapless maid deposited the laden trolley beside her.

'Yes, my lady.' Tilly parked the trolley and did her best to adjust her cap before fleeing from the room.

'Honestly. If it weren't so hard to get staff these days,' Lady Sarah muttered. 'Millicent, my dear, would you pour? I feel quite at sixes and sevens myself.'

Mrs Craven dutifully obeyed her relative. Kitty rose to assist her while Bertie looked hopefully at the plate of biscuits that accompanied the tea.

As the tea was served they heard the study door open and the heavy tread of footsteps in the hall. Mr Conway came into the drawing room looking quite disgruntled and rather red in the face.

'My dear Mr Conway, do come and join us for tea,' Lady Sarah commanded.

'Is everything all right, Pa?' Ruby peered anxiously at her father. 'We thought we heard raised voices.'

'Everything is perfectly fine, honey, don't worry. Just a little misunderstanding with the inspector. All cleared up now.' Mr Conway sat down on one of the upright occasional chairs. Kitty handed him a cup of tea.

She wondered if the inspector had believed him about paying Agnes for information. It had sounded a most uncom-fortable interview. After all, the American now seemed to have a motive for killing the girl.

'Where is Amelia? I suppose she's closeted in the orangery daubing paint on something.' Lady Sarah sighed as she stirred her drink.

'I'll fetch her, Granny. You know how Mother is, she probably hasn't realised the time.' Sebastian went to find his mother while Mrs Craven retook her seat, holding her own cup and saucer.

'Matt has to go to London tomorrow for the day on another case. It is rather urgent and can't be put off.' Kitty looked at Ruby and Mr Conway.

'You'll still be here though, Kitty?' Ruby asked anxiously.

'Yes, Bertie and I will remain here,' Kitty assured her.

'I shall be back around dinner time,' Matt said.

'I see. So long as someone is watching over the place,' Mr Conway said. 'At least until whoever killed that girl is behind bars. I was tempted to suggest we went back to London, but that danged policeman wants everyone to stay here for now.' He glared at the door of the drawing room as if Inspector Lewis might be just the other side in the hall.

Lady Amelia had a smudge of blue paint on her cheek as she followed Sebastian into the drawing room.

'The tea will be quite stewed by now,' Lady Sarah informed her daughter-in-law as she helped herself to a cup.

'I was busy on a piece. One has to make the most of the light,' Lady Amelia said as she took a seat and took the last biscuit from the plate.

Bertie gave a disappointed sigh and sank back down at Kitty's feet.

'Where is Henry? He's been gone all day and I thought he would have returned by now,' Lady Sarah said.

'I haven't heard from him.' Lady Amelia gave a slight shrug of her shoulders. 'I daresay he'll be back for dinner.'

'That reminds me, Rupert won't be in tonight, he's staying

at the Cox-Herberts in Chudleigh. He telephoned just as we arrived back this afternoon,' Sebastian said.

Kitty suspected this news would not please Inspector Lewis when he discovered Rupert had left the estate. Not after he had told the Conways to stay at the house.

It seemed her suspicions were correct. Inspector Lewis was not at all happy at dinner. Sir Henry, however, had returned and seemed in a brighter mood. If he had been to see his creditors it seemed the news of Sebastian's engagement had assisted his fortunes.

The atmosphere around the table was uncomfortable with Inspector Lewis surveying the family through narrowed eyes. Conversation was limited to offers to pass the salt or the weather for the next day. Kitty was relieved when the meal was finished, and they could all retire from the dining room.

Sir Henry and Mr Conway went to play billiards, while Ruby and Sebastian went out for a late evening stroll around the garden. Lady Sarah declared herself fatigued and went to bed early and Lady Amelia drifted off back to her studio to check on her painting.

'Well, that was helpful, everyone going off like that. Where has the inspector gone?' Mrs Craven asked once Mrs Putnam had delivered the after-dinner coffee.

'He didn't say. I presume he must be working,' Kitty said as she took a sip of her coffee.

'Did he tell you if he found out anything in the village?' Mrs Craven asked.

'No, he was in a frightfully bad mood. Then, of course, he spoke to Mr Conway.' Kitty told her about the note and what Ruby's father had said.

'No wonder he was displeased, and we heard raised voices.

I knew there had to be something important in that box of Agnes's,' Mrs Craven said, looking smug.

Kitty, who knew full well that the older woman had forgotten all about the box until she had reminded her, bit her tongue and said nothing.

'I hope you'll be all right here tomorrow, Kitty.' Matt looked at his wife.

'I'm sure it will be fine. I told you I have Bertie and Mrs Craven is here,' Kitty said.

'Of course, I can supervise Kitty's sleuthing and you'll only be gone for a few hours. What can possibly happen in such a short time?' Mrs Craven asked.

Kitty hoped she was right.

CHAPTER EIGHTEEN

Kitty drove Matt to the railway station early the next day before breakfast and dropped him off.

'Please be careful, darling, I don't like leaving you at Markham with a murderer still at large.' Matt kissed her goodbye and got out of the car.

'Bertie and I will be fine,' Kitty assured him and gave a cheery farewell wave of her hand before setting off back to the Hall.

She had just turned off the road to enter the long drive leading to the house when she saw a horse-drawn cart trotting towards her. She slowed down to avoid spooking the horse so that it could pass her safely. As it drew nearer she saw Tilly sitting up front on the cart beside the driver. What looked like the girl's trunk was in the back along with what appeared to be some sacks of foodstuffs.

The cart passed her by, and Kitty continued on her way to the Hall. It seemed as if Tilly had resigned her position. Perhaps that was what had been on the girl's mind yesterday. Kitty parked her car and extracted Bertie from his place on the rear seat. She hoped there would still be some breakfast available as she was quite hungry, and lunch was a long way off.

She hurried inside the house and headed for the dining room. The room was deserted but it was clear that others had already eaten, the used crockery still on the table. Kitty helped herself to sausages and bacon and shared some with Bertie. She didn't like to ring for more tea or toast.

Mrs Putnam and her sister would have far too much to do if Tilly had in fact departed. Quite how they would manage now was anyone's guess. The housekeeper looked startled when she entered the dining room to discover Kitty finishing her breakfast.

'I'm sorry, Mrs Bryant, I thought everyone had finished.' The housekeeper started to clear the used plates and turned off the burners under the hot plates on the sideboard.

'I'm late, I'm afraid. I just took my husband to the station. I thought I passed Tilly leaving on the driveway as I came back in,' Kitty said.

Mrs Putnam's already pursed lips grew tighter. 'Yes, Tilly's father has fetched her away. He seems to believe she isn't safe to stay here anymore with what happened to Agnes. He bundled her up and took her off.'

'Oh dear, that's going to make it very difficult for you and your sister. Will you be able to get more help from the village do you think?' Kitty asked in a sympathetic tone.

Mrs Putnam made a dismissive noise. 'If Lady Faversham would pay then we could, but that well has run dry. No one will work here unless they are paid upfront. My sister and I are only waiting ourselves for what's owing to us.'

Kitty finished eating and placed her cutlery on her plate. She then jumped up and started to assist the housekeeper to stack the dishes. 'I hadn't realised things were quite so bad. Are you owed much money?'

'We are both owed four months.' Mrs Putnam's expression was grim. 'Lady Sarah borrowed money from Mrs Craven to pay the butcher, the grocer and the wine merchant.'

'I presume when Sebastian's wedding goes ahead you will get your money? And I suppose Mrs Craven will get her money too?' Kitty suggested.

'Allegedly.' Mrs Putnam made no objection to Kitty assisting her to clear the breakfast dishes.

'You argued with Agnes the morning she disappeared.' Kitty looked at the housekeeper.

'I told the little madam off. Back-answering me she was and gloating about how she was going to be leaving here soon now she had some money in her pocket.' Mrs Putnam shook her head. 'I told her she still had chores to do else she'd find herself out the door with no reference and then where would she be?'

'What did she say to that?' Kitty asked.

'She laughed and said she weren't bothered. I hadn't the time nor the patience to deal with her. She knew as she had the whip hand. We needed her to keep things ticking over. Then after lunch she disappeared. I thought at first as she'd gone to do the bedrooms. When she didn't come for her tea on the afternoon, I was worried. I sent young Tilly to check if her things were still in their room. You know, in case as she'd done a flit after what she'd said to me on the morning. When she said everything was there, I thought perhaps she had just taken herself off for a bit.' Mrs Putnam sighed. 'I never for a moment thought as anything had happened to her.'

'What happened when she didn't arrive in time to help with dinner?' Kitty placed the dirty dishes on the trolley ready for them to be taken to the kitchen.

'We were all quite cross. Well, more'n cross really, furious at her thoughtlessness. It being a big thing having the Conways here for the second time. She knew as there was a lot riding on

Master Sebastian wedding the American lass. It was too hectic to worry about finding out where she might have gone. We still thought as she'd gone off gallivanting and would show up later that night all smirking and pleased with herself. Young Tilly left a light burning for her in the kitchen thinking as she'd come in the back way.'

'And obviously she didn't return,' Kitty said.

Mrs Putnam shook her head. 'No, young Tilly told my sister first thing the next day. Tilly had got up to do the fires and start things off and saw that Agnes's bed hadn't been slept in.'

'What happened then?' Kitty asked as she continued to assist the housekeeper.

'I had to let Lady Sarah know.' The housekeeper's shoulders slumped. 'She were neither use nor ornament. She said we just had to get through the weekend, and we could worry about where Agnes might be once the Conways had gone. I kept thinking the girl would turn up or would send word for her box. I thought she had maybe gone to her sister in Dartmouth.'

'But then Dora contacted you asking where Agnes was?' Kitty could see how the events surrounding Agnes's murder had unravelled.

'That's right. We feel so guilty now, me and Emily, that's my sister. I think we knew deep down as something must be wrong, but it seemed so unlikely.' Mrs Putnam paused, her hands on the handle of the trolley ready to wheel everything off to the kitchens. 'I mean, murder, it just didn't seem possible.'

Kitty went to follow the housekeeper. 'Do let me come and give you a little assistance, Mrs Putnam. My husband will be gone all day, and your workload is so large.' Bertie stretched and stood at Kitty's heels.

'I don't know, Mrs Bryant, Lady Sarah won't like it.'

She could see the housekeeper was torn about accepting her offer. 'Bertie will be no problem, and Lady Sarah need not know I am helping you. I was a hotelier, and I have done every job you can think of within a hotel so I promise I can be useful. Although my husband would tell you not to allow me to cook,' Kitty added with a smile.

Kitty had her own reasons for wishing to help beyond assisting the house to run smoothly. She was anxious to talk to Mrs Gray, Mrs Putnam's sister.

Mrs Putnam still looked dubious but gave a brief nod of her head. Kitty and Bertie followed the housekeeper out of the dining room and through the baize-covered door into the servants' part of the house.

* * *

Matt alighted from the steam train at Paddington station and headed out into the city. He had a good idea of where the hospital was and determined he had time for a quick lunch before finding a taxi to take him to visit Samuel Jobbins.

He could only hope the man would be both well enough and willing to speak to him. Matt ate his lunch at a small café near the station, then stopped to buy a few gifts to take to the hospital. Jobbins would probably speak more freely if a present was involved.

The hospital was not one of the well-known buildings in the city. It was a small red-brick building in a poor part of town. It had started life as a workhouse in Queen Victoria's day. Now its soot-stained bricks and shabby entrance suggested a place nearing the end of its working life.

Matt stepped out of the taxi into the spring sunshine and followed a couple of uniformed nurses up the sandstone steps into the lobby of the building. The directions to the wards were engraved on metal signs on the cream-painted walls and he soon saw the one for Samuel Jobbins's ward. Up the flight of concrete steps to the first floor.

The hospital had the familiar scent of disinfectant mingled

with stale humanity. He queued outside the ward entrance with the other visitors waiting for the dark wood and glass doors to be opened and entry permitted.

At the stroke of two, a junior nurse in a grey uniform and white starched Sister Dora cap opened the doors. The visitors streamed inside clutching bunches of flowers and bags of grapes, eager to see their loved ones.

Matt followed more slowly, uncertain if he would recognise Samuel after all the years that had passed. He noticed one bed at the end of the ward without any visitors. As he drew nearer he saw a face he knew well. Older now, and very obviously ill. The man's once plump cheeks were thin and caved in, his skin holding a greyish unhealthy pallor.

'Mr Jobbins, I don't know if you'll remember me.' Matt removed his hat and drew a wooden chair closer to the man's bedside.

Jobbins surveyed him through rheumy eyes, his breath whistling noisily. 'Yes, I do know you. Captain Bryant, ain't it? You married Edith. I 'eard what 'appened and I'm right sorry about that. She were a good sort your Edith. What brings you 'ere now then?'

Matt saw no point in beating about the bush. He placed the bag of humbugs and the fruit he had bought for Jobbins on top of the bedside cabinet as he said, 'Redvers Palmerston.'

Jobbins's expression changed immediately from alert curiosity to a feigned blankness. 'Palmerston? I don't know as I properly recall 'im at all.'

'I'm sure you do. You were the one who helped him fake his own death in order to avoid being sent back to the front.' Matt spoke in a matter-of-fact tone. He had no wish to antagonise the man, or he would get nothing from him. This was his one chance to determine if what he and Kitty thought had happened was true.

'I don't know what you're talkin' about, Captain Bryant.

Palmerston is brown bread, dead.' Jobbins had small beads of sweat forming on his greying temples.

'We both know the man that was buried was not Redvers Palmerston. I have seen him and so has his wife. I don't think either of us has seen a ghost,' Matt said.

Jobbins passed his tongue over his cracked and parched lips. 'Could you pass me a drop of water, please, Captain. A man could die of thirst in 'ere.'

Matt poured some water from the jug that stood on the cabinet and handed Jobbins the glass. He steadied it so the man could drink.

'Thank you.' Jobbins lay back on his pillows as Matt replaced the glass on the cupboard.

'Now, about Redvers. I presume you assisted him to obtain civilian clothing and moved the body of another man into his bed?' Matt continued as if there had been no interruption to his questions.

'Captain, I'm an ill man, my memory ain't what it was.' Jobbins's scrawny fingers plucked anxiously at his blankets.

'Naturally Redvers paid you handsomely for this. He would have been shot as a deserter if he had tried a stunt like that back on the battlefield.' Matt ignored Jobbins's weak protestations.

'Suppose as, 'ypothetical like, you was right. What of it? The war's been over a long time. I mean, as I said, I'm an ill man. I ain't got that long left,' Jobbins said.

'All the more reason to clear your conscience with a full confession before you meet your maker.' Matt had a modicum of sympathy for the ill man but the mess that Redvers's fake demise had caused helped harden his heart.

Jobbins looked even more uncomfortable. 'Suppose as I did give 'im an 'and, well, it ain't done no 'arm to nobody.'

'His wife was left to raise their son on a widow's pension. His boy grieved the loss of his father,' Matt said.

'Better the boy think 'im dead than a coward,' Jobbins

muttered. ''Ow did you find me anyway? And why would you think it was me as 'elped 'im?'

'After I came face to face with a dead man I spoke to his widow and discovered she too had recently thought she had seen him. The boy is grown up now and married. There was a burglary at his home and all that was taken were the keepsakes Redvers gave to me shortly before his alleged death,' Matt said.

Jobbins shuffled uncomfortably on his pillows. 'Sounds like she done all right. 'E said as he would find 'er and tell 'er once it was all over. They could start again under another name, go abroad. I didn't see any 'arm.' Jobbins couldn't meet his gaze. 'Besides, I needed the money.'

'I see.' Matt rose and placed his seat back against the wall. 'Well, thank you for confirming my supposition.'

''Ere, what's going to 'appen now? You ain't going to turn me in? Not now, not after all this time. I don't want to spend my last few weeks in a prison 'ospital.' Jobbins started forward on his pillows before falling back in a paroxysm of coughing.

Matt looked at the dying man. 'I see no point in alerting the authorities. Not for your sake or Palmerston's, but for the sake of his wife and child.'

'Thank you, Captain Bryant.' Jobbins's eyes closed.

'I doubt we shall see one another again.' Matt picked up his hat and replaced it on his head. 'Goodbye, Mr Jobbins.' He strode purposefully away from the dying man, eager to be back outside the hospital and away from the scent of death and deception.

* * *

Mrs Gray's eyes widened when she saw Kitty and Bertie arriving in the kitchens accompanied by Mrs Putnam. Bertie flopped himself down on the red-tiled floor near the sink while Kitty explained her offer of assistance.

'We'd best find you an apron then, Mrs Bryant. You can't be ruining your lovely frock with kitchen grease.' Mrs Gray produced a large wrap-around pinafore which she assisted Kitty to put on. The cook was an older, plumper version of her sister. Her once dark hair had grey streaks and there were crow's feet at the corners of her eyes.

'If you are certain as you're happy to help, then I'm going to get the bedrooms done. Luckily Tilly did the fires afore her father turned up.' Mrs Putnam hurried from the room.

Kitty busied herself with filling the sink with hot soapy water and began the mammoth task of cleaning all the things used for breakfast. Bertie settled himself for a snooze not far from her feet.

Mrs Gray had her hands full preparing things for lunch. Kitty dealt with the glassware then moved on to the crockery, working as swiftly as she could. When the servants' bell rang, signifying someone required them in the drawing room, Mrs Gray sighed. 'That will be Lady Sarah wanting morning coffee and there's no one to take it.'

'Shall I run along and see what's wanted?' Kitty asked.

Mrs Gray looked alarmed as the bell jangled again. 'Oh no, Mrs Bryant, her ladyship will have conniptions if she sees you in that apron. I'll go. The kettle is on ready, can you tend to the trolley?'

Kitty dried her hands and set to work while the cook went to answer the bell. Mrs Gray returned just as the kettle was coming to the boil.

'Bless your heart. Lady Sarah wasn't best pleased at seeing me, but she couldn't say much with the Conways there.' The cook made the coffee and wheeled the trolley away.

Kitty went back to her final task of scrubbing out the heated chafing dishes with steel wool. Mrs Gray came back and placed a thick mug of coffee at her elbow just as she was finishing.

'Thank you, Mrs Gray.' Kitty let the water out of the sink

and gratefully took a sip from the mug. 'What can I do for you next? I am good at peeling and chopping,' she suggested.

The cook set her up with a pile of potatoes and two vast pots so they could prepare the ones for lunch and for dinner that evening.

'I'm right grateful for your help with this. You say you have a hotel?' Mrs Gray said as she expertly filleted fish to go into a pie.

'Yes, the Dolphin in Dartmouth. Where did you work before coming to Markham?' Kitty was keen to discover something of Mrs Gray and Mrs Putnam's backgrounds.

Mrs Gray kept her attention on her task. 'My sister has been in service all her life, from when she was a young girl. She was last with Lord Bervis but he was very ill and it looked as if his son was going to obviously take over the running of the castle. My sister never cared for the mistress. At the same time, my husband passed away and we lost our home. It was a tied cottage. He was a gardener and I was cook. My sister thought it would be nice if we could be together. When these posts come up here at Markham, we took them. Lydia came first and I followed a month or so after.'

'I understand that you and Mrs Putnam are owed a considerable amount in back wages from the Favershams,' Kitty said as she dropped the potato she had been peeling into one of the pots.

'That's right and I don't expect as we shall see any of it unless Miss Conway marries Master Sebastian. We don't have much choice except to wait it out. At least we have a roof over our heads and food in our bellies.' Mrs Gray gave a slight shrug of her shoulders. 'We can't interview for another post with no money to travel and we need the reference from Lady Sarah.'

'That's awful,' Kitty said. 'This business with poor Agnes, what do you think happened to her?' She was curious to discover the woman's thoughts on who may have killed the maid.

The cook paused and looked up from the fish. 'I don't rightly know, Mrs Bryant, but I think as there's a lot of secrets in this house.'

CHAPTER NINETEEN

They were forced to leave the conversation there when Mrs Putnam clattered back into the kitchen wheeling the coffee trolley.

'I've never made beds nor cleaned bathrooms and basins so quick in all my life. A lick and a polish is the best as I can manage,' she said as she speedily unloaded the used crockery into the sink.

The housekeeper then took over the potato peeling, while Kitty washed up the coffee things.

'You had best get back out there, Mrs Bryant, before they notice as you've been gone. Thank you for your help. We really do appreciate it,' Mrs Putnam said once the last things were clean, and the trolley had been reset ready for afternoon tea.

'Yes, thank you, it's been most kind,' her sister added with a grateful smile.

'If you need help this afternoon, come and find me. I have a little time before I need to collect Matt from the station,' Kitty said as she hung her apron back on its hook. Her spell in the kitchen had been most useful not just to the staff but also to the investigation.

She slipped back through the baize-covered door with Bertie following behind her, and headed for the drawing room.

'Kitty, we were just talking about you. Where have you been all morning?' Mrs Craven asked as she entered the room.

'Oh, I was out and about with Bertie. Has there been any news from the inspector yet?' Kitty asked as she took a seat. Ruby and Sebastian were playing cards at one of the tables, while Mrs Craven and Lady Sarah were seated on either side of the fireplace.

'Nothing. Pa and Sir Henry were hoping to speak to him this morning to find out if there was any progress,' Ruby said.

'Did Matthew get off to London all right?' Mrs Craven looked at Kitty.

'Yes, the train was on time I believe. I hope it will run to time this evening.' Kitty hoped Matt would get some answers from Mr Jobbins and wouldn't have had a fruitless journey. She also wondered if Rupert had returned to the house yet. There was no sign of Lady Amelia and Kitty assumed she must be in her art studio.

No mention was made of Tilly having gone and everything seemed as usual. Perhaps they hadn't seen the cart collect the girl and Mrs Gray or her sister may not have said anything yet to Lady Sarah. Kitty couldn't help feeling that the atmosphere in the house felt strained and tense though. She excused herself to take Bertie back upstairs and to quickly apply some of her rose-scented lotion to her work-reddened hands.

She left Bertie to snooze comfortably while she returned back down in time for the summons to lunch.

'Mrs Putnam, I have asked the vicar to tea this afternoon so we can make the arrangements for the wedding. We shall require a few treats. I trust you and Mrs Gray can manage that?' Lady Sarah said as she took her seat at the table.

'Yes, my lady,' Mrs Putnam agreed while looking at Kitty, an unspoken plea in her eyes.

Kitty gave a small nod of her head. She could assist with washing-up while the housekeeper and her sister prepared dainty sandwiches to satisfy Lady Sarah and the vicar at teatime. She wondered if the housekeeper had made the dowager lady aware of Tilly's absence. If she had, then it was thoughtless indeed to expect her staff to prepare a special tea.

'Splendid, splendid.' Sir Henry had returned for lunch and appeared in good humour.

'The end of June will be a lovely time to hold a wedding.' Mr Conway had torn himself away from his papers to come to lunch. He too seemed to be delighted at the prospect of a date for the nuptials being secured.

'Yes, most delightful,' Lady Amelia agreed vaguely, her mind still seemingly on her artworks.

Kitty noticed that neither the bride nor groom appeared to have much to say on the matter.

'Did you see the inspector this morning?' Ruby asked her father. 'We were wondering how the investigation was progressing.'

Mrs Putnam served the small summer salad which was the first course.

'Only very briefly, my dear. I rather think he still feels the girl must have been meeting someone when she was attacked.' Mr Conway poked the lettuce on his plate somewhat dubiously.

'A boyfriend then. I knew it,' Lady Sarah said in a triumphant voice.

'One can only presume that was what he was inferring. Although he has had men poking about in the woods for ages,' Sir Henry said.

'And in the house,' Lady Amelia added.

Everyone around the table looked at her in surprise.

'He's collected up all the walking sticks and umbrellas for some reason,' Lady Amelia explained.

'The croquet mallets too,' Sebastian said.

'Well really, the impertinence of the man. He's never asked permission.' Lady Sarah looked at her son. 'Did you know about this, Henry?'

Sir Henry, who had turned a plum colour when his wife had explained what the inspector was doing, spluttered an indignant response. 'No, I did not. Really, Amelia, and you gave him permission. What the devil is he up to?'

'I don't think I could refuse permission,' Lady Amelia said.

'I rather expect he's looking for the murder weapon,' Sebastian replied coolly as he set his cutlery on his empty plate.

The implications of what Sebastian had just said seemed to silence everyone and the housekeeper scurried around, clearing plates ready for the second course. Once everyone had been served with thinly fried potatoes and a cold collation of meats the conversation resumed.

'Why is the inspector looking for a murder weapon in the house?' Lady Sarah asked.

'It's pretty obvious why, Granny. He thinks one of us must have killed Aggie,' Sebastian said.

'Sebastian!' Sir Henry glared menacingly at his son.

'It can also exonerate everyone,' Mrs Craven pointed out. 'That is correct, isn't it, Kitty?'

Kitty wished the older woman hadn't dragged her into the conversation. 'I suppose it can determine if something from the house was used or not, as Mrs Craven has just said. The inspector does believe in being very thorough.'

'Well, I for one wish he would hurry up and find whoever is responsible for the girl's death. It really is most unpleasant having the police hanging about the place,' Lady Sarah grumbled.

'I agree,' Sir Henry said. 'She was just a maid, after all, and with what seems to be emerging about her behaviour, well, it's little wonder something happened to her.'

Kitty's brows rose and she attacked her slice of roast beef with unnecessary vigour.

'Really, what behaviour? Oh, the business of her having unaccounted-for money and her impertinence, I suppose. Or this secret lover she must have had.' Lady Sarah sniffed.

Kitty wondered what the Dowager Lady Faversham would have to say if she knew the full extent of Agnes's activities. Lunch concluded with a sorbet, and everyone drifted away from the table to resume their previous activities. The sun was shining so Ruby and Sebastian set off for a walk. Mrs Craven and Lady Sarah returned to the drawing room and Lady Amelia back to her art. Mr Conway had letters to write and Sir Henry said he intended to go out with his shotgun to scare the crows from his cereal crop.

Kitty spied her chance and slipped back to the kitchen. She put the apron back on and set about starting the washing-up. The sisters were engrossed with cutting up food for the unexpected teatime guest and finishing preparations for dinner.

'Does Lady Sarah know that Tilly has gone?' Kitty asked when she was up to her elbows in suds at the large stone Belfast sink.

'She knows as something is amiss because I took the morning coffee out,' Mrs Gray said. 'I didn't say anything to her though.'

'I haven't told her yet. You would have thought as she'd have come to ask if something was amiss,' Mrs Putnam said as she chopped up a cucumber with a large knife. 'Not just sat there, demanding fancy food for the vicar.'

'I see Rupert hasn't returned to the house,' Kitty observed.

'I heard him arguing with his father the day he went off to stay with his friends,' Mrs Putnam said.

'He has considerable gaming debts apparently.' Kitty placed the dinner plates in the wooden rack to drain.

'P'raps as that was it then. I know there was harsh words

being said. They haven't been getting on at all the last few weeks. Sir Henry didn't look best pleased when Master Rupert took off in that old car of his.' Mrs Putnam frowned. 'I'm surprised as Master Rupert would have gaming debts though.'

'Oh?' Kitty asked.

'He's always been the more staid of the two brothers. Now if it had been Master Sebastian I wouldn't have been surprised. Although he's been minding his p's and q's since Miss Conway came along. He was always the more reckless of the two of them, especially where the ladies are concerned. No thought of consequences. Apparently, he got in some right scrapes when he were younger,' Mrs Putnam said.

Kitty continued with her voluntary tasks and stored the information away to discuss with Matt later when he returned. She had just completed all the clearing away and was ready to hang up her apron when there was a knock at the back door.

'Oh, Inspector Lewis, come on in, is there something as we can do for you?' Mrs Putnam asked as she opened the door.

The inspector removed his hat as he came inside, not noticing Kitty at the sink on the far side of the room. Kitty thought the policeman looked tired and dispirited as he wiped his feet on the coconut matting.

'I'm sorry to trouble you, Mrs Putnam, but I wondered if you could oblige me with a cup of tea? I also wanted to ask you both a couple of questions,' the inspector said.

The housekeeper showed him to the scrubbed pine work-table where he sank down on a chair with a weary sigh. Mrs Gray put the kettle back on to boil and set out some earthenware cups and saucers.

Kitty removed her apron and hung it back on its peg. Inspector Lewis still appeared not to have noticed her presence in the kitchen and she wondered how someone so unobservant could have risen to become an inspector.

Mrs Putnam made tea while Mrs Gray produced a tin with

some fruitcake and cut them all a generous slice. Inspector Lewis looked up from contemplating the tabletop when Kitty took a seat at the table.

'Good heavens, Mrs Bryant! What are you doing in here?' He frowned at her, clearly confused at discovering her in the kitchen.

'Mrs Bryant has very kindly been lending us a hand. Tilly, our maid, has quit on us, fetched home this morning by her father,' Mrs Putnam explained as she poured the tea.

Inspector Lewis gave Kitty a sour look as he accepted his drink and a slice of cake.

'I thought I would make myself useful,' Kitty said sweetly. She was tempted to add that at least he couldn't say she was interfering with his investigation. Not while she was busy washing up or peeling potatoes.

'Now, you said you had some things you wished to ask us?' Mrs Putnam said.

The inspector glanced at Kitty, clearly wishing she wasn't there. 'Yes, I wanted to double-check with you both that Agnes gave no indication of having a lover?'

Both women shook their heads. 'No, sir, and that is something Agnes wouldn't have kept to herself. Not if it were anything serious. She would have bragged about it. She were being secretive about other things, like where the money she had in her purse had come from, but she would have boasted on having an admirer,' Mrs Gray said.

'That's why when she disappeared, at first we couldn't quite work out where she could have gone. We thought it had to be a man, probably because that was the only way we could make sense of it.' Mrs Putnam's brow furrowed. 'But she was in her uniform and she hadn't even changed the ribbon in her hair or put none of her perfume on. You always knew when she had her scent on as it were quite strong.'

'But no one raised the alarm? Not even when her sister

contacted you?' The inspector persisted. 'Did you raise this with your master or Lady Sarah?'

Kitty sipped her tea and listened attentively to the responses. These were all questions she and Matt had tried to get answers to.

Mrs Putnam and Mrs Gray exchanged uneasy glances. 'We did, sir, yes. Tilly was worried. She shared with Aggie and she kept saying as Agnes wouldn't have just gone off and not said anything. Lady Sarah said that we were just to box her things up and no doubt Agnes would send for them when she was settled.' Mrs Putnam coloured. 'I'm afraid we took that to mean as Lady Sarah might have dismissed the girl in disgrace and Agnes, being headstrong, had just took off.'

Inspector Lewis's eyes narrowed. 'By in disgrace you thought perhaps she may have become pregnant?'

Kitty couldn't see how that could be with no boyfriend, unless there had been something secret between the dead girl and one of the sons of the house. They both certainly spoke affectionately of her and admired her prettiness.

'No, not so much that. It was the money she had, we thought maybe she had stolen something,' Mrs Gray said.

'She liked pretty things,' Mrs Putnam added.

'Lady Sarah is quite old-fashioned and can be ruthless. She would have turned her out with no time to take her things,' Mrs Gray explained. 'She wouldn't have told us knowing how short-staffed we are. She wants everything kept on an even keel until this wedding takes place.'

Kitty could see that this made much more sense.

'Truth be told, even though we were uneasy, we've been kept so busy there was no time to fret about Agnes,' Mrs Putnam said.

'And it weren't our place to go to the police or anything. What would we have said? Lady Sarah and Sir Henry wouldn't have been pleased especially with the Conways visiting,' Mrs Gray added, looking at her sister.

Kitty could see that the inspector was not so certain about the staff's explanation of events.

'You admit you argued with the girl on the day she disappeared.' Inspector Lewis looked at Mrs Putnam.

'Yes, I told her off. She was back-answering and slacking about her work. Short-staffed or not I won't be disrespected. It were nothing out of the ordinary in the running of a house. 'Tis my place to correct the staff and make sure as they pull their weight. She were a bad influence on young Tilly.' Mrs Putnam pursed her lips as her sister nodded in agreement with her sister's stance.

'Did Agnes quarrel with anyone else that day? Or in the days before she disappeared?' Inspector Lewis asked.

'Lady Sarah was sharp with her. Mind you, her ladyship is sharp with everyone.' Mrs Gray frowned as she thought about the question.

'There was something about Lady Amelia. She told Agnes off for moving things in the orangery. You know Lady Amelia does her arty things in there and by and large we just ignore it. Agnes said as she'd gone in there to sweep it out. At the time I didn't give it no mind, but perhaps there was something. Lady Amelia is a very placid lady, she doesn't usually get het up about anything,' Mrs Putnam said.

Kitty wondered what could have ruffled Lady Amelia's feathers. Had Agnes been snooping and been caught?

CHAPTER TWENTY

Once Inspector Lewis had finished his tea and departed, Kitty went upstairs to take Bertie out again. She applied more lotion to her hands and decided a stroll around the terrace might be pleasant for both her and Bertie. It was almost time for the vicar to arrive to discuss the wedding arrangements with the Favershams and the Conways, so it was better that she absented herself.

The air outside in the garden was refreshing after being cooped up in the kitchen for so long. She wandered along the terrace enjoying the afternoon sunshine. Bertie trotted about happily sniffing and inspecting everything.

Inspector Lewis hadn't said where he planned to go next, and she wondered if he would speak to Lady Amelia. She hoped he would wait until after the meeting with the vicar was concluded. Lady Sarah would not be happy if he disturbed the wedding planning.

Kitty dawdled along and then decided to venture down onto the grass so that Bertie could have a good romp around the lawn. The ground was still slightly damp underfoot despite the sunshine and the air smelt fresh and clean. A couple of butterflies flitted over the roses which looked a little battered after the recent storm.

She pottered aimlessly around the edge of the lawn before starting to head back closer to the house. It had been so quiet and deserted in the garden that she couldn't help startling when she heard a sharp and insistent 'Psst,' from behind the croquet shed.

'Mrs Craven, what are you doing?' Kitty asked once her heart had stopped racing, and she realised who was lurking in amongst the laurel bushes.

'Looking for clues, obviously.' Mrs Craven emerged from the bushes and brushed a few stray leaves from the skirts of her elegant navy-print frock. 'The police seem to have drawn a blank discovering the murder weapon so I thought I might take a look around. Especially after Sebastian said the inspector had taken the croquet mallets. Sarah is busy with the vicar and the Conways, so I spied my chance to slip away. Where have you been all day?'

'I thought I should talk to some of the staff while Matt was in London. Just to see if there was anything we may have missed.' Kitty refrained from telling Mrs Craven that she had been working in the kitchen. She knew the other woman would have been horrified.

'Well, I've had no luck out here and Inspector Lewis has taken a lot of things from the house already. To no avail though it seems. It appears he's now returned almost everything.' Mrs Craven fell into step beside Kitty. 'Did you find anything out from the staff?'

Kitty told her what Mrs Putnam had said about being surprised that Rupert was the one in trouble over gaming debts. She also mentioned Lady Amelia having words with Agnes a few days before the girl had vanished.

'Yes, now you've come to mention it, it is surprising about Rupert. Sarah always said Sebastian was the wilder one of the two boys. Still, his father told her he had spoken to him about it. Rupert hasn't returned to Markham either from staying with his friends. Do you think he is avoiding the inspector?' Mrs Craven put her hand on Kitty's arm and gripped her tightly. 'What if he is the one who killed Agnes?'

Kitty paused for a minute and Mrs Craven released her grasp.

'It's possible but what motive would he have?' Kitty asked.

Mrs Craven thought for a moment while Bertie started to excavate a hole under the shrubbery. 'Well, she could have been the one who discovered his gambling and told his father. He could have been so angry that he struck her down in a fit of rage.'

Kitty considered the suggestion. 'He could but there are others in the house with stronger motives and there is no mention of him and Agnes having quarrelled.' She moved forward and called to Bertie to stop digging.

'My dear Kitty, much as I hate the idea that Rupert may be the culprit, who else do you suspect?' Mrs Craven asked as Kitty went to drag her disobedient dog from his excavations.

'Everyone,' Kitty said as she grabbed hold of Bertie's collar.

'Nonsense, surely you don't think Lady Sarah, for instance, could have done it?' Mrs Craven protested.

'Why not? She has far more motive. She is desperate to retain the estate by promoting this match between Ruby and Sebastian. If she had discovered Agnes snooping about and then taunting her with whatever she had discovered, I think she would be ruthless enough to strike out.' Kitty tugged at Bertie's collar to try and get him out from under the bush.

Mrs Craven looked horrified by Kitty's suggestion. 'Nonsense, Lady Sarah is older than I am and a dear friend.'

'Sir Henry then,' Kitty said. 'He has a lot riding on this marriage.'

'Well yes, but surely he wouldn't harm Agnes. He never takes any notice of the staff, Sarah does all of that.'

Kitty managed to persuade her dog out of the shrubbery. 'Sebastian too may have secrets which he might not have wanted Ruby to discover. Especially since you say he is the wilder of the two boys,' Kitty said as she kept an eye on her unrepentant dog.

'Really, Kitty. Next you'll tell me that this argument with Lady Amelia gives her a motive too.' Mrs Craven chuckled.

Kitty looked at her companion. 'Of course it may. We need to know what they quarrelled about. It may not be significant, but we can't be certain. Lady Amelia is as invested as Lady Sarah in saving Markham to preserve her son's heritage. I know this is difficult since Peregrine was related to the Favershams, but you can't trust any of them. Not until Agnes's killer is caught.'

Mrs Craven looked affronted. 'If you had only known what it used to be like here, Kitty. Peregrine spent some of his boyhood here and when we were first married we would come for weekends.' She sighed and looked around the neglected garden. 'It was so beautiful. Sarah and her husband, Sir Norman, were wonderful hosts and then when they had the boys, we came for the christenings and birthday balls. It was a tragedy when Arthur was killed and, of course, Sarah had lost her dear husband just before the start of the war.'

'That was when Sir Henry inherited the title and the estate?' Kitty asked.

'Yes, my dear. Henry was in a reserved occupation so wasn't called to fight. There were two lots of death duties in quick succession and I don't think the estate really recovered. Henry too is not a good manager. Sarah has told me privately that he has made some very poor financial decisions over the last ten years. Bad investments on the stock market, bad land management decisions.' Mrs Craven shook her head and gazed up at the house. 'I do hope Sebastian can turn things around, there is so much history here. With Ruby's help, of course,' she added quickly.

Kitty stopped herself from saying it was Ruby's money which was needed to save the Faversham and Markham. They walked slowly up the shallow flight of stone steps onto the terrace with Bertie running ahead, his tail high as he trotted around.

They avoided the French doors to the drawing room not wishing to disturb the discussions taking place with the vicar. Instead, they strolled in the direction of the ballroom and further on towards the large and ornate orangery where Lady Amelia did her art.

As they drew nearer to the orangery they became aware of raised voices. Kitty immediately recognised Inspector Lewis's hectoring tones and Lady Amelia's softer, well-modulated voice. She quickened her pace to get closer in the hope of catching some of what was being said.

Mrs Craven scurried after her, a horrified expression on her face.

'Kitty!'

'Shh, we don't want to be heard,' Kitty warned her.

'This is most unladylike.' Mrs Craven tutted but she dropped her voice and came closer to Kitty so that she too might be able to hear what was being said. The windows of the orangery were open, so it was easy to hear the conversation inside.

'I must say, I find this whole conversation most distasteful.' Lady Amelia's soft tones floated out through the open top lights.

'I'm afraid murder is most distasteful, your ladyship, and I need to ask questions if I am to uncover the person responsible.' There was an irritated note in the inspector's voice and for once Kitty felt a little sympathy for the policeman.

'Yes, but I fail to see what a conversation I had with Agnes some days before her death could possibly have to do with her killer,' Lady Amelia said.

'I shall be the judge of whether your quarrel with the girl was relevant or not. Frankly, I find it most odd that you didn't think to mention it before to me,' Inspector Lewis said.

'Because I fail to see why it mattered.' Lady Amelia's tone sharpened.

'Then you can have no hesitation in telling me what it was about,' the inspector countered.

'The conversation was not pertinent to her death,' Lady Amelia insisted.

'Then you have no reason not to tell me what your quarrel was over as I've just said. I shall be the judge if it is pertinent or not. So, for the last time, what did you and Agnes argue about?' Inspector Lewis sounded angry, and Kitty could picture the scene. Mrs Craven leaned in a little closer and Kitty steadied the older woman by placing her hand on her arm.

'I had discovered Agnes snooping in my studio. She had moved several of my art pieces on the pretext that she was cleaning. I found her reading a piece of private correspondence so I confronted her.' Lady Amelia's voice became a little muffled and Kitty guessed the woman was walking about the room.

'What did she have to say for herself on the matter?' Inspector Lewis asked.

'She was, to be frank, quite insolent. She said that she knew things about the family and there were people who were willing to pay her for what she knew. I reminded her that she had a duty of loyalty to this house,' Lady Amelia said and Mrs Craven nodded.

'And what was the girl's response?' Inspector Lewis continued with his questions.

'She said her loyalty wouldn't pay her bills and we owed her several months' wages. I was appalled at this.' Lady Amelia sounded uncertain.

Kitty exchanged glances with Mrs Craven. It sounded as if Lady Amelia had been unaware that the staff had not been paid.

'You didn't know the staff were owed money?' Inspector Lewis asked.

'No. I knew that finances were tight, but my mother-in-law manages the household. Henry gives her a budget. I thought the girl must have been lying.' There was a bewildered note now in Lady Amelia's tone.

'Did you accuse her of lying?' Inspector Lewis's voice had a sharp edge to it.

'I said she must have been mistaken. I asked if she had applied to Lady Sarah for her wages. She laughed and said there was no money to pay any of them and if the wedding didn't come off, then the staff would all be gone.'

'Did you ask her what she supposedly knew about members of the family?' Inspector Lewis continued.

'I said that there were no secrets in our household, and she laughed again. She said I must be blind and that even my own husband and children were deceiving me.' Lady Amelia's voice trembled.

'Had you any idea what she meant by that?' the inspector asked.

There was a pause and Kitty looked around to make sure Bertie was still near them on the terrace. She had no wish for her naughty little dog to somehow worm his way into the orangery and disrupt what was a most promising conversation.

Lady Amelia's reply was quieter and Kitty had to strain to hear. 'I know that there is something wrong. I know that our financial situation is bad. My husband tries his best to reassure me, but I am not stupid. Even so, I didn't believe her when she said that they were keeping secrets from me. I worry about them you know, all of them. Rupert has been behaving so oddly since he returned from university. Sebastian too has not been himself.

I thought perhaps it was because we needed him to face up to his duties to make a good match and take over the estate from Henry. I don't know though. Now I keep thinking, what if it's more than that? His and Ruby's engagement is not primarily a love match, but they seem fond of each other. My own marriage began in a very similar fashion.' Her voice tailed off.

Kitty gave Mrs Craven a questioning look. She hadn't realised that Lady Amelia's marriage to Sir Henry had also been one made of practicalities. Mrs Craven gave a faint nod to indicate that she had been aware of the background.

'And you are certain that she said nothing else that could give you an idea what she meant by these secrets?' Inspector Lewis asked.

'No, none whatsoever. Now, you must excuse me, Inspector, I am wanted in the drawing room. I need to attend this meeting with the vicar before Mr Conway gets carried away and tries arranging for the marriage to take place at Exeter Cathedral.'

The conversation died away and Kitty assumed they must have both left the orangery. She moved quickly away from where they had been crouched near the wall of the house. Mrs Craven's face was avid with excitement. 'That was rather interesting,' she said. 'What secrets do you think Agnes meant?'

Kitty was thoughtful as they made their way back along the terrace to take a seat at one of the outdoor tables. 'I don't know. Perhaps this business of Rupert's gambling?' she suggested.

'Yes, that could be something. We know that Sir Henry had confronted him, but he and Lady Sarah have kept it from Lady Amelia.' Mrs Craven took the chair opposite to Kitty. Bertie flumped down under the table.

'It seems to me that Agnes was a very different person here to what her sister believed,' Kitty said.

'Yes, although Dora does tend to always think the best of people. I have to watch her, or she'd be swindled by every dishonest trader,' Mrs Craven said. 'She falls for all the sob stories the doorstep peddlers give her. Heaven only knows how many dusters she's bought from them over the years.'

'You knew that Sir Henry and Lady Amelia's marriage was not a love match?' Kitty asked.

'Oh, my dear, when one has an estate such as this there are obligations. One cannot afford very often to marry just for some notion of love. Liking and respect are important and once the matter of an heir or two has been met, then the couple may choose to conduct their marriage as they wish.' Mrs Craven looked at Kitty's horrified expression. 'It works very well, my dear. Ruby and Sebastian will probably be very happy together. He has a good regard for her.'

'And her money,' Kitty remarked drily.

'Of course, but she knows she will gain a title and a secure background for any children they have. She will have a passport into respectable society and she will be free to undertake anything she is interested in. In return the estate is secured for the future. Ruby knows this, I'm sure. Her father will have made certain her fortune is safe, and she will be protected against any fortune hunters and swindlers. It is eminently sensible,' Mrs Craven said.

Kitty was not so certain. Still, she had no doubt that Mrs Craven knew far more about this kind of thing than she did. She wondered if the interview with Lady Amelia had assisted or confused the inspector.

CHAPTER TWENTY-ONE

Kitty pulled her car to a halt outside the station and waited for Matt to arrive. The large plume of smoke and sound of the approaching steam engine told her the train was on time. There would be just enough time to get back to Markham, scramble into evening attire and head for the dining room. Lady Sarah had graciously allowed dinner to be slightly delayed. Something which Kitty hoped would assist the beleaguered kitchen staff.

Matt looked exhausted as he opened the passenger door and slid into his seat. Bertie, who had come along for the ride, gave a small woof of welcome from the back of the car. Kitty hoped his day had gone well.

'How was London?' she asked once Matt was settled in his seat and had greeted their dog. 'Did you manage to see Mr Jobbins?'

'London was busy, noisy and, yes, I saw him.' Matt gave her a tired smile as she expertly swung her car out of the small parking area.

'And what did he say about Redvers? Was he the one who assisted him to fake his own death?' she asked as she pulled out onto the main road.

'Yes, he finally admitted it. He seemed quite unrepentant about it all. He was more concerned that he might face some consequences for what he'd done.' Matt adjusted his position on the seat to stretch out his legs a fraction more.

'At least we now know for certain that the man in that grave is not Redvers Palmerston. The awful thing is there may be a family grieving for their loved one not knowing he is buried under another name here in England,' Kitty said.

'That's very true, but we have no way of discovering who he might be. Jobbins and Redvers seem to have switched identities and done away with that poor soul's ID. Then we also have to think about Redvers's wife. She is remarried and Redvers is still it seems very much alive, despite the death certificate.' Matt glanced at Kitty.

'Ugh, what a mess,' Kitty agreed as she turned into the lane leading to Markham.

'What has been happening here today? Have you been all right?' Matt asked as the house came into view.

Kitty quickly told him what had happened and how she had spent her day.

'My poor darling, all that washing-up in order to further our investigation.' Matt grinned at her as she pulled her car to a stop.

'I felt so sorry for Mrs Putnam and Mrs Gray being left to struggle with everything. Plus, it was the perfect way to find out more of what life is like here. It's a house so full of secrets,' Kitty said.

Matt took Bertie from the back of the car, before linking his arm through Kitty's ready to go inside the house. 'You've certainly been busy.'

'I also inducted Mrs C into the finer art of eavesdropping.' Kitty flashed a mischievous smile as she told him what they had overheard earlier outside the orangery.

'Hmm, Agnes was clearly not the sweet, innocent girl

Dora believed her to be. It sounds as if she got a taste for money and decided to try a little blackmail on various people after Mr Conway started paying her for information,' Matt said.

'Exactly, and she must have tried it on the wrong person,' Kitty agreed as they hurried inside and up the stairs to their room to quickly dress for dinner.

Kitty was touched to discover that despite the pressures of being so short-staffed Mrs Putnam had still found time to place a dish of meat for Bertie. His water bowl had also been refilled. They hurriedly changed and were just descending the stairs when the gong sounded for dinner.

'In the nick of time it seems,' Matt murmured in her ear as they greeted the rest of the household on their way to take their places at the table.

They had just sat down when the dining room door opened, and Inspector Lewis appeared. He apologised for his late arrival and took a seat at the table next to Kitty. Lady Sarah glared at him and Lady Amelia also appeared none too pleased that he had joined them.

The first course was a consommé which Mrs Putnam served speedily and efficiently. Kitty wondered if Lady Sarah had yet been made aware that Tilly had gone.

'Did you manage to set a date with the vicar for the wedding?' Kitty asked Ruby as she buttered her bread roll.

The American girl blushed. 'Yes, the last Saturday in June, so not far away really.'

'How lovely,' Kitty said. 'I hope you'll be able to get all the arrangements made in time.'

'Perfect timing to get the banns read. Millicent has volunteered to assist us with all of the preparations. Fortunately, she has a great many contacts.' Lady Sarah smiled at Mrs Craven.

Kitty noticed that Rupert was still absent from the table and wondered how much longer he intended to stay with his friends. It seemed strange to her that he would be gone at such a busy time for his family.

'The church on the estate sure looks most charming and as you say more personal than the cathedral. I saw it earlier today with Sir Henry.' Mr Conway took a sip of his wine.

'The family have, of course, always supported the church. Many of our younger sons in previous generations were members of the clergy,' Lady Sarah informed him.

It was clear that some gentle persuasion had been applied to deter Mr Conway from his vision of seeing his daughter married at Exeter.

'Oh yes, the church here is delightful, it adds a much nicer, more personal touch, to a wedding,' Mrs Craven agreed.

'How goes your investigation, Inspector? It would be nice to have things cleared away before Sebastian and Ruby's marriage.' Sir Henry looked at Inspector Lewis.

'I believe I am making progress. These things take time, I'm afraid, and several people have unfortunately been less than forthcoming with information.' The inspector glanced at Lady Amelia.

An awkward silence fell across the table with various people exchanging glances or focusing on their soup. Mrs Putnam re-emerged to clear dishes and served the fish pie Kitty had seen being prepared earlier.

Mrs Craven cleared her throat. 'So, are you close to making an arrest?' she asked.

The inspector looked around the diners. 'I believe I may be getting very close.'

Kitty noticed his gaze didn't seem to linger on any particular person and she wondered if he was on a fishing expedition to see if he could rattle anyone into thinking they were close to being arrested.

'That's good to hear. The sooner the bounder is caught the better, eh?' Sir Henry said.

There was a subdued murmur of assent from around the table as everyone concentrated on their dinner. The main course was followed by egg custard tart, then Lady Sarah requested coffee to be served in the drawing room.

It seemed to Kitty that everyone was keen to escape from the dining room and from Inspector Lewis's presence. The inspector didn't join them, pleading pressure of paperwork, and there was a palpable sense of relief once he had departed.

'How much longer does he expect to stay here?' Lady Sarah demanded once he was out of earshot, and she was ensconced in her favourite armchair.

'I suppose until he has arrested whoever killed Agnes.' Lady Amelia started to serve coffee from the trolley and Ruby went to assist her.

'Well, if you ask me, he's overstayed his welcome. Not that he was terribly welcome in the first place. Such a dreadful fuss over a servant,' Lady Sarah grumbled, and Kitty's neatly arched eyebrows rose at this outrageous statement.

'How did your journey to London go, Captain Bryant? You said that you and Kitty were engaged on another case?' Ruby asked.

'Very well, thank you. I managed to get the confirmation we had been seeking to tie up a loose end,' Matt said.

'Is it a murder case like the one here?' Ruby glanced up from adding milk to the cups.

Lady Amelia's hand shook as she picked up a saucer and she spilled a little coffee as she passed it to Mrs Craven.

'In a manner of speaking. It's about someone who faked their own death several years ago,' Matt said.

'How'd he manage that then? That must be a tricky thing to pull off,' Sir Henry asked.

'It was,' Matt responded in a light, but firm tone, and Kitty knew he would not divulge any more details about their case.

'Do you think it would be hard to escape like that?' Ruby

mused. 'To just disappear and start all over again as a new person?'

'It's harder than you think. You'd spend the rest of your life looking over your shoulder in case someone recognised you,' Kitty said. 'And people do, you know. It's surprising, you can run into people you know in the queerest of places.' She wondered if Ruby was having cold feet again about the wedding after setting the date.

'I suppose the best bet would be to go abroad,' Sebastian suggested.

'Then you have to leave the country before anyone realises you're missing. If the police, for instance, were searching for you, they can look for tickets and passports. There is always a clue to be found somewhere,' Matt said.

'Like that Crippen fellow, wasn't that how he and his mistress were caught?' Mr Conway said, referring to a notorious murder case from several years ago.

Lady Sarah shuddered. 'Ugh, most distasteful. Let us hope the inspector is correct and he arrests the culprit soon. Then at least he will be out of our way, and we can focus on the wedding.'

* * *

Matt and Kitty retired upstairs early. Matt having pleaded weariness from his journey in order for them to escape. By the time he returned to their bedroom after taking Bertie for one last trot around the garden before bed, Kitty was already changed.

'What did you make of the inspector's announcement this evening? Saying that he was close to making an arrest?' Matt asked as Bertie settled back on the fireside rug with a sigh.

'Personally, I thought he was bluffing. I thought he was perhaps trying to rattle everyone to see if someone would let something slip.' Kitty dropped her ruby earrings into the small dish on the dressing table.

Matt grinned at her as he sat on the armchair and slipped off his evening shoes. 'I agree. I don't think he's any further forward with this case than we are.'

Kitty swivelled round on the dressing-table stool to face him. 'I'm bothered about Rupert. It's jolly odd, don't you think, the way he just took off like that to stay with friends and hasn't come back. He knows how important this weekend is and with the murder you would have thought he would have stuck around.'

'Well, he argued with his father, didn't he, just before he left? That may be why he's in no hurry to return,' Matt said as he hung up his jacket in the large wardrobe.

'Or he may be avoiding the inspector,' Kitty said. 'I mean he is where he says he is, I suppose. I wonder if anyone has heard from him since he went to Chudleigh? Or if the police have checked on him,' Kitty said.

'You think he may have tried to do a disappearing act?' Matt asked as he finished preparing for bed.

'I think it was on my mind before this evening's conversation but there has been a lot of talk tonight about disappearing and then death,' Kitty remarked with a shiver.

'That's very true. Did you want to try and track him down tomorrow? We know who these friends of his are. They were some of the people at the ball. It may be that Sebastian has spoken to him since they seem close. We can try to find out at breakfast in the morning,' Matt suggested. He dropped a kiss on top of Kitty's blonde curls. 'Come to bed and stop fretting. We can look into things tomorrow.'

He got into bed and as Kitty snuggled up beside him he wondered if she was right. It was odd that Rupert had stayed away from Markham. Perhaps it was nothing to do with Agnes's death and more to do with these gambling debts and the argument with Sir Henry. Even so, Kitty had a point. It would be good to try and discover exactly what was going on.

They couldn't really extend their stay at the Hall for much longer. They were already trespassing on the Favershams' kindness. Ruby was definitely less anxious than she had been, which was why they had been asked to stay on in the first place. Was that because she had decided to marry Sebastian after all? Had her idea of stealing her own jewellery and disappearing finally been put to rest?

His own trip to London had answered a good many questions about their other case but he still had to decide what they needed to do next on that matter. Seeing Jobbins again after all this time had stirred up a lot of memories and not all of them good.

* * *

Breakfast the following morning was a sparser affair than before. Only one covered dish was on the burners. Bertie, however, who had accompanied them downstairs was delighted to discover it contained eggs and bacon.

Kitty gave him some on a plate beneath the table before anyone else appeared. They hadn't been seated long before a harassed-looking Mrs Putnam deposited tea and toast on the table and scurried off again with only a brief good morning as she left.

'I do feel bad for them,' Kitty said as the housekeeper vanished in the direction of the kitchen.

'I know what you mean. From what you said they are in a tricky position,' Matt agreed.

Sebastian strolled into the room and bid them good morning, before going to the sideboard to fill his plate with food.

'Not much on this morning,' he remarked with a frown as

he studied the contents of the dish before coming to sit with them at the table.

'I expect they are doing their best. Tilly left yesterday so it's just Mrs Putnam and Mrs Gray doing all the work now. They will have to cut back somewhere if they are to manage,' Kitty said.

'Oh dear. I expect Granny will have to try and get a girl in from the village to help out for a bit.' Sebastian sounded unconcerned, and Kitty guessed he had very little idea of how much work was involved in running a house the size of Markham.

'Have you heard from your brother at all? He's staying not far away, isn't he, with friends?' Kitty asked.

Sebastian looked surprised. 'Yes, that's right, with the Cox-Herberts over at Chudleigh at the old rectory. He often disappears over there when he and Father have locked horns.'

'I expect Inspector Lewis has probably contacted him there if he has any more questions for him,' Kitty said as she cut up her bacon.

'Yes, I suppose so.' Sebastian appeared a little discomfited by her questions and she wondered if she had hit a nerve.

'You and Ruby will have a hectic few weeks now the date has been booked. I expect the first banns will be called this weekend,' Matt said, helping himself to toast.

'That's right. Ruby will be staying here now until after the wedding. Although, for propriety's sake, Granny has insisted she use the dower house as her address.' Sebastian gave a small shrug of his shoulders at his grandmother's whim.

'I suppose there is a formality to these things. Will it be a big wedding?' Matt asked.

'No, I don't think so. The same people that were invited to the engagement ball pretty much and a few distant relatives I suppose. I don't think Ruby has anyone much except her friend, Jennifer, who is going to stand up for her as bridesmaid. Granny is talking about having the gardener's granddaughter as flower girl, but I don't know if Ruby is terribly keen on the idea.'

Kitty finished her breakfast and saw that Matt too was done. 'Gosh, it all sounds very exciting. We had better get on and leave you to enjoy your breakfast.'

Kitty led the way out of the dining room with Bertie following reluctantly behind them.

'Well?' she asked once they were further down the hall.

'I think you're right. A trip to Chudleigh may be in order, if only to check that Rupert is where he says he is,' Matt agreed.

'It's not terribly far away and it sounds as if the old rectory is quite a well-known house so we should be able to find it. I'll just get my bag.' Kitty collected her things while Matt let Bertie have another good roam around the terrace, before bundling the spaniel onto the rear seat of the car.

Inspector Lewis's police car was parked beside Kitty's, and she noticed it had a shiny new tyre on the front-right wheel. She assumed that must have been the one that was damaged on the night of the storm.

Matt looked up the route to Chudleigh on the map that Kitty kept in her glovebox, and they set off down the drive. It was another fine spring day with bright blue skies and warm sunshine.

Kitty wished she could shake off the uneasy feeling that had been bothering her ever since Matt had returned from London. She hoped that Rupert was where he had said, and they would find all was well at his friend's home.

CHAPTER TWENTY-TWO

At least the drive along the country lanes on the edges of the moors was pleasant. They were away from the oppressive atmosphere of Markham Hall and the Favershams with their secrets. It had been quite a few years since Kitty had been to Chudleigh. It was a small, very old village with a charming stone church and several very fine buildings.

'Sebastian said Rupert was at the old rectory,' Kitty said as she paused her car by the church. 'That implies there must be a newer one.'

'Let's try further along the street just past those cottages. A rectory is normally close to the church it serves,' Matt suggested.

'Oh, I see it, and that looks like Rupert's car parked at the side of the house.' Kitty parked her car at the kerb and Matt extracted Bertie from his seat. The old rectory was a large cream-painted building in the late-Georgian style. It looked like a larger version of a child's doll's house with symmetrical sash windows. A couple of tall, stone mushrooms surrounded by a pretty tangle of forget-me-nots were set in the tiny patch of lawn on either side of the front path.

Kitty followed Matt and Bertie in through the small

wrought-iron front gate and up the path to the slightly faded dark-blue front door. Matt pushed the polished-brass button for the doorbell, and they waited for a reply.

A moment later a plump, rosy-cheeked maid in a smart black uniform with a white cap and apron answered the door.

'We're sorry to disturb you but we wondered if Mr Rupert Faversham was at home. We understand he is staying here with the family at present.' Matt presented the girl with his card.

She eyed both the card and Matt and Kitty dubiously before replying. 'I'm sorry, sir, miss, but Mr Faversham is not available today.'

Kitty went to speak but the door was closed promptly and firmly in her face.

'Well!' she remarked.

'I suppose we should have had our story ready. If Rupert is here and is hiding out from his creditors, the girl could have believed we were here to collect his debts,' Matt said as he looked at her chagrined expression.

'I'm quite certain he is here. He wouldn't have gone far without his car.' Kitty looked at the house.

'Uh-oh, what are you thinking?' Matt asked, a note of alarm in his voice.

Kitty slipped past the front window of the house and down the side towards where Rupert's car was parked. Behind the car was a taller wrought-iron rail fence with a gate. Through the railings she could see the house had an extensive garden and she was certain she could hear voices.

'Kitty!' Matt had followed her.

'I'm just going to take a quick peek.' She tried the gate and discovered it was unlocked. Before Matt could stop her, she let herself into the back garden of the rectory.

'I'll be quick, and I'll stay out of sight of the windows. If anyone sees me let Bertie in and we can claim I was looking for him,' Kitty said and hurried off, keeping well to the side of the grounds.

Unlike Markham the garden was well maintained with a neat lawn and flower gardens followed by a vegetable area and a small orchard. The voices and laughter were louder now, and Kitty glimpsed a small group of people at the far end of the grounds playing quoits.

There appeared to be two young women and two men. She didn't recognise the girls or the one man, but the other one was definitely Rupert Faversham. At least her worst fears had not been realised, and Rupert was in fact alive and well. It had crossed her mind that he could have been murdered as well since no one had heard from him once he had come to Chudleigh.

Her heart thumped in her chest, and she straightened her shoulders. She'd come this far and didn't intend to be thwarted now. Why was Rupert hiding out at the old rectory and was it indeed to do with his gambling debts or something darker? She strode purposefully across the grass towards the quoits players.

The group paused in their play as they saw her approach and she saw curiosity writ large on the expressions of the young women and the other man. Rupert's face, however, told a different story.

'Mrs Bryant, Kitty, what brings you here?' He scurried towards her before she could get too close to the rest of the group.

'Good morning, Rupert. I wasn't certain if you were at home. The staff at the house seemed a little confused on the matter,' Kitty said once he was beside her.

'Are you here alone?' Rupert had lowered his voice as he glanced towards the side of the house.

Kitty followed his gaze but couldn't see any sign of Matt or Bertie. 'No, I'm here with my husband and the dog,' she said.

She wasn't sure if she imagined it, but his shoulders seemed to sag a little with relief. He had started to stroll in the direction of the gate where she had entered the garden, and she realised he seemed to be trying to escort her out.

'I see, well it's quite the surprise you calling here. There is nothing wrong at home, I hope? Has the inspector made an arrest yet?' Rupert asked.

'Everything seems much the same except that Tilly has resigned so the house is extremely short-staffed. The inspector seems to feel he is close to discovering who may have killed Agnes. However, I am not so certain that is in fact the case.' Kitty stopped dead, forcing Rupert to also halt.

'Oh?' The nervousness that had marked his features when he had first spotted her returned and she could almost feel his unease.

'Yes, he's been asking a lot of questions and of course they are still looking for the murder weapon,' Kitty said. 'I presume Inspector Lewis has already questioned you?'

'Oh yes, he was very thorough. I dealt with all of that before leaving the house to come here.' Rupert glanced back to where his friends were still watching them from a distance.

'Your father seemed to feel that you had some financial problems. Something to do with gambling?' Kitty said.

'Um, it's nothing much. Father is prone to exaggeration.' Rupert didn't meet her gaze.

'Are you certain? He seemed to think there were creditors looking for you and obviously the family are unable to help you in meeting your debts. Is that what you argued with him about when you left Markham?' Kitty was determined to get an answer.

'Look, Mrs Bryant, Kitty, I don't know why you are here or what you think this has to do with anything, but things are not how they seem.' Rupert ran his hand distractedly through his hair and looked towards the gate.

'It looks as if you are hiding here for some reason. That is how it looks. Now, it may be from creditors, or it could be that you killed Agnes and are avoiding speaking to the inspector,' Kitty said. She watched his expression keenly.

There was something he wasn't telling her, she was sure of it. 'Or is it something else?' she said.

Rupert swallowed hard, the Adam's apple in his throat bobbed just above his striped silk cravat. 'You don't understand. Really, I promise I did not kill Agnes. It's just...' He paused.

Kitty saw that Matt and Bertie had come through the gate and were just inside the garden.

'Just what?' Kitty asked. 'This is important, Rupert. If you didn't kill Agnes, do you know who did?'

Rupert didn't reply. Instead, he strode towards Matt and Bertie, a determined look on his face. Kitty trotted after him, her shorter legs struggling to keep pace with his much longer strides.

Matt watched as Rupert opened the gate and went to his car, lifting the boot. 'Here, see for yourself. I promise I found this in the hallstand before the inspector started searching the house looking for a weapon. I panicked and didn't know what to do.'

Kitty and Matt peered inside the boot to see a walking stick with a silver fox head handle. A handle that was smeared with a brownish-red substance that looked suspiciously like dried blood.

'Whose cane is it?' Matt asked.

Rupert's gaze was locked on the walking stick. 'It lives in the stick stand near the front door along with the umbrellas. Father uses it and so does Sebastian and even Mother at times. Anyone could have used it. I found it by chance when the storm was on. I was after an umbrella to go outside to check the guttering. The rain was forcing it to overflow above the scullery. I snatched it up and hid it in the car boot while I tried to think what to do.'

'Why didn't you tell the inspector?' Kitty asked. 'Why bring it with you here?'

She wondered that he hadn't cleaned it or thrown it in a bush somewhere to dispose of it. It seemed odd to her that he had carried it to Chudleigh in his car.

'Like I said, I panicked. I knew it would cause more suspicion to fall on the house and we need Seb and Ruby's wedding to go ahead. I thought if I just moved it, then perhaps the inspector would find proof that whoever killed Aggie was a servant or a tramp like Granny kept saying. That whatever was on this stick wasn't what I thought it was.' Rupert swallowed once more. He glanced at the cane and looked away again.

'You think you know who killed her, don't you? You know it's someone in the house. And you're worried that the killer knows that you suspect them,' Kitty said. It was either that or Rupert was the murderer.

Matt took a large clean handkerchief from his pocket, and he used it to extract the cane from the car. He placed it in the boot of Kitty's car while Bertie watched with interest.

'I don't know who killed Aggie, I swear. It wasn't me though, you have to believe me.' Rupert looked at them.

'You realise this doesn't look good,' Kitty warned. 'You're hiding here, avoiding the inspector. What appears to be the murder weapon is in the boot of your car. You have motivation to kill her.'

'No, no I don't. What motivation did I have to harm Agnes?' Rupert asked. Panic was written large now on his expressive aristocratic features.

'You have a gambling problem and owe a great deal of money. Something that would not be good for the Conways to know. It would be yet another problem that Ruby's money might be needed for. Agnes may well have tried to blackmail you about it. She was reporting all kinds of things about the family to Stanley Conway in return for money,' Matt said as he closed the lid on the boot of Kitty's car.

'No, that's not it at all!' Rupert collapsed down on a nearby garden bench clutching his head in his hands.

'Then I think you had better tell us exactly what's going on. Otherwise, when we pass this stick on to Inspector Lewis you may well find yourself inside a cell,' Kitty said.

Rupert groaned. 'The gambling debts, they aren't mine. I just let Father say they were because the truth would have derailed the wedding. Ruby was already having doubts about agreeing to marry Seb. She told me after I found her studying the safe in Father's study. You know she was the one who tried to break into it I suppose?' Rupert asked as he lifted his head to look directly at Kitty.

'Yes, she confessed to us,' Matt said.

'Whose debts are they? Are they Sebastian's?' Kitty asked. She was beginning to have a good idea of who might be responsible for Agnes's murder.

Rupert's body slumped and he dropped his gaze. 'No, not Seb's. They're Father's. He was desperate to get some money together. Except, he was as bad at poker as he was at managing the estate. The last lot of money he raised from selling Granny's diamond necklace went in about an hour and then the financial hole he was digging just got deeper. If Stanley Conway had discovered the gaming debts were Father's, then he would have definitely called off the engagement. Without the wedding and Ruby's money, Markham would be taken by the bank. Five hundred years or so of history gone.'

'What did your father say to you the morning you left Markham?' Kitty asked.

'He said I had better say nothing about the gambling. Leave him to deal with everything as he had almost sorted out all the problems.' Rupert ran his hands through his hair once more and looked at Kitty. 'The way he spoke, his eyes were so dark and cold. I admit, it scared me.'

Matt looked at Kitty. 'I think we need to return to Markham as quickly as possible to find the inspector.'

Kitty nodded. 'Did Sir Henry know you had discovered the blood on the walking stick?' She looked at Rupert.

'I told him I was leaving to stay with friends. That if the inspector asked me again about the gaming debts that I couldn't lie anymore. He didn't mention the stick but I think he knew I'd found it. I'd moved it just before the inspector had begun to gather up any possible weapons from the house. I'd overheard the inspector on the telephone so I knew what he had planned,' Rupert said.

'And you asked the staff here not to say you were at home in case your father came after you?' Kitty continued as Matt lifted Bertie into the rear seat of her car.

'I didn't want to think what I was thinking. It was the way he looked at me, something in his expression. I thought it was better if I just got out and stayed away. He came looking for me the other day but I managed to avoid him.' Rupert had risen to his feet. 'Look, I'll come back too. It's better if I face the music and explain myself to the inspector.'

Kitty glanced at Matt.

'No, stay here for now, it may not be safe for you at Markham. The inspector can come to you, or we can telephone to let you know. You must remain here, however.' Matt's tone was firm.

Rupert was pale, but he agreed. 'You have my word as a gentleman.'

There was no time to debate the matter. Rupert's friends walked up to join him. They left him inside the gate and hurried to Kitty's car. She jumped into the driver's seat and started the car engine.

'We must get back and find Inspector Lewis,' she said as she sped along the country lanes, the wind tugging at the brim of her straw hat.

'Yes, and Sir Henry,' Matt agreed.

'We need to tread carefully. There is no telling what he may do if he thinks we have spoken to Rupert,' Kitty said as she overtook a horse and cart, leaving a cloud of dust and the annoyed shout of the driver behind her.

'I wonder where the inspector may have gone this morning?' Matt said.

'I don't know. Perhaps to Bovey Tracey again?' Kitty hazarded a guess. 'Or he may be still on the estate somewhere. I hope he hasn't gone back to Exeter. What time is it, by the way?'

Matt glanced at his watch. 'Half past eleven. We have a little time before lunch to find them both.'

'I hope we find the inspector first. I don't want to sit down to luncheon with a murderer,' Kitty said as she turned into the long driveway that led to the house.

Matt laughed. 'Darling, we've dined with plenty of killers.'

'Yes, but we haven't known they were murderers. I don't know that I can do it,' Kitty pointed out. How could they sit there making idle conversation over the soup knowing that their host was almost certainly responsible for the death of his maid.

CHAPTER TWENTY-THREE

'We must appear calm and unruffled. We don't wish to arouse any suspicions,' Matt warned her as she pulled up the hand-brake at the side of the house. The inspector's car was missing.

She switched off the engine as Matt got out and took Bertie from the back seat of the car. The sun was much warmer now and she could hear the distant sound of voices and laughter on the terrace. They made their way around the house to where Lady Sarah was seated with Ruby and Mr Conway. They had clearly taken their morning tea outside and were sitting in the shade of a rather tattered-looking umbrella.

'Captain Bryant, Kitty, we wondered where everyone had gone on such a fine day.' Mr Conway stood as they approached, clearly ready to find Kitty a seat.

'Oh, we just went for a little run out in the car. It is such a glorious day,' Kitty agreed as she accepted the offer of a chair. Matt pulled a vacant seat closer to the table.

Her heart hammered in her chest as she tried to look unconcerned and as if they were simply making small talk. All the while she longed to demand to know where the inspector and Sir Henry might be.

'It is glorious, isn't it? I wonder what the inspector is doing this morning? We didn't see him at breakfast.' Matt's tone was casual, and Kitty marvelled at how cool he sounded.

'I think he has gone to talk to the gardener's boy again,' Mr Conway said. 'I passed him in the hall earlier as he was on his way out.'

'It's about time he pulled his finger out, if you ask me. Really, I don't know what else he thinks the gardener's boy can tell him,' Lady Sarah declared with a disparaging sniff.

Kitty's gaze locked with Matt's, and she tried to recall where on the estate the garden staff's cottages were located. She knew they were down a track since that was where the inspector had acquired his puncture during the storm.

'Sebastian should be finished with the estate manager soon. They went out to inspect the crops.' Ruby fanned her face with a languid hand.

'Did Sir Henry go with them?' Kitty asked.

'Oh no, I think Henry has gone down to the lake with Millicent. He has his shotgun with him as usual, I rather think he has been trying to take out some of the pigeons. Millicent, of course, wanted to poke around near the mausoleum. Ghoulish, I call it. Still, she will insist that she is trying to assist the police in their investigation,' Lady Sarah said.

Kitty's grip on the rattan arms of her chair tightened and she forced herself to calm her breathing.

'I wonder if we should take Bertie for another quick walk before lunch,' Matt suggested, looking at Kitty.

'He has been in the car a lot this morning,' Kitty agreed and jumped up quickly, anxious to be off.

Bertie, who was always ready for exercise, was also on his feet and ready to go after hearing the mention of a walk.

Lady Sarah looked a little affronted at the haste of their departure. 'Well, do make sure you are back on time. Mrs Putnam is being most disobliging at present.'

They hurried away from the terrace and headed back towards Kitty's car. 'We need to find the inspector and quickly,' Kitty said. 'Do you think Mrs C is safe with Sir Henry?'

'I don't see why not. I mean she doesn't suspect anything, does she?' Matt asked.

'I don't think so, but he has a guilty conscience, and she may inadvertently say the wrong thing.' Kitty bit her lip. She wasn't very fond of Mrs Craven, but she had no desire to see her harmed.

'Listen, you take the car and drive around to the gardener's cottage. It's back along the way we came in, a small track to the right. Be careful, I don't want you coming a cropper like the inspector did the night of the storm. Tell Inspector Lewis what we've learned. I'll walk down towards the lake with Bertie and see if I can get Mrs C back up to the house,' Matt said.

'Very well, but do take care, darling. Sir Henry has his shotgun with him.' Kitty kissed Matt quickly on the cheek and hopped into her car. She set off along the drive and took the bumpy, rutted trackway which led down behind the woods towards the estate workers' cottages which lay a half mile or so further on.

Her pulse was racing, and she forced herself to slow her speed, not wishing to lose a wheel in any of the deeper potholes that littered the track. Eventually she saw the small row of lime-washed cottages ahead. She sighed with relief at the sight of the inspector's car parked outside the end cottage. She parked alongside the black police vehicle and climbed out, looking around for any sign of the inspector.

There were no signs of life from any of the three houses in the row, so she decided to try the one closest to the police car first. The front garden was neat and tidy, filled with rows of vegetables. She hammered on the door and desperately hoped the inspector was inside.

The door opened and the gardener who had cut the lawns shortly after their arrival goggled at her in surprise.

'Is Inspector Lewis here? He is wanted urgently,' Kitty said.

The inspector and the gardener's assistant, a boy of about fourteen, appeared in the tiny hallway.

'Mrs Bryant, is something wrong?' Inspector Lewis asked.

* * *

Matt made his way as swiftly as he could down through the woods towards the lake. He kept Bertie on his leash, not willing to allow the dog to run free if Sir Henry was shooting. He hoped Kitty would be successful in locating Inspector Lewis. He sensed time was of the essence now.

He reached the far side of the wood without encountering either Sir Henry or Mrs Craven on the path. There was no sign of either of them around the margin of the wood, so he headed towards the mausoleum with Bertie trotting ahead, his nose to the ground.

There was still no indication that anyone had passed that way. He jogged up the steps to the mausoleum and found the door had been firmly secured to prevent anyone entering. He stood on the terrace and scanned the area below. Suddenly a movement on the water caught his eye and a small rowing boat emerged from the back of the tiny ornamental island and diving platform.

Sir Henry appeared to have the oars and Mrs Craven was seated comfortably in the prow of the boat, a small pink parasol above her head shielding her from the sun. Matt breathed a sigh of relief and walked back down the steps and headed for the boathouse.

At least Mrs Craven appeared to be perfectly safe and enjoying a morning boating in the sunshine. He waited near the old wooden jetty expecting Sir Henry to steer towards it ready for them to disembark.

Bertie tugged impatiently on his leash having sighted the mother duck and the ducklings swimming in the reeds nearby. Sir Henry and Mrs Craven appeared oblivious to his presence in the shadow of the boathouse. They had stopped rowing in the deeper part of the lake. Matt could see Mrs Craven gesticulating towards the mausoleum.

Sir Henry had rested his oars across the rowlocks of the boat and seemed to be leaning in, listening to whatever Mrs Craven was telling him. Matt watched as he leaned back and reached under his seat to produce his shotgun.

Horrified, Matt saw him raise the barrel of the gun, pointing it directly at Mrs Craven.

'Sir Henry! Stop!' Matt's shout startled the nearby ducks, and the drake flew out of the reeds in the direction of the boat, quacking loudly.

Mrs Craven was quick to take advantage of Sir Henry's momentary distraction and Matt watched as she brought her parasol down smartly on Sir Henry's head. The movement brought up his arm and the gun discharged its shot upwards, narrowly missing Mrs Craven's hat.

Sir Henry lunged forward, and the oars slipped free of the rowlocks falling into the lake with a splash. Mrs Craven ducked down and hit out at the enraged peer. Matt looked around the outside of the boathouse for a lifebelt or some rope.

The boat was too far out for him to attempt to reach them, and he saw no sign of any other vessel. The struggle continued in the small boat, and he could see it rocking perilously to and fro. It was drifting over towards a large bed of reeds on the far side and Matt started off around the edge in that direction.

'Sir Henry, stop!' he shouted again, waving his arms, hoping the peer would come to his senses before disaster could strike.

Mrs Craven's pink parasol appeared worse for wear now.

Matt could see the material had come away from one of the spokes. She tried to fend Sir Henry off with it once more, poking him hard in the ribs. Sir Henry roared with rage and wrested it from her, tossing it into the water.

Matt stumbled as he hurried around the water's edge, discovering the path was overgrown with brambles and nettles. Bertie barked with excitement, thrilled by this new game. In the meantime, the boat was drifting further towards the reeds.

Sir Henry appeared to be trying to throttle Mrs Craven – his hands were about her throat. Matt feared for the worst but then Mrs Craven appeared to bring up her leg kneeing her attacker with some force. The movement made the boat, already unstable, tip, sending both occupants into the water.

Matt found a weathered post which held a loose coil of fraying rope. He could only hope it would hold without breaking as he looped it free from the hook.

'Swim away from the reeds!' he called from the bank. The diving platform was in the deeper water but there was less chance of them becoming entangled if they could make it there.

The boat was upside down now and drifting into the reeds. He could see Mrs Craven's hat, the bright pink flowers which adorned the rim making an incongruous sight on the water. Sir Henry, despite a great deal of splashing, was still attempting to reach Mrs Craven.

Mrs Craven, for her part, seemed to have heard Matt's instructions and was striking out for the diving platform. To his astonishment she swam extremely well. Sir Henry splashed noisily after her seemingly trying to grab at her feet. The ducks in the reeds, disturbed and alarmed by the noise, flew out onto the water preventing Sir Henry from catching hold of his quarry.

Sir Henry seemed to flounder in the water, his head disappearing beneath the lake surface before popping up again. Mrs Craven had taken advantage of her assailant's problems and was heading for the platform at a steady pace. Matt could see Sir Henry was having difficulties and he guessed he had fallen foul of the weeds.

'Sir Henry, tread water, I'll throw you a rope,' Matt called.

He tossed the end of the rope as far out as he could manage in the peer's direction. He kept the other end looped firmly around his shoulder and his chest. Bertie stood on the edge of the water barking in excitement, his plumed tail wagging like a flag.

Sir Henry finally appeared to hear him and lunged for the rope. Matt could only watch as he missed and disappeared beneath the water once more. Mrs Craven had reached the platform and was holding on to the edge trying to regain her breath.

Sir Henry resurfaced once more and made another vain attempt to get to the lifeline that Matt had thrown.

'My foot is caught! The weeds!' Sir Henry tried to grab at the rope.

Matt couldn't see how he could get it any closer to the stricken man. There were too many reeds and weeds in the way.

'Reach out!' he called from the bank. There was no way he could enter the water from that point. It was far too dangerous and it would take too long to run back around and swim out from the other bank.

Sir Henry made another desperate lunge for the lifeline but missed and sank once more beneath the surface. Matt could see the man's strength was failing.

'Sir Henry!' Matt called once more, hoping to see the man reappear.

Mrs Craven had hauled herself up onto the diving platform. 'Matthew! Assistance is coming!'

Matt glanced away from the spot where he had last seen Sir Henry to see Inspector Lewis, Kitty, the gardener and his boy all emerging from the woods and running towards the lake. He looked back to where he had last seen Sir Henry and could see no sign that he had re-emerged.

'Help! Over here!' Mrs Craven waved and called to the party who were running towards the lake. Bertie had his paws in the water and the ducks were still quacking as Matt frantically scanned the area where he had last seen Sir Henry.

'Matt!' He heard Kitty call his name and he let go of Bertie's leash, knowing the dog would run to her.

The gardener and his boy opened up the boathouse and retrieved a long wooden pole with a hook on the end. They rushed around to where Matt was standing.

'Sir Henry has his foot caught in the weeds. He's just gone under,' Matt said. He assisted the gardener to lower the hooked end of the pole into the water. Together they started to probe, trying to find where Sir Henry had gone down.

* * *

Kitty caught hold of Bertie's leash as her dog scampered eagerly towards her. She could see a very soggy Mrs Craven shivering on the diving platform. The boat appeared to have turned turtle and was drifting now towards her side of the lake. Out on the water she could see the oars floating where they must have come out of the rowlocks.

She could only watch helplessly as Matt and the gardener used the boathook to probe below the lake surface where she guessed Sir Henry must have last been seen. The gardener's boy had gone back inside the dilapidated shed and found a faded lifebelt, more rope and some spare oars.

Inspector Lewis rushed over to where the rowing boat was now coming very close to the lake shore, and he waded in to retrieve it. The boy rushed over to help him. Between them they managed to haul the heavy wooden boat to the edge and righted it. Gallons of lake water streamed from the boat and ran down back into the lake. Swirls of mud eddied up from the bottom and the inspector's ruined shoes squelched as he moved.

Kitty looked back to where Matt and the gardener were still probing the water with the boathook. There was no sign of Sir Henry. It seemed there was little more that she could do. The inspector and the boy seemed to be preparing to rescue Mrs Craven from her sodden perch on the diving platform.

It occurred to Kitty the most useful thing she could do was to hurry back to the house to fetch towels, blankets and brandy for the rescuers and Mrs Craven. Now she knew Matt was safe she took Bertie and scurried away up through the woods towards Markham.

She had a nasty stitch in her side and was out of breath by the time she ran across the lawn towards the terrace steps.

'Kitty, what's wrong?' Ruby was on her feet as soon as she saw her approaching. Lady Amelia had joined the group on the terrace.

'There's been an accident at the lake. Need blankets, brandy,' Kitty gasped as soon as she was in calling distance.

'Good heavens, we wondered what was going on when we saw you all go rushing off into the woods. Amelia, hurry and find Mrs Putnam.' Lady Sarah sprang up and chivvied her daughter-in-law to go inside the house.

Sebastian was also on his feet and rushed to assist his mother, grabbing the things Kitty had requested from her.

'Quickly, go down to the lake. The inspector is there with Matt,' Kitty gasped as Sebastian ran down the steps to where Kitty was trying to regain her breath.

He nodded and hurried away through the woods. Ruby came down to offer Kitty her arm as Bertie danced about her feet.

'Kitty, come and sit down, tell us what has happened,' Ruby urged as Mr Conway hurried past them following Sebastian.

'I'm not entirely certain. When we got there the rowing

boat was upside down on the lake and Mrs Craven was on the diving platform calling for help,' Kitty said as she sank down gratefully on one of the rattan chairs. Bertie flopped at her feet.

Lady Sarah teetered slightly and sat down on her chair, her hands gripping tightly to the arms. 'Where was Henry?'

'I didn't see him. I presume he must have gone into the water. Matt and the gardener are searching for him now. The inspector has retrieved the boat,' Kitty said just as Lady Amelia emerged back onto the terrace clutching a decanter and glasses.

She set the things down on the table with a shaking hand. 'Did you say Henry had fallen into the lake?'

'I don't know. I presume that is what's happened,' Kitty said.

'Let me take that.' Ruby took a crystal goblet from Lady Amelia's other hand and poured some into the glass to give to Kitty. 'Sip this. It looks as if you're suffering with a stitch.'

Kitty accepted gratefully. The pain in her side was quite acute. She took a sip and winced.

Lady Amelia had gone quite pale. 'Henry is not a good swimmer. Why were they on the lake? We thought we heard a shot?' she asked as she peered towards the woods.

'I don't know. We got there after the accident must have happened,' Kitty said. At least her breathing was easier now and the ache in her side began to recede. She had her own ideas about what may have happened at the lake but now was not the time to speculate.

They would discover more once everyone returned to the house.

CHAPTER TWENTY-FOUR

After another ten minutes a couple of figures emerged from the edge of the wood and began to walk up the lawn towards the house.

'It's Matt and Mrs Craven.' Kitty got to her feet ready to go and meet her husband.

Mrs Craven was swathed in a blanket and seemed to be leaning heavily on Matt's arm. Bertie too jumped up and looked to see his master approaching, his tail wagging a welcome.

'Good grief, poor Millicent looks completely drenched,' Lady Sarah said as they drew closer.

'There is no sign of Henry.' Lady Amelia wrung her hands together, her face anxious as she scanned the edge of the wood for more people.

Kitty and Ruby went down the stone steps to assist Mrs Craven up to the terrace. Kitty looked at Matt and he gave a faint shake of his head. Clearly they had not managed to save Sir Henry.

'Oh, my dear, come and sit down. Amelia, more brandy.' Lady Sarah moved a seat so that Mrs Craven could rest for a moment. Mrs Craven sank down on the chair, water pooling onto the stone flags around her feet from her sodden clothing.

Lady Amelia moved to obey her mother-in-law and poured more shots of brandy into the glasses she had brought outside.

'Where is Henry? What's happened?' Lady Amelia asked as she passed the goblets across.

'I'm terribly sorry but I'm afraid it looks as if Sir Henry is dead, drowned,' Matt said in a gentle tone. Lady Amelia's knees buckled, her face paper-white at his words. Matt caught her and assisted her into a chair.

'Dead? Henry is dead?' Lady Sarah asked, looking at Mrs Craven.

'Yes, my dear. I'm afraid it seems so. He got into trouble in the weeds in the lake and couldn't get free.' Mrs Craven took a sip of her drink. Her teeth chattered on the edge of the glass.

Kitty could see she looked grey and weary. Her usually immaculate hair was wet and plastered to her head.

'I don't understand. Why was he in the water?' Lady Amelia looked as if she was about to collapse.

'The inspector is coming. We may know more in a moment,' Ruby said as more figures emerged from the woods.

First the inspector, then Sebastian and Mr Conway. All three walked slowly and looked dejected as they started across the grass to the terrace.

Ruby went to her father as he drew closer and then to Sebastian, placing her hand in his as they followed the inspector up the steps.

'I'm very sorry, Lady Amelia, Lady Sarah. I'm sure Captain Bryant and Mrs Craven have told you that Sir Henry is dead,' Inspector Lewis said.

Lady Amelia gasped, her hand covering her mouth at having the news officially confirmed. Lady Sarah's face was white, and she helped herself to brandy.

'I think, Inspector, you had better tell us what happened,' Lady Sarah said once she had taken a drink.

Mr Conway sat down heavily on one of the vacant seats. Ruby placed one of her arms around her father's shoulders. Her other hand was still holding on to Sebastian's as he took a chair near his fiancée.

Inspector Lewis slipped off his wet shoes and wrapped his lower legs in one of the spare towels that had been placed nearby.

'I regret to say that Sir Henry seems to be the person responsible for the murder of Agnes Jones. His death today, whilst accidental, was as a result of an attack upon Mrs Craven here.' He looked at Mrs Craven who was trying to dry her hair with one of the towels.

Tears were running down Lady Amelia's face. 'I don't understand. That's impossible. Why? Why would he do that?'

'To save Markham and five hundred years of history,' Lady Sarah said. 'That's why, isn't it, Inspector?' Her voice was dull.

'I'm afraid that does seem to be the case, my lady,' Inspector Lewis said.

'What happened on the lake?' Lady Amelia looked at Mrs Craven.

'We had been for a walk in the woods, and we ended up at the lake. Henry had taken a potshot at some of the pigeons to keep them from the crops.' Mrs Craven sighed and took another sip from her brandy before continuing. 'I said that I had been assisting Kitty and Matthew with their investigations and that it was strange the murder weapon had not yet been discovered.'

'Go on,' Lady Amelia urged when Mrs Craven paused again.

'I... I suggested that perhaps we might get a different perspective on the case from the water. Henry offered to row us out onto the lake. It was such a pleasant day, I didn't see any harm in it.' She dabbed at her cheeks with the towel.

'That was when I came down to the lakeside,' Matt said.

Mrs Craven nodded and Kitty could see she was deeply upset by what had then happened. It was also clear to Kitty that she was too distressed for a moment to continue so Matt took over.

'I saw them in the boat on the far side of the lake. They had stopped and Mrs Craven was pointing to something by the mausoleum. That was when I saw Sir Henry place down the oars and pick up his gun. He pointed it directly at Mrs Craven.' He stopped and looked at the older woman who nodded.

'Yes, I had said I wondered how the girl had come to be there that afternoon. She must have been meeting someone, perhaps to pass on information or to blackmail the killer.' Mrs Craven's voice shook.

'I presume he must have thought that you had guessed that he was the person Agnes was meeting,' Kitty said. 'He must have arranged to meet her there away from prying eyes. She thought he would pay her and he went with the intention of silencing her forever.'

Mrs Craven nodded. 'I suppose so. He set down the oars as if listening to me, then picked up the gun. He pointed it at me, and I saw his expression had altered. I said don't be silly, do put that away.' She paused again and closed her eyes as if trying to gain enough courage to continue.

'That was when I shouted a warning to you. I thought it would make him stop when he knew I was there,' Matt said.

'It took him by surprise when the ducks flew up towards us. It gave me sufficient time to hit him with my parasol. The gun went off, fortunately missing me.' Mrs Craven shuddered.

'We heard the shot as we got out of the cars,' Kitty said. 'We hurried down through the wood as fast as we could to try and find you.'

'Mrs Craven was trying to get Sir Henry to stop, but he continued to try and attack her. The oars had fallen into the water and the boat had drifted closer to the side of the lake which is most overgrown. I ran around there to try and get to them, but the boat overturned in the struggle,' Matt explained.

'I tried to swim away from the reeds to get to the diving platform and to escape Henry. He was still trying to grab me to pull me under. I felt his hand on my foot, and I kicked him away.' Mrs Craven shook as she spoke. 'It was awful, so frightening.'

'Mrs Craven headed for the platform, and I could see Sir Henry was struggling. I'd found a rope so threw it out to him but he couldn't reach it. He said his foot was caught in the weeds,' Matt said.

'He had gone under when we arrived at the lakeside. The gardener fetched a boathook and we tried to find him to get him out,' Inspector Lewis said. 'I waded in to retrieve the boat to rescue Mrs Craven.'

'I was a swimming champion in my youth. I've swum many times in that lake. I know there is a current from the river that feeds it and weeds near the reed bed,' Mrs Craven said. 'That probably saved my life today.'

'Why were you there, Inspector? I mean what made you go to the lake?' Mr Conway looked at Inspector Lewis. 'You said Sir Henry killed the maid.'

'We found the murder weapon. It was the walking stick Sir Henry liked to use, the one with the silver handle,' Kitty said. 'I'd gone to the gardener's house to tell the inspector.'

'But the inspector had examined all the things in the house that he thought might be a weapon,' Ruby said.

'It seems Rupert had discovered the stick, hidden in the hallstand. This was before Inspector Lewis had collected up potential weapons. Sir Henry's fingerprints would be on the stick. He placed it in the boot of his car and took it with him when he left for Chudleigh,' Kitty said. 'His father had said that Rupert had gaming debts and that was why he was lying low to escape his creditors.'

'Gaming debts? Rupert? Did you know about this?' Lady Amelia looked at her mother-in-law.

'It wasn't true. It wasn't Rupert at all. It was Sir Henry who had gambled the last of the money he had raised from the sale of Lady Sarah's diamond necklace. He lost and then lost even more. This was what Agnes was threatening to tell Mr Conway,' Matt said.

'It was Henry, not Rupert? That was why he said not to tell Amelia. He knew she would have asked Rupert and I suppose he would have told her the truth.' Lady Sarah looked bewildered.

'I don't understand. Why would Rupert try to shield him? Did he know his father had killed Agnes?' Ruby asked.

'He suspected it, we think. I believe he didn't want to think his father was capable of murder, but he was afraid. He panicked when he found the stick, but he knew that the only way to save Markham was if your marriage to Sebastian went ahead. He argued with Sir Henry the morning he left. I believe he was frightened of his father and what he might do at that point,' Matt explained.

Ruby looked dazed by the revelations. 'That's awful.' She turned to look at Sebastian. 'Did you know that was why Rupert had gone to Chudleigh?'

Sebastian looked ill. He shook his head slowly. 'No, I knew something wasn't right. Rupert and I have always been close. I'd never known him to have a gambling habit. He would have told me if he was in trouble of that sort.'

'I can't believe it.' Lady Sarah looked as if she had aged twenty years in the last few minutes.

'Why would Rupert not just have gone to the inspector?' Mr Conway asked.

'Loyalty to his father. Fear that his suspicions might be correct. Worry about his brother's future and the future of

Markham Hall. I don't think he was thinking straight,' Kitty explained.

'Where is Henry now?' Lady Amelia too appeared as if she had shrunk down into herself.

'The gardener and his boy are at the lakeside, they are still attempting a recovery. If you will excuse me, I need to make some telephone calls.' Inspector Lewis rose and squelched away inside the house leaving silence behind him.

Ruby was the first to break the silence. 'What will happen now?' she asked in a quiet tone.

Kitty saw that she was still holding Sebastian's hand.

Her question seemed to galvanise her father into action. 'Well, it seems to me that this marriage can no longer go ahead. I think it's best that Ruby and I pack up and leave here as soon as the inspector says we may go.' He looked at his daughter who removed her arm from his shoulders. 'We can go back to London for a spell.'

Ruby stared at him. 'I don't understand. You have made the commitments.'

Kitty guessed she was referring to the legal documents that Mr Conway and Sir Henry had drawn up and signed regarding Ruby's finances.

'Ruby, honey, if Sir Henry has done what the inspector said then how can you still think about marrying into the family. There has to be some streak of, well, mental illness. If you have children, well...' Mr Conway didn't trouble to spare the feelings of the Favershams.

'Pa, you are being ridiculous. I have given my word to Sebastian.' Ruby's eyes flashed with defiance behind her spectacles.

'If you hope for Ruby to marry into any aristocratic household in England that doesn't have a touch of madness somewhere along the line, then you will be greatly disappointed. Even our own dear royal family has had its moments.' Lady Sarah gave Mr Conway a hard stare. His comment appeared to have rallied her from the profound shock of what had just occurred.

'Ruby, if you wish to be released from our engagement after what has happened then I quite understand. For my part, I would hope you will stay and not for any money you might bring to the estate, but for yourself.' Sebastian looked at Ruby and moved to cover her hand where she was holding his with his other hand. 'I know our engagement didn't begin as a love match but I have come to love you, my dear, as we've spent more time together.'

Kitty found her eyes filling with tears. She could see that Sebastian appeared sincere. She had noticed for herself over the last few days that the young couple had grown close.

'I'm sorry, Pa, but if you want to go back to London then you'll have to go alone. My place is here now.' Ruby smiled at Sebastian, and he squeezed her hand affectionately.

'Ruby, I beg you to rethink. This is foolhardy, come with me, have some space to see how you feel away from here.' Mr Conway looked at his daughter.

The girl shook her head. 'No. I'm sorry, my mind is made up. I'm needed here.'

'You are very welcome to remain here, Ruby, as indeed are you, Mr Conway. I should be sorry to see our acquaintance at an end.' Lady Sarah looked at the American.

Mr Conway glanced at his daughter's resolute expression, then at the Dowager Lady Faversham and seemed to accept he was defeated. 'Very well, if you are certain, Ruby, honey, that this is what you want.'

'Thank you.' Ruby extracted her hand from her fiancé's and hugged her father, kissing him tenderly on the cheek.

'I think I feel able to go and change now,' Mrs Craven said. Her colour seemed restored after the brandy and the dreadful shock of what had happened at the lake.

'I'll help you upstairs,' Kitty offered. 'A hot bath will revive you.'

'Thank you, Kitty.' Mrs Craven accepted her offer and took Kitty's arm to leave the terrace.

Kitty escorted the older woman upstairs to her room and started to draw her bath, adding some of the rose-scented bath salts she found in the room.

'I'm sorry about Sir Henry,' Kitty said as she laid out fresh towels.

'So am I. I always knew he was... well, unpredictable, even as a child. Still, it is a bitter pill for Sarah and indeed Amelia,' Mrs Craven agreed. 'It was very fortunate that Matthew came down to the lake when he did. Still, who knew my prowess as a swimmer would have come in useful after all this time.' She shook her head ruefully and closed the bathroom door.

CHAPTER TWENTY-FIVE

Kitty and Matt decided to leave Markham as soon as possible once Sir Henry's body had been retrieved from the lake. Inspector Lewis and his constables took their statements and Rupert returned to Markham and his family. Mrs Craven insisted that she wished to remain for a few more days to support Lady Sarah, refusing their offer to take her back to Dartmouth.

Ruby and Mr Conway had both thanked them for their help and support and gave them a generous tip. Largely, Kitty suspected, at Ruby's behest. Ruby was also intent on rewarding the staff for their loyalty and recruiting more assistance.

Rupert confirmed all the suggestions Kitty and Matt had made about why he had stayed silent about his suspicions. Despite his horror at being correct about his father, he was clearly distressed by Sir Henry's death. He and Sebastian had also been very fond of Agnes and intended to send kind messages and flowers to Dora expressing their sorrow at her death.

'I can't say that I'm not glad to be going home and leaving

the Favershams behind,' Kitty declared with feeling as they drove along the driveway away from the house.

'I know what you mean. At least Dora will know now exactly what happened to her sister,' Matt said.

'Poor Dora, it will be such a shock to discover Sir Henry was responsible for Agnes's murder.' Kitty halted at the junction before pulling out onto the public road.

'And to find out why she was killed. I wonder what she hoped to gain from Sir Henry? I mean, she knew he had no money as that was why he needed Sebastian to marry Ruby,' Matt mused.

'It was probably the promise of future money once the marriage was fixed,' Kitty said. 'She was already being paid by Stanley Conway so some money afterwards to avert scandal would have been tempting.'

'I suppose so. It's strange, I had thought the days of the dollar princesses, where American heiresses came to marry impoverished aristocrats, was gone,' Matt said.

'I suppose a genuine title and an estate going back hundreds of years is something you can't normally obtain unless you already belong to those circles. Mr Conway knows that Ruby's money makes her a target for fortune hunters so I suppose by trying to secure her a husband where she will be moving in the top circles of society is attractive. He has taken care to ensure that she will call all the financial shots.' Kitty had been giving the matter some thought.

'They seem well matched too. Ruby and Sebastian clearly have come to really care for one another it seems. I hope the estate can withstand a further round of death duties. Sebastian has the title now so Ruby will be the next Lady Faversham rather more swiftly than Mr Conway anticipated.' Matt smiled at Kitty.

'After her earlier cold feet where she was trying to take her own jewels from the safe so she could run away.' Kitty smiled back at her husband. 'I hope things go well for her and Sebastian. Rupert too, he seemed fond of that girl at Chudleigh. I think I spy another romance looming there.'

'Let's hope Lady Sarah is also able to repay Mrs Craven the money she borrowed after the wedding,' Matt said.

'I hope Mrs Putnam and Mrs Gray receive their wages. They deserve a hefty bonus and some more help in the house,' Kitty replied with feeling.

Matt laughed. 'Ruby seems determined to ensure they will be well looked after. And at least you won't be assisting them with more washing-up.'

Kitty gave her husband a mildly reproachful glance which made him laugh even harder.

'I suppose Inspector Lewis will take the credit for solving the case,' Kitty said as she changed gear to go up one of the hills.

'If it helps him obtain that promotion he's been chasing, then that may not be a bad thing. He can stay in Exeter and Chief Inspector Greville may get a new man back in Torquay,' Matt suggested.

Kitty's spirits lifted at Matt's suggestion. 'That would be rather nice.'

'We should call in at the office on our way home. There may be more post waiting for us as we have been away longer than we planned,' Matt suggested once they had cleared the city and were heading for the coast.

'That's a good idea,' Kitty agreed. 'It will give us a head start then on deciding what to do with the Palmerston case if we know if there is more work in the offing.' She knew that they often became busier over the summer months with the increase in visitors to the bay. The wealthy clientele often also attracted jewel thieves and scoundrels keen to take advantage.

It was late in the day and the shops were either closed or closing when Kitty parked her car outside the door that led up to their office. Their business was situated above a gentleman's outfitters in Torquay on the main street. Matt lifted Bertie from the back of the car, and they went up to the office together.

They shared the landing with a company that manufactured and fitted false teeth, so their part of the floor was quite small but eminently suitable for its purpose. A small outer office come waiting room and a square space to interview clients and hold meetings.

The post was lying on the tiles inside the door as Matt unlocked the waiting room. Kitty stooped to pick it up while Matt went to check that all was well in the main office. Bertie sat and waited patiently, aware that he rarely received treats when they came to the office.

'Anything interesting?' Matt asked as he closed the main door behind him and came to join her.

'A couple of bills I think and an advertising flyer for a new art gallery. Just one envelope that appears promising.' She waved the thin white envelope enticingly under his nose.

'Come on, we can open it at home. I know you are longing to see your darling cat.' Matt shook his head at her.

'Yes, poor little Rascal, although I am certain he will have been most royally spoiled by Grams and will be as fat as a barrel. She was going to take him to the house ready for our return,' Kitty agreed as Matt locked the offices up once more.

'I must admit, I'm dying for a cup of tea,' Matt said as they got back into the car to set off for their white modern villa at Churston.

Kitty too was glad to be back at home. She parked her car next to Matt's Sunbeam motorcycle and stretched as Matt opened the house and got Bertie. She went straight through to the kitchen to put the kettle on, while Matt carried in their luggage. She would deal with that later once they had said hello to their cat.

Kitty smiled as Rascal twined around her feet purring a welcome as soon as she entered the kitchen. Bertie had bounded straight out into the back garden as Kitty had opened the back door. Mrs Smith, their housekeeper, had left them a cold supper in the pantry with an apple pie and clotted cream for dessert.

Kitty made a tray of tea and carried it out to the small table in the garden under the apple tree. It was a favourite spot that offered glimpses of the sea from their seats. Matt came to join her carrying the rest of the post that Mrs Smith had placed on the hall table.

Once they were seated and the tea poured, Rascal jumped up onto Kitty's lap, purring contentedly.

'Oh, it is so nice to be home.' Kitty gazed around her happily.

Matt smiled as he started to sort the post. 'I agree. Not much here, darling. I think there is a letter from Lucy.' He handed her a small cream envelope.

Kitty's cousin Lucy now lived in Yorkshire with her husband and baby son. Kitty opened her letter using the small cake knife she had brought out with her to slit the envelope open.

'Oh, how lovely, Lucy says William has his first tooth.' She read on. 'And do you remember Hattie, that distant cousin of my uncle's?'

'Yes, of course, she came to Lucy's wedding and ours and she always stays at your aunt and uncle's for Christmas,' Matt said.

Hattie was one of the poor relations amongst Kitty's uncle's family. A spinster in her late fifties she had no money or settled home of her own but moved about between the family, staying for various lengths of time. She did small jobs and ran errands to pay her way.

Kitty liked her and could even overlook Hattie's habit of acquiring small silver objects that didn't belong to her during her visits. The family all knew to count the teaspoons and quietly remove them from her luggage at the end of one of her stays.

'This is quite lovely. Lucy says that Hattie has unexpectedly been left a small legacy from another distant cousin. A cottage and a sum of money. Isn't that wonderful?' Kitty looked at her husband who was sorting through the household bills.

'It is wonderful. She will be delighted to finally have her own home after all these years,' Matt agreed.

Kitty folded up the letter and returned it to its envelope. 'Let's see what that letter that came to the office is about.' She produced the post from the pocket of her dress. She used the small cake knife once more to slit the envelope open.

'Curious, there seems to be a letter and a photograph.'

Matt set aside the bills. 'Who is it from?'

'A Mrs Weston. She wants us to look for her husband. She says he has gone missing and thinks he may be in Torbay.' Kitty scanned the letter, frowning as she read the contents. 'Listen to this.'

Dear Sirs,

I am writing to request your aid in looking for my husband, Robert Weston. We have been married for only three months, and he has gone missing from our home. I am most concerned since he is a veteran of the Great War and suffered much in that conflict. No one of my acquaintance has seen him and the local constabulary have not been much help. I am also missing some money and jewellery and fear something bad has befallen him. He was last seen by a gentleman I know on a train heading for the southwest. I know he has some connections there, hence my writing to you. I enclose a photograph of us at our wedding. It is the only one I have and is not the best quality. Any help you can give me would be much appreciated.

Mrs Jane Weston

'She has listed his physical characteristics too in case they might help us to trace him. Six foot two, greying hair and moustache, oh...' Kitty broke off and looked at Matt. 'Take a look at the photograph,' she urged.

Matt picked the picture up from the table. His eyes widened as he studied it and he released a low whistle. 'Let me guess, the next characteristic this poor lady mentions, is it that he is missing part of his ear?'

Kitty nodded. 'It's him, isn't it? Redvers Palmerston. He has bigamously married this lady under a false name and now it sounds as if he has absconded with her money and possessions.'

'It is definitely him. The picture is poor, but I doubt he would have wished one to be taken so probably moved on purpose to try to conceal his features.' Matt gave the picture back to Kitty.

She studied it carefully, keen to get her first look at this mysterious man who seemed to be causing chaos everywhere he went. Redvers was tall and good-looking for his age. His top hat shadowed his face, and his new bride beamed happily at the photographer. She was a small plump woman, well dressed and clearly wearing her finest clothes for her wedding.

'Oh, Matt, this is dreadful. That poor woman. What can be done? We have to try to track him down.' Kitty stared at Redvers's face, committing it to her memory.

'Indeed. He has to be stopped. I think this must be our priority before he can deceive anyone else,' Matt agreed.

'Then we need to visit Mrs Weston and get as much information as we can. It seems we will have our work cut out for us.' Kitty placed the photograph down carefully on the table.

'We have succeeded in all of our other cases,' Matt pointed out. She could see the glint of determination in her husband's bright blue eyes. 'And this case is personal.'

A LETTER FROM HELEN

Dear reader,

I want to say a huge thank you for choosing to read *Murder at the English Manor*. If you did enjoy it, and want to keep up to date with all my latest releases, just sign up at the following link. Your email address will never be shared and you can unsubscribe at any time.

www.bookouture.com/helena-dixon

I hope you loved *Murder at the English Manor* and if you did I would be very grateful if you could write a review. I'd love to hear what you think, and it makes such a difference helping new readers to discover one of my books for the first time.

I love hearing from my readers – you can get in touch through social media or my website.

Thanks,

Helena Dixon

www.nelldixon.com

facebook.com/nelldixonauthor

x.com/NellDixon

ACKNOWLEDGEMENTS

My thanks to all of my Torbay friends for all their help, support and knowledge. Special love to the Tuesday zoomers and the Coffee Crew who help support me and my craziness in so many ways. Thank you to my brilliant and hard-working agent, Kate Nash, who always knows just what to say when I'm having a moment! Who knew when I first pitched *Murder at the Dolphin Hotel* that we would now be on book twenty! I had ideas for the first twelve books and then Kitty and Matt just took off with a life of their own. My thanks to my fabulous family too who are always there for me. Finally, much love and extra special thanks to everyone at Bookouture on Team Kitty who all work incredibly hard to make the books the best that they can be. An extra shout-out to Jane Eastgate and Shirley Khan my brilliant expert eyes. I appreciate each and every one of you. Here's to the next round of adventures for Kitty and Matt!

PUBLISHING TEAM

Turning a manuscript into a book requires the efforts of many people. The publishing team at Bookouture would like to acknowledge everyone who contributed to this publication.

Audio
Alba Proko
Sinead O'Connor
Melissa Tran

Commercial
Lauren Morrissette
Hannah Richmond
Imogen Allport

Cover design
Debbie Clement

Data and analysis
Mark Alder
Mohamed Bussuri

Editorial
Cerys Hadwin-Owen
Charlotte Hegley